THE WOMAN IN MY HOME

A compelling and emotional domestic psychological thriller

C.R. HOWELL

JOFFE BOOKS

Joffe Books, London
www.joffebooks.com

First published in Great Britain in 2024

Cover art by Imogen Buchanan

ISBN: 978-1-83526-587-1

Dedicated to the memory of two brilliant women who loved books.

Caitlin O'Keeffe Roe, 1988–2020

Jenny O'Sullivan, 1988–2016

PROLOGUE

She wasn't crying. That was the terrifying part. Tears I was used to — how very many of them I had wiped from your faces, held you wet-cheeked and wailing after an injury or injustice that meant nothing in the world but everything to you. *Crying is good*, a doctor told me once. *Crying is what we want.* I knew what he meant, that my children's sobbing, frantic as it made me, was vital and healthy, a sign of struggle and strength in the face of sickness or pain.

I tried to hold on to this. With every meltdown and head bump and red-faced fever — in the course of our chaotic lives, when tears were relentless and routine — I said to myself: *Crying is good. Crying is what we want.*

I was never okay with it, though. I still wanted it to stop.

Then came the accident.

It started with a scream that brought me rushing outside. It was you, howling in terror, alerting me. I didn't notice your sister. Only you, and the strange, acrid smell in the air.

"What happened?" I said.

It was your birthday.

I studied your face, searched your arms and legs, bare in the warm summer evening. Behind you, the sun was vanishing behind the mountains, the sky lurid and beaten like a terrible warning.

"Where's Catrin?" I said. "Where's your sister?"

Your face turned dark. You pointed, wordlessly, at her body, out of my sightline until I turned my head. I ran to her. The bucket lay on its side next to her, the lethal liquid soaking the concrete. Stunned, I got down on my knees, unable to make sense of the slow-seeping disaster.

The smell was overpowering.

Sometimes I smell it now, when a tiny detail, like the colour of the sky, conjures the hateful stench, and the fear of that moment shakes me, the stacked cards of memory reshuffled. And I'm there again, your sister's toddler figure, so agile and defiant in the normal run of things, lifeless on the ground like one of her dolls. And me, trapped in the silence, longing for the tyranny of tears.

ONE

The day I came home, I hadn't seen you for ten months. That's why I'm telling you my side. It hurts me that you don't know. You were five when I left. Catrin was two and a half. I left when she was very ill. That's one of the worst things about it. As I drove north I was trying not to think about that, remembering instead how your sister had smelled of rash cream and pull-ups, mingled with the sweetness of her toddler skin, and how her hair was fine and easy to wash, a few jugs of bathwater rinsing it clean and her curls bouncing back into place as she ran around the bedroom, naked and giggling.

But your hair was as dark and heavy as your father's, hanging on to shampoo like your clothes held on to stains.

"It's nearly done," I would sing in my television voice. You saw right through me.

"Mummy, it's in my eyes!"

My arm ached with the effort of lifting water. I ached all the time then. The pain of motherhood didn't stop after the birth. It went on and on. And so I would plead with you. "This would be a lot quicker if you just put your head under the water. Just lean back, like Mummy does!"

"I don't want to!"

So I would fill the jug and let the water slip through your hair again, angling my other hand to protect your eyes, then sigh when I ran my hand over the back of your head to find bubbles forming again.

* * *

Driving home, the sun was bright, the sky cloudless and blue. Fields sailed by, vivid as a painting, and rapeseed shone, an expanse of yellow. But the air was edged with the death-chill of winter, and the wind tugged at the crops until their yellow heads danced.

When I reached the north, it was overcast, a bruised skin of grey shutting out the light. The fear I felt coming back to the village, your father, your nain — it was worse than I expected.

A few miles from the house a fullness came over me, like air ballooning inside my head. I slowed into a long lay-by and got out of the car. Mountains rose in the distance. The road stretched ahead. A lorry thundered past, shaking the ground, then a flurry of motorbikes behind it. Mist hung over the mountains. Overhead, a flock of birds moved in a perfect circle before swooping down onto a field and dispersing.

I did an exercise Ben taught me while I was away, naming each thing I could see. "Mountain, sky, hedge, bird." I was talking to myself, aloud, on the side of the road. But it helped.

Then I was back in the car, moving deeper into the mountains. The land turned dark, the deep green of the woodlands, black slate sheening the hillsides. On either side of the road the terrain was coarse and uneven, scrubby ground sweeping out to meet sheer rock. Heather and fern grew in thick patches. Rubble walls ran through the wild grass. Nettles spilled over wind-bent fences. Sheep huddled dangerously close to passing cars. So many times, before I left, I had slowed to let a stray scuttle across the road.

I saw the house, a white speck against the vast backdrop. Coming from this direction, it was the first house you saw belonging to the village. I turned up the track, the car bouncing over ridges hard enough to burst a tyre. As I moved closer to the house, forgotten details swung into view — a pile of cracked tiles at the gate, the tree growing out of the front wall, the gas tank alone on the drive. A gust of wind rocked the car and I remembered how, when I first moved in, mountain gales made the windows rattle and the world outside seemed to howl.

* * *

Your father's van was parked in the drive, facing the low stone wall between the house and next door's farm. When I walked over to the wall, the sheep lifted their heads. Beyond them, a woman was fixing twine to a gate. Her hair was tied back but strands had come loose and blew wildly in the wind. I knew this woman. She and her father lived on the farm. Watching her, I found it extraordinary that she was still here, though it wasn't surprising at all, given her family had owned the farm for decades. As I stood at the wall, she looked up as though she had sensed me there. She didn't smile or wave but stared in quiet wonder across the sheep-scattered field.

Walking past the van, I saw your father's flask beside the handbrake, his fleece on the passenger seat. On the floor were a pair of shears and an industrial-size bottle of weed-killer, overspill from the back where he stored his landscaping supplies. I was reminded how often he came home from work smelling of chemicals. Even after showering, a trace remained.

* * *

There was a dog in the window. The second I pressed the bell it appeared, as though it had been waiting in the shadows until the electronic melody vibrated in the walls. It was a Dobermann, tall and black with tan markings and uncropped ears. It panicked me, this dog. What if you'd moved? What if a new family lived here and I had no idea where you were? But your father would never sell this house. Then I remembered his van parked behind me.

My palms were itchy with sweat. I wiped them on my jeans. The door opened. I looked back at the window. The Dobermann had disappeared. Within seconds, it was in the hall, staring at me from behind the figure in the doorway. Your father. The dog was still, not trying to move past him to charge up to me. It stood quietly in the shadows. It was only to be expected, if your father had bought a dog, that he would have trained it. But the dog's stillness seemed unnatural somehow.

"Sit," said your father. Behind him, the dog did as it was told.

Your father looked out at me from the dark hall. He had been distracted at first, looking past me with mild impatience when he opened the door. But as he fixed his gaze on me, the realisation passed over his eyes like a shadow in water. As though sensing the change in your father's mood, the dog growled, a low rumble reverberating into the mountain air.

"Jesus," said your father, shaking his head. "What's the matter with you? Have you not heard of a phone?"

I nearly laughed. It was him all over. No pleasantries, no sigh of relief. Just his knee-jerk, offhand contempt. Without another word he shut the door in my face. Inside, it was silent, even the dog didn't make a sound. I listened like a deer in the woods and it did cross my mind — a crazy, whirring thought — that he might be opening the cellar door, unlocking his safe, taking out his shotgun.

I had no idea what he was doing, if he was coming back. Maybe he would leave me there in the hope I might disappear again.

But he came back. When the door opened again, he was shaken, his hands trembling. I was surprised to see him like that. So human. He stepped out, pulling the door half-closed behind him. Our bodies were close enough for him to put his arms around me. But he didn't. On his breath I could smell coffee, like the old days. Bitter, like him. I never liked it.

"What do you want?" he said.

The wind was strong, whipping the backs of my trousers. The sleeves of his top rippled.

"I would have rung first, but—"

"What do you want?" he said again.

He was trying to stay level, but fury trembled through his voice. I looked over at the sheep, the grassy slopes rising behind them, and again I remembered how it had felt to move here when I was young enough to think I could leave certain parts of myself behind. The question he had asked, twice, hung in the air.

I looked back at him. "I want to see my children."

TWO

Let me tell you something about my life before I met your father. I know children don't like to think of their parents that way, how I wandered around, carefree, nobody's mother. But it will help you understand. My mother didn't want me. That's one thing. Neither did my father. That's another. I never knew my parents' names. There's no way of explaining what it's like to live with this, having been created only to be discarded. What I do know is I was taken in at the age of two by a woman called Jude, a full-time foster mother with a messy house full of unwanted kids. The kids came and went. We didn't know when and often we didn't know why. Kids were brought to us in the very early hours of the morning after a night-time raid. The authorities knew Jude, and if the phone rang in the middle of the night we knew another child was coming, like a puppy at Christmas.

You've probably heard by now what people say about foster parents, that they do it for the money. That wasn't true of Jude. She did it because she cared. But it's also true that she never adopted me, admitting freely that the constraints were financial.

"I can't afford it," she said. "I wish I could. But I can't."

It wasn't her choice and she hated that I could be taken from her any time, if my birth parents came looking for me or someone decided to adopt me. But she was lucky. No one ever did.

* * *

This is the other thing I want to tell you. After I left school, I was filled with emptiness. There was a hole in the middle of me that I hadn't noticed until then. I grew up in a small town in south Wales. My friends went to college, or they got a job and had kids, or they got a job and didn't have kids, or they just had kids. I wanted to do something, too. But there was nothing I wanted. I had part-time work at a dress shop in town, helping older women find an outfit for a special occasion — a christening or a wedding. I liked the quiet of the shop, a break from the chaos of home, and I liked those women; they were nice to me and made me feel safe. There was a rhythm to my life. Jude didn't want me to move out. I was a big help to her with the younger kids by then. "No rush, is there?" she said.

But I knew my time was up. I couldn't carry on as I was. I needed to do something. Everyone has to do something, that's the problem.

* * *

One day, I was at the petrol station, filling up Jude's people carrier that she drove all these kids around in. I had taken two of the kids to the shops. They were in the back, swinging their legs and watching me through the blackened windows as I lifted the pump, petrol dripping from the nozzle. When I had finished filling the tank, one of them tapped the glass, shouting to me that she needed the toilet. I replaced the nozzle and pulled open the back door.

"Can't you wait until we get home?"

She shook her head. She was three. If she wet the car seat, Jude would be cross. Of course, then the other one complained he didn't want to be left alone in the car. So I carried the girl into the shop while the boy walked beside me, holding my hand. The toilet wasn't for customers but they let us use it.

While I had the girl on the toilet with her pants down, smiling at me as she relieved herself, the boy unlocked the door quietly behind me. By the time I'd turned around, he was gone. Foster kids do this a lot. They run off, climb trees, go out windows. I swore to myself, pulled up the girl's pants and ran with her in my arms back into the shop, frantically scanning the aisles. We were on the outskirts of town. The road outside was a busy and fast dual carriageway. I began to panic, tears filling my eyes as I shouted like a mad person to the staff and customers.

"Have you seen a little boy? He's five. He's only five!"

A man looked over at me, open-mouthed, holding a packet of rice. Everyone was helping then, searching, abandoning their shopping and pumps and cars to look. As I rushed round in circles, still holding the girl, a woman said to me, "You just stay put. We'll find him. Look after that one." She pointed at the girl, who was clinging to my neck and watching the scene in quiet wonder. I sat down on the cold hard kerb by the newspapers, thinking what I'd tell Jude, the police, social services.

Then I heard footsteps. I looked up and there he was. Your father, holding the boy's hand, bringing him back to me.

* * *

I can't say I was in love with him. I find this a stupid way to describe how you feel when you meet someone who affects you. The only people you love straight away are your children — and even then, it's complicated. I'll explain more about this. I'll try. But I did feel something, things I probably should have been wary of. Admiration, I suppose. The possibility of rescue. A better life. An end to the emptiness. But I didn't want him to know me. The shame I felt about my life, where I came from, it was deep in me. I didn't want him to see. I should have been wary of that, too. How can you make a life with someone if they don't know you? I didn't understand this, not then. I wanted to go into the world new, like a snake shedding its skin. But it was more like cutting out a vital organ, thinking it would allow me to survive.

* * *

I didn't want him to meet Jude, nor Chris, my brother — Jude's own kid — and definitely not Abi, my foster sister. I didn't want him to see the little kids screaming the house down. He wouldn't understand them. He didn't especially want to meet them either. It was inconvenient for him, for one thing, as he lived in the north. I'd been to stay with him but he'd never come back down. This made sense, practically, as he had a house of his own. He was a grown-up. But when I told Jude I was moving in with him, she lost her mind.

"Over my dead body are you running off to live with a man I've never even met!"

She wasn't just angry, she was hurt, betrayed. Now that I have children of my own, I understand this. If you did the same thing, I would be devastated. But even after living with Jude my whole life, I didn't think of her that way. It had always felt temporary, at least to me.

"I'll just come down and meet her," your father said. "Don't worry — I'm good with mams."

"It's not that," I said. "I know you'd be great. It's just the house, the kids—"

"Don't worry about it. It'll be fine."

He didn't understand. People like your father have never seen homes like the one I came from. The chaos, the shouting, the unwashed clothes on the kitchen counters, the McDonald's boxes on the living room floor, ketchup packets ripped open.

11

And among all this, babies — actual babies — kicking their legs and crawling through the rubbish.

The next time I stayed with him we agreed he'd drive me back down on the Sunday and spend the afternoon with Jude. The night before, I couldn't sleep. It was excessive, how frightened I felt. Or maybe it wasn't. It seemed a real possibility to me that once he saw where I came from he would no longer want me.

"Maybe we should all go into town?" I said to him as we drove back down. "There's a fish and chip shop. There's a café, too."

He laughed. "Stop worrying."

As we walked up the front path, I glanced at him, studying his reaction to the sandpit littered with crisp packets, the broken toys. His face gave nothing away. As I turned my key in the lock, the sounds of the children inside were fainter than usual. I opened the door, stepped into the porch. I looked around. The hall, normally a mess of toys and coats, was clear. It seemed to have a new floor, too. Then I realised — I had hardly ever seen the floor, not like this. The children's shoes had been pushed into the corner and their coats hung up above. I glanced into the living room. There were cushions on the couch — cushions! — and the carpet was hoovered. The television was off.

And there was something else. The children were gone.

Jude appeared, holding one of the new girls, a two-year-old sucking a dummy and staring at your father. Jude looked at me. "Your face!" she laughed. "I do know how to clean, you know!"

* * *

It wasn't the plan for me to go back with him that same day. But your father didn't want to drive four hours home only to come back down to collect me later.

"Why not just come back with me now?" he said. "What's the difference?"

He had a point. But the difference, to Jude, was huge. She felt ambushed. She thought we had planned it that way.

"You're not even packed!" she said.

"It won't take long," I said, but I didn't like the rushing much, either. Your father was right, I told myself. It wasn't fair to make him drive back down.

Yet something was wrong.

I put my clothes in carrier bags. I didn't own a suitcase and I had very few things. As I loaded the bags into the boot of his car your father eyed them.

"I don't have a suitcase," I explained. He nodded. But he looked unhappy about the carrier bags.

Your father was perfectly nice — he had been the whole time — and when we left, he kissed Jude lightly on the cheek and said, "I'll look after her. Don't worry."

Jude looked at him. She was cool but I knew she disliked him. He hadn't won her over, not at all. I didn't expect to care but I did. It made me worry. It made the something-wrong feeling get bigger as your father climbed into the driver's seat and turned on the engine.

I gave Jude a long hug. She began to cry.

"I'll come back and visit soon," I said.

"I don't know why you're doing this," she said. "Have I done something?"

"No!" I said. "Not at all. I'm not leaving you. I'm just leaving. I will see you soon. I promise."

"What will I do without you?" she said.

"You'll manage," I said, and it sounded colder than I intended.

She looked at me. "It's too fast," she said.

* * *

As we began the long drive north, a feeling overcame me, like I was not so much travelling forward with the movement of the car as rising from my seat. What was taking place in the car — your father's light chatter, the music on the radio

— did not feel real. When I looked at the objects around me, I could not connect them to myself. I glanced down at the water bottle in the drinks' holder between us. I imagined touching it, lifting it to my lips. But I sensed it would vanish in my fingers. I could not seem to connect with my body. I didn't know if I was hot or cold, hungry or full. There was only my mind, expanding.

THREE

When you hear a mother has left her children — particularly if they were young at the time — you think she must be insane. A friend of mine once told me about a man she knew whose wife left him and their young children. Years later, one of the children committed suicide. The mother came back for the funeral. My friend was at the funeral, too, and when she saw her, the mother said, "This is all my fault." My friend didn't contradict her. "I wanted to," she said. "But I couldn't."

* * *

Your father let me in — for no other reason, I thought, than he didn't know what else to do. He couldn't force me to leave. He also knew — as I did — that if I walked over to the farm, Nia and John would let me in. Not because they didn't despise me for leaving my children, but because this wasn't a community to turn away a mother. I was still a mother.

But he was thinking hard. From the second I stepped into the house he was thinking about what he was going to do. Your father was a clever man. And he was not a man who liked to lose.

Following him into the living room, I didn't sit down. Neither did he.

"David—"

"I don't want to hear it," he said.

"Okay. Can we talk about the girls?"

"The ones you abandoned?"

I had anticipated all this — the scolding and blaming, the intense moral authority that had withered me long before the accident. I had never been good enough for him. I had never been as good as him. Your father was taught, probably before he could speak, that he was special and good. I was taught the opposite. While I was away, I had come to understand that this belief about myself informed not just the things I did but how readily I believed everything your father told me. I took it all at face value because I had already bought into the premise. Confirmation bias, Ben called it. "We have certain beliefs about ourselves, formed when we are very young. We spend our lives looking for evidence to support them." This revelation had stunned me. I tried to hold its implications at the forefront of my mind as I travelled home — the things your father said were not necessarily true. My instinct to believe him was not necessarily reliable. I needed to struggle against both.

I thought about what he'd just said, about abandoning the girls. There was a contradiction here, and it needed exposing.

"Wasn't that what you wanted?" I said.

"I beg your pardon?"

"At the hospital, when you told me I had nearly killed our daughter. When you said Catrin nearly died because of me. When you said I wasn't fit to look after our children. What exactly did you expect me to do?"

He watched me carefully. "I didn't expect you to abandon them, on top of everything else you'd done."

"But why would you want me here — why would you want me around them — if you didn't think I was capable of keeping them safe? Surely it was better for everyone that I left?"

He sighed. "You don't just run away from your responsibilities, Elin. That's not how it works."

I nodded slowly, trying to hold on to the fragile threads of my mind, so easily entangled with his. But all my convictions were dwindling under his gaze.

"It doesn't make sense," I said. "If you really thought it was my fault—"

"I didn't *think* it was your fault. It *was* your fault. That was pretty clear to everyone involved."

"So then why would you want me to look after them?"

He sighed. "I'm not doing this, Elin. It was painful enough at the time."

"How are they?" I said.

"It's none of your business."

"You have to let me see them."

"I don't have to do anything."

"Yes, you do. You know you do." A familiar keening entered my voice and I despised it, as I knew he did. Though it was he who made me this way — weaker, less sure of myself — he also hated me for it. That was the unfairness — and the stupidity.

"And what if they don't want to see you?"

"They will. I'm their mother."

"Now you're their mother," he muttered, walking into the kitchen. I heard him turning on the tap, popping open the lid of the kettle. "I need coffee."

"Coffee would be good," I said, though he hadn't offered. "Black with one sugar, please."

He came back a few minutes later, carrying two mugs and pushing one into my hand. "I know how you have your coffee."

* * *

All around there were photos of you, new ones that had been put up in my absence. I wanted to look at them. I don't think you'll understand until you have children of your own what it was like to be away from you, the pain of waking each morning to stillness and silence, no one crying out for me from a nearby room or climbing into bed beside me, that urgent daily rush of love and want — gone. I wanted to look at the photos. But I couldn't.

"Where are you planning to stay?" he asked.

Honestly, I hadn't thought about it, and it's the kind of thing — it was always the kind of thing — that drove your father crazy. The lack of planning. The last-minute decisions. What he would describe as recklessness. He had never found it endearing. It was always careless, thoughtless, inconsiderate. He was right, in a way.

"Maybe at Tŷ Gwyn?"

He shook his head, putting down his mug. "There's no way they'll have room. It's the school holidays."

"Is it?"

He sighed. "Yes."

"So where are the girls?"

He looked at me, wearied by my question, my cluelessness, my existence. I had been home no more than twenty minutes.

"They're with my mother."

"Oh. Of course."

"She's taken Catrin to a hospital appointment."

"Why?" I said. "What's wrong?"

That look of tired disdain again, but elevated to utter contempt. I felt a familiar humiliation. It was all in his eyes. And it was inside me, the core of myself ripe for degradation. A direct line existed between us. It was what connected us. Yet somehow I had thought I could come back here and override it with the things I had learned about myself, while far away from him, in the last ten months. There was one thing he was right about — I had always been naive.

"Are you really asking that?" he said.

"Yes. Why? What do you mean?" A hollow feeling slipped through me. "You mean because of the accident?"

He placed his hands comically on his cheeks, his face contorted in mimicry. "*You mean because of the accident?*" His expression turned back to cool disregard. "I suppose you left before you had to deal with any actual consequences."

"I just thought that once she'd been treated then, you know, she just . . . I don't know—"

He watched me impassively. My mind whirred. The pressure that had been building in my head all morning intensified, turning to a searing pain at my temples. I brought my fingertips to my forehead, closing my eyes. As the pain deepened, my body seemed to recede, get lighter. I was swaying, my body full of air, my head reeling. Somehow I moved over to the couch and held on.

"Help me," I heard myself say.

Far away I heard your father swear under his breath. Then his hands were on me. I struggled against him. He pushed harder, the heat of his body behind me.

"Stop resisting," he said.

He forced me across the living room into the kitchen, the track lights painfully bright, and down into a chair, pressing my head between my knees. I drew in gulps of air that seemed to evaporate before they reached my lungs.

* * *

When I had calmed down enough, he led me upstairs, holding my hand as I stumbled behind him like a child.

"Where are you taking me?"

"To lie down."

"I don't want to. I'm fine."

He ignored me. At the top of the stairs he opened the door to the nursery — what had been your room as a baby, and still your sister's when I'd left. I stared into the small room and looked at your father.

"Why are we in here?"

"It's the spare room."

"It's not Catrin's anymore?"

"She's three and a half, Elin. Do you think she's still in the cot?"

"No," I said. "I just thought you'd put a bed in here."

"She's in the other room now, next to Rhiannon."

"Why?"

"She wanted to be next to her sister. Elin, do you want to see the girls or not?"

"Yes. But I can stay somewhere else, it's fine."

"There is nowhere else. I told you."

"I don't mean holiday places. I can stay with Ema or . . . There are loads of people!"

He looked at me evenly.

"Have you spoken to any of those people recently?"

He shut the door behind him, enclosing us in the baby room. It had once been no more than a storage space, by far the smallest room upstairs. But I wanted you next door to us, not down the landing, so I had the dilapidated shelves removed, painted the walls, filled it with soft toys and sheepskin rugs. The cot was still here, bare and emptied of bedding. The mobile hung above it, a pale wooden circle dangling felt stars and crescent moons. I had installed the hook myself when I was pregnant with you, reaching up from the ladder as I twisted it into the ceiling, plaster dust falling into my eyes. I remembered vividly how I had stepped down and stared at that mobile, feeling sad and chilled to know that twirling shapes could not ease the loneliness of infancy, alone in a cot with no beating heart but your own.

"Elin." Your father moved closer to me. "There is no one who will take you in. Not after what you did. None of those people want to see you."

* * *

Beside the cot was the futon I had slept on a hundred times when you or Catrin were poorly or unsettled or in one of those dreaded sleep regressions where you wanted to feed through the night like a newborn. Your father brought me blankets and I lay down on the rough fabric, falling asleep and dreaming instantly about your sister. Even in the depths of sleep, I recognised the scene and tried desperately to wake up. But my dream-mind was busy, conjuring a memory — real but distorted. Catrin was a toddler, uneasy on her feet. She wore denim dungarees, which, even as I slept, I knew was not right. Though I remembered nothing about the accident itself, I knew I had put her down in the cot beforehand, dressed in a clean nappy and a sleepsuit.

In the dream she pulled idly at leaves, tugged the heads of flowers off their stalks and put them in her mouth. She plunged a chubby hand into soil that was squirming, in the dream, with worms. She pulled one out and brought it to her face, studying it carefully. A bucket was there, a metre or so from her. She hadn't noticed it yet. It was large and metallic, weighed down by the heavy liquid inside.

Now it caught her eye. She moved over, gravitating towards an unknown object, full of possibility. As she approached, she craned her neck, reached out her hands.

* * *

I woke to voices. You were in the garden with your sister, the dog barking frantically while you laughed. Downstairs your nain was talking to your father, outraged, demanding to know exactly what my intentions were. She wasn't trying to keep her voice down. They were in the hall. I moved over to the door to hear more clearly. "What are you planning to tell the girls?" she kept asking your father. I didn't understand the question.

As though he sensed I was awake and listening, your father said, "Let's go in there."

A door closed. They were in the living room. That was the only room that led off from the hall.

I checked my phone. It was quarter to four. The clouds were low outside the window. I went onto the landing. The stairs running down to the darkened hall were dangerously steep. I lost track of the number of times you had tripped, running up or down them with overexcitement, and more

21

than once after moving in I had banged my head on the stooped ceiling that slanted above them. Slowly, I moved down the stairs, leaning against the slack wooden banister to make my footsteps light. As I reached the point where the wall receded, leaving only the banister between myself and the closed living room door, the conversation grew clearer.

"It's hard to believe she vanished for ten months and then reappeared out of nowhere," your nain was saying.

"Well, that's what's happened."

"Where has she been?"

"We didn't get that far."

There was a silence.

"After you texted me," she said briskly, "I rang Nia from the farm. I wanted to ask her—"

"Jesus, Mam. What are you doing ringing the neighbours? They think you're a lunatic."

"They certainly do not think I'm a lunatic! And let me tell you, they were my neighbours before they were yours. Anyway, what Nia did say is that she was out in the field when Elin drove up here, and when she saw her get out of the car, she thought it was someone else. You know, a visitor or something. It didn't even occur to her it was Elin."

"Fascinating, Mam. Maybe we should get Nia round here?"

"This is serious, David!"

"I'm aware."

They fell quiet again. I remembered a time after you were born when your father was on the phone to your nain. They talked a lot on the phone, though he never rang her. She called him, sometimes several times a day, wanting to know how he was, if he needed anything. New socks? Hay fever tablets? Groceries? Things he could acquire for himself. But she thought of him as a child, that was how she was. Anyway, you were a tiny baby. I was a new mother. I had just got back to the house, pushing you in the pram that she had bought for us. I had taken you for a walk along the track. It was October, the weather light but tipping into autumn, damp leaves piling on the ground. You were four months. I had felt desperate when I left the house, you writhing with tiredness, spitting out your dummy. But the walk settled you, the air clean and fresh against your hot baby skin. It settled me, too. When we got back, I parked the pram in the hall, you sound asleep under the hood, and I heard them in the kitchen, your nain on speakerphone while your father made his coffee.

"There's something not right about how she is with the baby," said your nain. "She acts like she's not even her mother."

Those were her words. It's hard to describe how I felt. Devastated, yes. You were my baby; how dare anyone say I didn't feel it? At the same time, I felt exposed. She was right, in a way. I didn't know how to play the role, not how I was supposed to. Particularly not with other people around. In fact, I was embarrassed — ashamed — by the intensity of what I felt, the contradictions, the high-strung alertness, the drowning exhaustion, the irrational defensiveness if anyone seemed to criticise you. It was as raw and primitive as the birth and breastfeeding and everything that had come with this induction to motherhood — and that had nothing to do with the soft maternal image imposed from afar, telling you to love your children the right way, the uncomplicated way, the unthreatening way, making you wonder why you were feeling it wrong.

Anyway, she said it so casually. I remember that. And your father didn't defend me. I remember that, too.

* * *

I felt that same feeling of exposure now, my integrity undermined by Nia's throwaway comment. I didn't even know what your nain meant by sharing it with your father. So Nia hadn't recognised me — so what? My hair was shorter. I had lost a lot of weight while I had been away. She had only seen me from a distance.

"Well," your nain was saying. "She's got a lot of explaining to do. Child desertion is a crime, you know." She was

23

breathless with indignation now. "She has no right to be anywhere near those girls. Especially Catrin."

Your father sighed. "Speaking of the girls, I need to go and get something for their tea."

"Oh, please, David, you're not going to tell them their mother's home?"

Your father raised his voice. "That is what I'm going to tell them because that is, in fact, the case."

If I were your nain, I would have excused myself at this point. But still she went on.

"Please try to think clearly, David. You mustn't get their hopes up when you don't know what she's planning. What if she doesn't stay? I think you should tell her to leave before the girls know anything about it. Once she's got a firm plan then we can see, can't we? You mustn't let her think it's okay to just turn up like this. The last ten months have been hell for those girls. Who does she think she is?"

Your father laughed. But his voice turned cold. "You'd better go now. I appreciate your input. Not to mention Nia's. But I need to be alone with the girls tonight."

"David," she said, as though starting to cry. So often she would break down in the face of his coldness and I should have sympathised — I knew how it felt — but to me her tears were ridiculous, theatrical. And in your father, of course, it only ever provoked disgust. "I really think I ought to be here," she was saying. "The girls are going to be very confused. I'm not sure you're in the right state of mind to look after their needs—"

The living room door handle turned and I scrambled upstairs, hiding in the nursery doorway as your father stepped into the hall, his keys jingling.

"I'd like you to be gone when I'm back," he said.

She was at his heels. From the garden I could hear you shrieking happily, Catrin giggling, the dog still barking. Crouched in the shadows, I saw your father's work boots moving towards the front door. Your nain's shoes clipped the tiles behind him. Before she could say anything else, he opened the front door and slammed it behind him, leaving her panting like an old dog. In the silence I sensed she knew where I was. I had always felt, with your nain, that her instincts were heightened in this way. Her feet shuffled. I shrank further into the shadows. But she didn't climb the stairs. Nor did she leave, as your father had asked. Instead she turned on her heels and headed back into the house.

FOUR

While I was away, I saw a therapist called Ben. I knew nothing about him beforehand except that he was Dr Benjamin Curtis, a psychologist at a clinic I was referred to not long after leaving you. He introduced himself as Ben, letting me know I could call him that, though I never really had cause to use his name. He used mine all the time. "Elin," he would say, before making an observation or asking a question, and I felt he had probably been taught to do that, a technique to demonstrate his attentiveness.

The room was light and airy and smelled of citronella, as did the corridors and waiting room beyond. The window was open. Ben caught me looking at it as our session started.

"I can close it, if you prefer?" he said.

"It's fine," I said.

"I opened it to get some air into the room. They must have put fresh diffusers in the sockets this morning." He was talking about the citronella smell. "I don't mean to be rude but it stank when I got in this morning."

I laughed.

"Let me know if you want me to close the window," he said again. "It's not a problem."

I couldn't understand why he was talking to me this way, with so much concern for my comfort. It was disorientating and it made me suspicious at first. But as the sessions went on I realised it was genuine, this wish that I be comfortable. It wasn't a trick. The other thing that struck me about Ben was how gentle-mannered he was. He was tender and softly spoken, and his eyes were cool and blue. I knew it was a common experience — maybe even a cliché — that your therapist can evoke in you a certain longing. I had felt that longing as a child, when I watched films with particular actors whose good looks I mistook for decency and kindness. Later on, when things came out online and in the papers about some of those men — how they had cheated on their wives, humiliated women on purpose, even touched women who didn't want to be touched — I experienced a ripping apart of the world as I had believed it to be. Sometimes I think you are growing up in a very different world to the one I grew up in. Other times I think it's no different at all.

* * *

In the sessions I was guarded at first, as he would eventually say I was with all people. It was uncomfortable, feeling his complete focus, how he listened to every word I said. There was no phone in his hand. He wasn't half watching television or thinking about something else, and while feeling grateful for this attention, I also had a prickly sense of exposure, like a creature uncovered in the grass.

During our second appointment, the pressure of what I was concealing from him became unbearable and I blurted it out. "You know I have children, don't you?"

As he looked at me, I felt a sting of remorse. I didn't want him to hate me. Though I had only known him an hour and a half in total, I felt it would have crushed me. During this time away from you I was incredibly vulnerable, surprised to find that, as difficult as parenting had been, you had been a shield for me, in some important way, from all the things I had been hiding from. Without you, there was nothing around me. And it was terrible, like falling through space and time with no promise of landing. But I needed to go through it.

Anyway, I think this was why I was so irrational about Ben, feeling that if he disliked me I would die. But he didn't flinch. If he was shocked or appalled, he didn't show it. If I were him, I would have said, "You didn't mention them last week when I asked about your family." But if I were him, I would have been trained not to say such things.

"I didn't know that," he said. "What are their names?"

"Rhiannon and Catrin."

"Would you like to talk about them?"

The room was no quieter than usual but I became aware of my breath, which sounded intrusively loud. I tried not to focus on it, knowing if I did its rhythm would change and Ben would think I was upset by the mention of my children, that something was wrong.

"I know what you must think," I said.

"What must I think?"

"That I'm a terrible person. A terrible mother. A monster, really."

"Is that what you think about yourself?"

Beyond him, the window was open and the large sycamore outside, darkly leafy, was wet with rain. You could smell the dampness of the leaves. I looked back at Ben. He was watching me. I didn't want to talk about what I thought about myself. That will sound stupid, I know, as this was therapy. But I really didn't.

FIVE

Living with your father, I had certain things for the first time in my life. It's nice to have things. Don't let anyone pretend it doesn't make a difference. I'm not saying you should spend your life trying to have them, just that it's no good pretending they don't mean anything. Growing up with Jude, I was never hungry. I'm grateful for that. I knew kids who were. Jude knew how to make the money she had go a long way, that a big pot of chilli or spaghetti bolognese cost little to make, and she took the time to make those things. When I became a parent I looked back in wonder at Jude finding the time and energy and organisation to cook wholesome meals for the fleet of children in her care. I struggled to do it for two.

So at mealtimes we had as much as we wanted and on Saturdays we went to McDonald's for a treat, littering the back of the car with dropped chips and Happy Meal boxes. And the house was warm in winter — that was another thing. We were never hungry and never cold.

We just didn't have anything else. I'm not complaining about that. I'm just explaining the novelty and the thrill of being with your father, who bought takeaway coffee and sourdough bread from the artisan bakery like it was nothing, and gave me a present whenever he felt like it. Jewellery, underwear, perfume. None of it was my taste, exactly. But I didn't have taste. You need money for that.

One Saturday, he took me shopping. He'd been wanting to do this for a while. My clothes were pretty awful by his standards, though I hadn't really thought about it before I met him. I had two or three items of clothing that were respectable, all of them hand-me-downs from Jude. But once I moved in, he saw how little I had and how cheap and worn out were my everyday clothes.

As we walked between the rails at the department store a two-hour drive away, I realised he knew what he was looking for. I was reminded of a story I'd heard from a friend of Jude's about a church minister who married a young Spanish woman who wore floral dresses and tube tops with tight jeans. The minister found her clothing inappropriate and the woman agreed to change. Soon she began to wear the same clothes as the minister. Often, they wore an exactly matching outfit. As your father and I walked among the clothes, I had a strange thought that maybe this was about to happen to me, too, and I wanted to laugh. My head felt airy, my body light.

"There are so many clothes in these places," I said.

He squeezed my hip. "Leave it to me."

I wandered among the make-up, picking up tester lipsticks and rolling them along my hand. A shop assistant watched me and I felt immediately, as I always had, that she was waiting for me to steal. When your father found me, he was holding a selection of clothes over his arm.

"How do you know my size?" I said.

"Easy."

* * *

The changing rooms were endless, swirling with mirrors and floral curtains. I took the clothes while your father sat on a couch in the waiting area. The cubicle felt warm and airless. There was an itching at my temples. There were three mirrors, swallowing me with the image of myself. I hung the clothes on the back of the door and tried on one dress after another. It was a tremendous effort, taking off each item and bringing the next one down over my body, lifting my arms, bending my knees. The clothes were dusty pastel colours I had never worn, the fabrics soft and delicate. I couldn't help but think of the old ladies I had not long ago been dressing for their weddings and christenings, and though I had enjoyed it, making them feel they would look their best, I felt ridiculous now, like a child.

The tightness in my chest turned to a tugging sensation. There was pressure in my head. When I stepped out into the waiting area, back in my old clothes, your father was on the couch with his legs spread wide, his arm draped over the back.

He smiled. "Well?"

I opened my mouth then hesitated.

"Listen," he said, holding up his hand. "You don't have to worry about the cost."

"I know," I said, glancing at the nearby shop assistant, who was pretending not to listen. "I mean, thanks."

I sat down next to him, thinking about how, since I was very young, I had been able to make myself like things I didn't like. I don't mean pretend to like them but truly like them. I was a blank slate that anyone could draw on and I understood, early, that it was possible to like and be whatever others wanted. This was how I could eat all my food while the other kids threw theirs on the floor, and say thank you for my birthday present and smile gratefully, even if it wasn't really what I wanted.

I didn't like the clothes in my hands but I would.

"I'll have them all," I told your father.

* * *

Your father brought up children for the first time at the café we went to on Saturday mornings. It was on the air

31

ambulance base, glass walls overlooking a landing strip where red helicopters rose into the sky, rotors spinning, then vanished into the distance.

"That's the mistake they always make," he was saying.

I turned my head to see him looking at a little girl, aged two or three, hiding beneath a chair, her lips stained with chocolate. Her mother was chiding her lazily, her heart not really in it as she gossiped with the friend opposite her.

Quietly, your father did an unflattering impression. *"This is your last chance. I'm not telling you again."*

These observations became routine and I was amazed his views on parenting were so evolved, given he had never had children. He hated dummies, he said, and safety harnesses. "It's all just a way of getting out of parenting your kid. If you want them to sleep, rock them. If you don't want them to run in the road, hold their hand. Why do people have kids if they can't be bothered to look after them?"

I listened carefully and I was surprised by my impulse to argue. Your father didn't know the responsibilities I'd had, growing up. The truth was I had looked after every age and temperament of child and I knew the value of dummies and safety harnesses, and anything — God, anything — that lets you make it through the day with none of them harmed.

I knew your father would want children. He didn't have to tell me. I also knew I wasn't ready. Even with this life we were living together, I couldn't get rid of a longing to go backwards, to retrieve whatever I had lost that might allow me to assume the grown-up existence awaiting me. But this was impossible. And anyway, I didn't understand what was missing.

* * *

A few weeks later, I woke up next to your father and walked into the bathroom. It was a Sunday. Looking in the mirror, I had that suspended morning feeling, a kind of humming fear that hadn't attached itself to anything because the day hadn't begun. After I'd been to the toilet and washed my hands, I opened the drawer beneath the sink, as I did every morning, to find that my pills were missing. I pulled everything out of the drawer, reaching into the back. I looked in the cupboard below and the shelves above the sink, rummaging between your father's razors and dental floss. But I wouldn't find them there. I knew what had happened to them.

I walked back into the bedroom. Your father was asleep, his mouth open as he breathed into his pillow. Through the window, the sun was edging up, spreading an orange glow through the pale light above the mountains. With no uncertainty I knew he had taken them. I think a part of me had expected him to. Strangely, I wasn't angry. In a way, I was relieved. The decision had been made for me. I didn't have to agonise. I didn't have a choice. A month later, I was pregnant.

SIX

Nothing could prepare me for seeing you again. There were mornings before I left when seeing you after a night apart — a night when you'd been asleep just down the landing — made me tearful. I'd be overwhelmed by the fact of your existence, the relief that you were safe and here and still mine, and it awakened in me daily the pulsing fear that I might lose you. It was constant heartache to love you as I did.

And now this.

Months apart and somehow I would have to walk back into your orbit with some kind of composure. Ten months is an eternity in the life of a child. Not only to be missing your mother but the changes I knew you would have been through. I had never been able to accept the speed with which you changed. People could tell me as much as they liked — *They grow so fast!* — it made no difference. All I could do was take each day as it came, try not to think about the march of time, the future or the past. I would scroll through my phone while you were sleeping, look at pictures and videos taken only months earlier, and be amazed by your tottering movements, your plumper face, the immaturity of your speech. You had renewed, in a matter of months, as surely as a starfish regrowing lost limbs.

34

I didn't like it.

Not the fact you had changed — you were meant to, I knew that — but that I had grown apart from the old you, it didn't feel as close and familiar as the newer version. One day I told myself to stop looking back.

* * *

I went out into the garden. Your nain was still here. I wasn't surprised. Why would she leave you with me? Why had he asked her to? Still, I wished she wasn't watching. The two of you were playing beneath the apple trees. You had a mud kitchen. Your father must have built it for you. Your nain was on the bench beneath the kitchen window, her long skirt almost touching the patio floor. She watched me like a cat as I moved towards you. Your sister was laughing, a fallen apple in her hands, touching the tip of her tongue to it.

"Na, Catrin!" you said. "*Paid a twtsiad. Ych!*" You were telling her not to touch the apples on the ground, that they were dirty. But it was only making her laugh and you laughed with her. "Look," you said, reaching up towards the branches, showing her the fresh apples growing there. "*Byta rhain yn lle,*" you said. *Eat these instead.* "But let's wash them, *iawn*? Catrin!"

I stood on the patio, watching. I couldn't get my head round the sight of either of you, so familiar to me and so head-spinningly new. You were taller and slimmer, less puppy fat on your arms and belly. This had been a gradual process since you were a baby, but the change was drastic and shocking to me now. Your hair was as thick and dark as ever but longer, tied in a neat plait at the nape of your neck. You wore white trainers and dark leggings and a T-shirt with a red dragon breathing flames.

People had always liked to tell me how much you looked like your father, and you were as pointedly like him as ever. But I was struck by features I didn't recognise and I wondered, as I had in the past, about all the people in your blood whom you — and I — had never even met. My mother

35

and father, for example. Your father's father, whose name we knew, but little else. All the ghosts in our DNA, estranged but living inside us.

The change in Catrin was more dramatic. She was so much bigger than she had been ten months before, her wispy, light-brown hair straighter and shoulder-length now rather than curling boyishly around her ears. She was taller, of course, and sturdier on her feet. Her style of clothing had not changed. She wore a multicoloured tutu over rose-patterned leggings and an Elsa vest, as she would call it, with a picture of the sisters from *Frozen*. Not long before I left, she had reached the point of refusing to wear anything but her Elsa dress (which, I assumed, she had finally now outgrown). However dirty and food-stained it was, she would take it from the washing basket, saying, "I want Elsa!" So I bought her another one. But within two days — sometimes, one day — they were both dirty. She needed ten Elsa dresses.

What really shocked me was her scar. The day I left she was in a hospital cot, bandaged from her head to her waist. But somehow I hadn't expected what was in front of me now: my three-year-old girl, her toddler skin once pure and unblemished, now disfigured by a tangled mess of swollen, inflamed flesh. The scarring deformed one side of her face, her ear misshapen, the skin cratered and coarse, and spread down over her shoulder and arm. She was really and truly maimed. Why hadn't I expected it? Why had I deluded myself that the burns would quickly heal?

While I was crushed by seeing her like this, you and she were acting like it was nothing, just carefree children playing with apples. She scampered in delight beneath the tree, the fallen apple in her hands. You tugged a fresh one from its stem. As you held it out to her, you saw me on the patio and stared across the grass in confusion before a darker expression crossed your face. I stayed still. I didn't want to frighten you. It was too late. You started to scream.

* * *

"She thought you were a ghost," said your nain. "What did you expect would happen, creeping up on them like that?"

She was holding you in her lap, brushing your damp, tangled fringe off your forehead with her fingertips. You had your arms around her neck, head resting on her shoulder. Your limbs looked so gangly to me, too long for your body.

"I wasn't creeping up on them. I just wanted to see them."

"You should have waited for David to come home. I'm sure he will have wanted to sit the girls down and prepare them first. Oh, well. Too late now."

Your sister was standing on her chair at the kitchen table, licking a biscuit.

"*Diod!*" she said, looking at your nain, demanding a drink.

Your sister was speaking more Welsh than she had been when I left and I wondered if your father had put her in Cylch, once I wasn't around to look after her. Your father rarely spoke Welsh to either of you, though he could speak it fluently, having grown up here. Your nain didn't speak it. Though she had moved here when she was a young woman, she had refused to learn, though she knew more than she let on.

"Just a minute, darling," she said to Catrin. "Your sister is still very shaken."

"I'll get it," I said.

Catrin stared at me in disbelief, as though she hadn't realised I had the power to make drinks.

"What would you like?" I said.

"Oren," she said.

"*Orange juice, please,*" said your nain to Catrin. "Give her apple," she said to me. "She shouldn't have orange so close to bedtime. And make sure it's heavily diluted."

I nodded, moving around the kitchen, finding the cups, letting the tap run until the water was clear and cold. It was like driving after a long break, I was rusty but I knew how. The time I had spent in this kitchen — countless repetitive hours taking your colourful plastic bowls out of the cupboard, filling them with cereal, crackers, cut-up fruit, sweeping spilled remains from the floor, rinsing the bowls, drying them, putting them away. It had seemed there would be no end to it.

"Does she still have milk before bed?" I asked. I wasn't sure why I asked it. It just popped into my head, as it was after five, that she might need a bottle. Your nain stared at me as though I had been unimaginably thoughtless. Maybe I had.

"No," she said. "She does not."

* * *

The front door opened, a chill drifting down the hall and into the kitchen. I was hovering near the fridge, wary of sitting at the table where you remained in your nain's lap, still recovering from the shock of seeing me. From where I was standing, I saw another figure in the doorway with your father. A petite woman, carrying shopping.

"I'll do their tea," she was saying. "You go shower."

"Are you sure?"

Catrin put down her juice, banging the bottle loudly on the table, and scrambled off her chair. Before Catrin got anywhere near the woman, the dog had belted from her position in the open back doorway and shot into the hall, jumping up at the woman. The woman dropped the bags on the floor and stumbled back a little, rubbing the dog's ears affectionately.

"*Beti!*" she cried. "*Dwi di gweld dy golli di!*" She was telling the dog she was happy to see her. On her hind legs, the dog — Beti — was the same height as the woman. Catrin was standing behind Beti, waiting her turn. Noticing her, the woman pushed the dog to the floor and crouched down to face your sister, opening out her arms.

"And who else did I miss?"

"Me!" shouted Catrin.

"*Tyd â hyg i fi!*" said the woman. *Give me a hug.* Catrin jumped into her lap, flinging her arms around her neck and knocking her over as she did. The woman laughed.

I found myself in a dumb kind of shock as I watched all this. When she pushed herself off the floor and walked over to me, saying matter-of-factly, "Hi, Elin, I'm Greta. It's nice to meet you," I couldn't even force a smile. I just stared at her. *But who actually are you?* I wanted to say. *Why are you here?* As she watched me, waiting for some kind of response, I studied her dark eyebrows and long eyelashes, the thick freckles on her cheeks. She wore a loose long-sleeved top and one of those scarves tied in a knot at the top of her head, a snatch of dark hair sneaking loose to frame her eyes. But what I noticed most of all was that she was young. Younger than me. Twenty-one, maybe. Twenty-two. A nanny, I thought. That was all she was. Your father had employed a nanny. But I wasn't sure. Your father had disappeared upstairs for his shower before I could ask him, failing to make introductions or even be here for this dizzying awkwardness.

When I didn't say anything, Greta half smiled and moved away, setting about putting away the shopping. In spite of my shock, I couldn't help but notice that her energy was light and lovely, brightening the room as she moved around it. There was a vulnerability that made her unthreatening in spite of her competence. Her trainers were a mess, I noticed, scuffed and broken and covered in scratches.

"How are you, Agatha?" she said, acknowledging your nain like a second thought.

"Oh, struggling along, you know me."

Greta nodded, her back turned as she adjusted the knobs of the oven. Spinning back round to face you and Catrin, she said, "Who wants sausage and chips?"

Catrin was playing with her doll pram near the patio doors, trying her best to fold an old muslin — one I had used to swaddle you both when you were babies — and place it over her doll. The pram was the one your father and I had given her for her second birthday, six months before I left, a lovely wicker carrycot on large wooden wheels. She had played with it constantly back then and apparently still did.

39

At the mention of sausages, Catrin looked up, flinging her arm wildly in the air. "Me! Me! Me!"

"Me, please," you said, so quietly it was hard to hear you. You were still in your nain's lap, head buried in her shoulder, clammy and shell-shocked.

Greta looked at you sadly and walked over, taking you — boldly, I thought — from your nain's lap and lifting you to her hip. You didn't resist. As Greta held you, I noticed again the gangliness of your arms and legs.

"*Ti'n iawn, cyw?*" said Greta softly. *Are you okay, little one?* There was a soothing quality to her voice, especially when she spoke her mother tongue. Before I left, I had noticed that when Catrin was crying or hurt, you would often switch to Welsh to calm her down, as though it was the natural language to console a child. I had never minded people speaking Welsh to my children. I liked the fact you were growing up bilingual. But now, watching this woman talk to you in a language I didn't speak, and only understood at its most basic level, I found it very upsetting. I felt threatened and excluded. I knew this was wrong, that I had no right. But it didn't change the feeling.

Greta held you close, whispering indecipherable phrases in your ear. In spite of my feelings, there was something mesmeric about it. As I watched, you glanced from Greta to your nain, and then to me, fighting back tears. You had never liked being watched.

Greta put you down gently on the floor, letting you wander over to Beti, who was curled up again by the back door. You sat on the floor next to her, stroking her head. You were still tearful, overwhelmed, and no one, it seemed, was addressing the elephant in the room — me, your mother. Yet I felt paralysed. I had already upset you with the clumsy way I had handled seeing you again and it was clear to me that you weren't so much pleased as traumatised by my reappearance. There were far more competent caregivers all around me, including a woman I had met five minutes ago. Any confidence or conviction I had felt coming back was quickly collapsing.

There was movement in the hall and I was startled by your father entering the room, his hair wet and skin damp from his shower, wearing the jogging bottoms and slippers that he changed into in the evenings.

"Daddy?" said Catrin, pushing her pram over to him. "Greta's making sausage and chips!"

"Sausage and chips?" he said, picking her up and swinging her into the air. She shrieked in delight. He held her against him, frowning. "Who do I know who likes sausage and chips?"

"Me!" shouted Catrin, giggling.

"Is it nain?" he said.

"No, it's me!" she shouted, laughing more.

He put her down on the floor and walked over to Greta. "Can I help?" he said.

"I think I've got it under control," she said, turning to him, smiling. She placed her hand on his chest and stood on her tiptoes to kiss his cheek as he moved his hands round her waist.

* * *

"Tŷ Gwyn is full," said your father. "As I thought."

We were on the stairs, passing each other as he came down from putting Catrin to bed.

"How do you know?"

"I messaged Sioned."

"Oh," I said, struck by an irrational jealousy that he had formed a relationship with one of the school mums. Sioned owned Tŷ Gwyn — a well-established local bed and breakfast — and a fleet of caravans behind it. She was also the most proactive and well-connected of the mothers at your school, sending updates to the messenger group about upcoming PTA meetings, changes in uniform policy, the afterschool club. "You didn't have to do that."

"It was no trouble. I was already messaging her about something else. Anyway, you'll have to stay here for now. It's not the best futon in the world—"

"It's fine," I said, wondering why his tone had softened so much in the few hours since we had argued in the living room. He was still curt, standoffish, but not now actively hostile. "Is Rhiannon okay?" I said.

"She's confused," he said. "Understandably."

I didn't mention Greta. Neither did he. But she spent the night and acted in every way as though she was accustomed to doing so. Before your father read Catrin her stories and put her to bed, Greta bathed her, the two of them alone in the bathroom, the door wide open as Greta splashed water, Catrin giggling. Greta washed her hair, wrapped her in a towel and carried her to her bedroom. I could hear them talking, playing with Catrin's dolls before your father took over and Greta left the room, going next door to your bedroom and asking if you needed anything, telling you your father would be in soon to tuck you in. When I saw Greta on the landing, I didn't intend to treat her like she was in charge. But she was so natural, so good at it.

"Can I do anything to help?" I said to her.

She smiled, not unkindly. "I think we've got it covered."

Later, through the thick wall separating the nursery from your father's bedroom — their bedroom — I heard them arguing.

* * *

In the middle of the night there was coughing. I heard it in my dream, the noise coming from the mouth of a black dog. Stuck inside the dream, I was disturbed to see the dog coughing like a human and I wanted to wake up, aware that I needed to anyway, that in real life someone needed help. Untangling myself from sleep, I lay in the pitch dark, taken back to the winters when you and Catrin were unwell with a string of viruses and infections and how I would wake, in the dead of night, to haunting coughs and gasps for breath that filled me with hollow dread.

I knew instantly it was Catrin. I wanted to go to her. But I lay in the stillness instead, the night light a muted gleam in the dark, and wondered how often she coughed at night like this and if anyone would come.

There was movement on the landing. The floorboards creaked. A crack of light appeared at the foot of my door.

"Daddy!" you were shouting. The urgency in your voice alarmed me.

"I'm coming," said your father, his voice rough with sleep. I got out of bed and went to the door, opening it and watching as he moved down the landing, clutching something in his hand. Catrin's bedroom door was open and you were waiting for him there in your pyjamas, your hair loose and fuzzy. You glanced at me, your eyes puffy with sleep. Beyond the open doorway Catrin's room was dark, no sign of life except her spluttering coughing and sleepy cries for help.

Help her, I thought. *Someone help her!*

Your father disappeared into Catrin's bedroom. You followed, leaving me alone on the landing. "Come on, darling," I heard him say.

There was a sharp sucking, like someone drawing air through a straw. An inhaler. That was what your father had been carrying. After the third or fourth inhalation, Catrin settled, crying gently while your father soothed her.

"Daddy?" I heard you say once things had calmed down.

"What?"

"I was thinking, why don't we keep Catrin's inhaler in her bed? She knows how to use it. You don't have to bring it to her."

"I don't think so, Rhiannon."

"But, Daddy, what if you don't wake up?"

"That won't happen."

"But what if it does?"

"Rhiannon," he said, his voice gently threatening. "Go back to bed."

SEVEN

Once pregnant I had no idea what to do. Your father told me
to ring the surgery, telling me there would be scans to book,
vitamins to take. The receptionist gave me the number for
the community midwife, a woman called Cadi who saw all
the expecting mothers in the area. She was maybe in her late
fifties, and I liked her a lot. Older midwives were nicer than
their juniors, I found, less prone to condescension.

At my first appointment, Cadi handed me a cardboard
jug and an empty test tube. I sat on the toilet and listened
to the spatter of my urine, aware of Cadi on the other side
of the door. When I handed her the tube, it was warm. She
unscrewed the lid and dipped in a white piece of card, telling
me my urine was clear. I didn't ask what this meant and she
didn't tell me.

She recorded my weight and measured my blood pressure, the cuff slowly tightening around my arm. Next, she
drew blood, wheeling over a trolley laid with needles. She
held my arm in her hand, twisting it so my palm faced up,
and prodded the underside of my elbow, her neatly filed nails
digging into my wrist.

Soon she was filling out forms in quick, illegible hand-
writing. She asked me if I smoked — I didn't — and how

much I drank — not much — and whether my partner hurt me.

"No?" I said, alarmed by the question.

She smiled apologetically. "We have to ask."

When we reached the family medical history, she yawned. "Excuse me," she said.

"It's fine," I said. I was tired, too. Pregnancy was extraordinarily tiring and this appointment wasn't helping.

"Let's start with Mam's side," she said. "Any history of heart problems?"

When I didn't answer, she glanced at me. She was behind her desk now, so I could no longer see her sheer tights and polished shoes, only her immaculate hair and the top half of her pristine uniform.

"Oh, these forms," she said. "They're over the top. It won't be much longer now."

A dull pain settled behind my eyes.

"I was in care," I said. "I don't know anything about . . ." I waved towards the forms, unable to finish the sentence.

"Oh!" she said, her eyes widening. "I didn't know." She looked at me for a few seconds. Then she placed her hands palm down over the forms, as though the sight of them had become offensive. "We haven't got hold of your medical records yet." She frowned. "Where did you say you were before?"

I told her. She nodded.

"I never registered with the surgery after I moved here. I kept meaning to."

She nodded more vigorously. For a couple of minutes, she was flustered, muttering to herself. Then she stopped and looked at me. "This is your first baby?"

I had told her this twice already. But this time — the third time asking — she didn't have the absent-minded air of routine questioning. She had a concern, I felt — one that had presented itself when I told her my history. Another question lingered. I waited. But whatever it was, she decided not to ask.

* * *

Your father had told me early in my pregnancy that although he didn't like the idea of abortion, he could not cope with having a child with serious health difficulties.

"Down's syndrome?" I said.

"Any of it," he replied.

I understood where he was coming from. But in reality, the thought of having an abortion in those circumstances distressed me. One of Jude's foster babies, Michael, had a cleft lip and a twisted stomach so that he cried every time he took a bottle. Jude did, too, especially as Michael struggled to gain weight. She was back and forth to the hospital with him. Michael was another child, like me, who Jude wanted to adopt but couldn't afford to, so I suppose I thought about him with a certain affinity, the way he was both wanted and unwanted, rescued but never fully. The idea that I would reject a child like him, before it had had a chance to enter the world and make a case for itself, I found too much to bear.

* * *

As we travelled to the hospital for the twenty-week scan, I was filled with dread. They would test for eleven conditions, so Cadi had told me. Was your father really going to make me get rid of the baby at this stage in the pregnancy? And how would we decide what to do if we disagreed?

I tried not to think about it. Scans were supposed to be happy occasions, so I understood.

In the waiting room, your father wrote an email. I tried to distract myself by watching the video playing on the television in the corner. A woman on the screen was demonstrating how to burp a newborn, cooing in the baby's ear, rubbing circles on its back. The baby was unimaginably tiny, its floppy head supported by her hand. A new video began, showing a woman with frizzy brown hair and a birthmark on her face. "My baby had colic and cried all the time," she said. "I thought I was losing my mind. I would never hurt her but there were times when I wanted to shake her. I couldn't help it."

"Jesus Christ," muttered your father, glancing up at the video.

The waiting room was big and draughty, a window at the back letting in the autumn wind. A chill ran over me. On the screen, a doctor appeared, smiling as she explained the damage shaking a baby did to its brain, which was still soft, she said, like jelly. "The advice I would give is to leave the room. It's far better to walk away and leave the baby to cry, take a few minutes to regain your patience."

* * *

The sonographer was young and pleasant. She squeezed the big tube over my belly, clear gel quivering on my skin, and its coldness shocked me, as it had at the first scan. Your father sat to my left, the sonographer boosted high on a chair that aligned her with the monitor in front of her.

I was relieved your father had put his phone away. But there was a sharp, almost acidic tension in the air that I felt was coming from him. It hadn't been there when I had come here alone. It was his silence as the sonographer chatted away, and the way he held his body. I looked over at him. He didn't smile. She moved the probe over my belly, apologising as she dug it into my pubic bone, sliding it over to the side and pushing hard there instead. Swirls moved on the big screen above the bed.

"What's wrong?" said your father, looking at the sonographer.

I stared at him then looked back at her.

"Nothing," she said. "It just takes a while sometimes."

He was angry with her, I realised, how she knew more about his baby than he did.

Finally, she sighed. "Ah ha!"

And there you were, the white outline of a huge head and tiny limbs, dipping in and out of view, swimming inside a black hole.

The cursor hovered over the image, the sonographer dragging the mouse to create yellow lines across your head and body. She was measuring you, making sure you added up. Still watching her own screen, she said, "Would you like to know the sex?"

I had forgotten all about that. I looked at your father. He nodded.

"Yes, please," I said.

"You understand we can't be sure?" she said.

I nodded.

"From what I can see, it looks to me like you're having a little girl." She beamed. "Is that what you wanted?"

"I didn't mind," I said. That was true.

She smiled. "If you want print-outs, you'll need cash."

I looked at your father. "I don't have any. Do you?"

He shook his head.

"There's a cash point on the first floor," said the sonographer. I waited for him to get up but instead he pulled out his phone. I stared at him for a minute then looked back at the sonographer, embarrassed. She was watching your father carefully, measuring him as diligently as she was assessing you.

* * *

On the way home, I sat in the passenger seat, the seat belt threaded below my belly as Cadi had told me to always do now. An invisible line had been drawn between your father and me, and I didn't feel I could bring up what had happened in the scan. The sonographer had taken pity on me, and given me the print-outs for free anyway. That wasn't really the point. Looking at your father, I said, "What's wrong? I thought this was what you wanted."

"It is," he said. But he was far away. Reaching over my lap, he opened the glove compartment and found his sunglasses. It was maybe five minutes later, after we had left the hospital grounds and driven past the out-of-town stores looming over the busy road, that he finally muttered, almost to himself, "It'll be fine."

EIGHT

I had always felt, from very soon after she was born, that Catrin belonged to me in a way you never had. I do not mean in the sense of ownership. I never felt you were possessions, the way that many people seemed to view their children, as though parents brought new life into the world to be in some way served by it. I mean that Catrin was devoted to me. That was just how she was. Before she could speak I felt that she would do anything for me and that I needed to be careful with this power.

You were different. You had your own mind, usually at odds with what was expected. As young as two you resented the natural authority of your parents. By three you were vocal in telling us. "Do as you're told," your father would say, and you would look at him as though it was he who had overstepped the mark. You made discipline feel pointless, given you had no fear and little remorse.

You frightened me. I will admit that. Parents are often scared of their children but ashamed to say so, particularly when they are young. But small children can be frightening in many ways. I feared your fearlessness, the way you thought yourself immune from harm. One thing Ben taught me was that it's good for children to test limits and defy you; it's a sign that they feel safe to do so. When they don't it may mean something is wrong. But children need boundaries, too. "How do you balance those things?" I asked Ben once. "Parenting is like a bridge," he said. "A child can run more freely with strong railings on either side, a barrier against the water below."

* * *

The next morning you and your sister were awake at the crack of dawn. Sunlight slipped into the nursery through the gaps in the blind. Outside the door I heard the patter of little feet, you telling your sister *taw!* — be quiet. You went downstairs together, no parent to supervise. I wanted to come with you but I didn't want to frighten you again. Anyway, you had it under control. I listened from my bed as you clattered in the kitchen, opening and closing cupboards, telling Catrin to sit still on her chair. When breakfast was done, you turned on the television, which came on loudly before you turned down the volume.

Once she was awake and dressed, Greta got you both ready. Upstairs was pandemonium for a while, the two of you running between rooms, laughing, arguing over the smallest triviality, refusing help then asking for it, misplacing the clothes and shoes Greta had carefully selected for you. I remembered this well. Greta was more patient than me, able to stay calm in the face of chaos. Before you left, Greta knocked on the nursery door. I was getting dressed myself and put my head round the door.

"We're meeting a friend of mine at the beach, yeah?" she said. "You can come if you want?"

"Oh. Thanks," I said. I was torn between wanting to go and knowing that she was only being polite. "I need to sort a few things out first, but maybe I could spend some time with them later this afternoon?"

She looked at me. "Of course you can," she said. "You're their mam."

* * *

Then I was alone. Your father had gone to work. The house was quiet, the mountains through the windows silent and still. I went into the bathroom and looked down at the driveway, empty except for my car.

I went downstairs.

I had forgotten all about Beti, who barked in mutual surprise when she saw me, leaping off her bed. She was Greta's, I now understood. She lived here because Greta did, they had come together. It was more obvious to me, now I was paying better attention, that another woman lived here. Her coats were hanging by the front door, several pairs of her shoes on the rack beneath. The house was clean and tidy in the way that your father expected but had never done anything about himself except suggesting we employ a cleaner. And here was her dog, another new member of the family, more at home in this house than me.

She didn't lie back down, watching me instead as I paused in the doorway. She let out a low, unwelcoming growl, as she had when I was on the doorstep the day before. I considered going back upstairs. But that would only tell her I was an intruder. Instead I held out my hand for her, talking gently.

"You know me," I said. "I was here yesterday. Remember?"

It made me strangely sad to think she had forgotten. But as I talked, her ears pricked and she trotted over happily, pushing her nose into my palm. I massaged her soft ears until she relaxed, her tail wagging.

I walked into the room and she went back to her bed, flopping down, watching at first then closing her eyes.

I made myself a bowl of cereal and went into the living room. Through the bay window the light was strong, and the mountains — grassy in patches, slate-covered elsewhere — were like a picture, unreal through the glass. The photographs I had not looked at yesterday were still there, mounting the side tables, the windowsill and the mantelpiece. This was your nain's doing, I thought. I had never got round to putting up photos. There was no way your father had done it.

I walked over to the windowsill. There were photos that I had printed myself, taking you all the way to Boots in town and printing them on a self-service machine only to leave them lying around the house indefinitely. It was just like your nain to correct this, get things in order. Mostly it was baby and toddler photos, framed side by side, almost all taken by me. But it was a school photo I found myself staring at in the silent room. Striking in its sharpness and clarity, it was last year's — the one I had missed. You were posed behind your sister, unimaginably grown-up, your hair drawn back in a high ponytail, your smile serious and mature. You wore your navy school jumper, the circular logo embroidered on your breast, your light-blue collar tucked over the neckline. The same uniform you had worn since the first day I took you to the classroom door, a day I felt I might die from the pain of it but could tell no one, not even your father — especially not your father — what I went through.

In front of you was little Catrin, her eyes shining with laughter and mischief. We had tried it the year before, letting her sit in on your school photo, but she was too little, unable to hold herself on the bench independently, and even when you managed to steady her she would wriggle free and topple off. The photographer tried to hold her attention, make her laugh, but she didn't like him and kept looking towards me, wanting to climb down and come to me. But in this photo, a year later, she was ready, a steadfast two-year-old committed to the project. Her light hair had been plaited in pigtails, strands loose and static against her jumper. Like her hair, her skin was lighter than yours — it always had been.

And clear as day on the side of her face angled towards the camera was her awful scarring, the intense light of the studio seeming to almost showcase it. Looking at the photo, I suddenly felt angry, furious with the photographer for so tactlessly exhibiting this disfigurement of her beautiful face. They didn't care if Catrin was ashamed or embarrassed. They didn't care what it symbolised to her, to us, the people who had been there. She was just another child.

But Catrin didn't look ashamed. Not at all. She was cheerful, full of light. It was me who was ashamed. Most likely, for your sister, the scarring meant nothing by now, it was just part of her, like her hands or her feet. I wondered how well she even remembered the accident, a year later. In these early years memory was so strange and unpredictable. Small children seemed to keep with them the most random and trivial details — the colour of a cup they had drunk from at a certain place a year before — but forgot big important events only a month earlier.

As I moved away, my eyes caught sight of another picture, close to the school photo. I leaned in closer, realising, with surprise, that it was a picture of me. Alone on a dry mud path, tall crops stretching behind me into a clear blue sky. I wore shorts, a big sun hat and green wellies. It must have been taken before you were born. But I couldn't remember it being taken and I was sure I had never seen the photograph. It was like looking at a picture of someone else.

* * *

The photos had shaken me. All of it had shaken me. I had no right to be here, I was realising, as I ate the cereal I had not bought and walked around this house that did not belong to me. Technically, your father and I were still married. This was my house, too. But not really. Your father had moved on. He was with someone else. That was fine. I wasn't here for him. But in a way, you had moved on, too, charged forward with your lives. It wasn't clear that Catrin remembered me at all.

* * *

I needed to learn more about Greta. Catrin adored her, that was obvious. It shouldn't be too difficult — everyone knew everyone around here and plenty about them, their secrets circulating like old stories. I had learned this soon after moving here, especially after having you. Befriending the mothers had got me to the heart of it all. They knew everything. They made it their business to know everything. Information was the capital they traded in.

But your father said they didn't want to know me any-more. I was ostracised now, like the sisters who lived in the farm behind the chapel, one of them mad, the other believing the village was to blame for everything that had gone wrong in their lives. There was the house, though. There would be information here that told me more about who she was, where she had been. You were still out at the beach with Greta and the friends you were meeting.

I went to your father's room. It was the lightest room in the house, big wide windows looking out over the mountains. At first, it didn't appear any different to when I had left. Sheepskin rugs on hardwood floors, white cotton bedsheets, pale oak furniture. A pretty bedroom bleached of colour. But then I noticed certain things had gone — my hand-painted jewellery box that your father hated, the woven basket with my bracelets and sunglasses. The chest of drawers where these items had been was now bare on top except for the radio.

I walked over to it and pulled out the left-hand drawer where I had kept my underwear. All of it was gone and replaced by hers. Instead of my plain cotton pants — the comfortable, oversized kind that I'd worn through those relentless years of pregnancy and childbirth and breastfeed-ing — the drawer was now filled with the finespun lingerie of a childless woman — lace bralettes, satin vests, thongs.

The house was eerily quiet, more so now I was trespass-ing. I walked over to the window and looked down again at the drive, still empty except for my car. Even knowing that I would hear a car or van coming up the track, crunching stones on the gravelly drive, I was terrified of getting caught. I knew nothing about your father's work plans today except that, working for himself, there tended to be change and flex-ibility in his schedule. I felt a chill and realised the window was open. I moved over to close it but changed my mind. It

54

was the kind of thing your father remembered, having left a window open.

In the far corner of the room was your father's tallboy, a narrow chest with seven shallow drawers. I walked over to it, opening the top drawer to find, as ever, the rolled-up winter socks he wore beneath his work boots. The next drawer down contained his boxer shorts. The third and fourth were unchanged, too, lined with the lidless containers — iPhone boxes, wood trays, soap dishes — in which he stored loose change, charging wires, cufflinks, batteries. In the fifth drawer were two shoeboxes stuffed with receipts he kept for his tax returns, records of tools and paint and, yes, the awful substance I couldn't think about without a terrible darkness rolling through my mind.

I went over to the wardrobe. Your father's check shirts and wool jumpers hung inside. My clothes were gone, replaced with Greta's sheer blouses, denim shirts and animal-print tops. At the far end of the rail, three tunics hung, hospital blue with white piping on the collars and sleeves. Midwife uniforms. In the dark space at the bottom of the wardrobe, several pairs of her shoes were piled messily beside a rope storage basket full of her make-up. Next to this, three white shoeboxes were stacked neatly. I got down on my knees and began to open them.

The first two contained shoes. The last one was light when I lifted it and I sat back on the carpet, bringing it into my lap. Opening it, I found papers — letters, photos, tickets, receipts. On top was a photograph of Greta and your father, her arms around his neck as she kissed his cheek and he looked at the camera. Folded beneath it was a cream sheet of paper that I could see from the letterhead was from the hospital. As I picked it up, I heard movement on the landing, the unmistakable creak of a floorboard. I froze, the letter in my hands, the opened shoebox in my lap, the photo of Greta and your father on the carpet beside me, wondering with a flash of panic if I had become too consumed in my thoughts to hear your father's van or Greta's car on the drive. This happened to me, losing all physical connection with the outside world. If one of them caught me like this there would be nothing I could say or do — no defence — and your father would use it against me in every way possible. And I would have no right to argue.

The door opened, brushing roughly against the carpet. I opened my mouth. What I was going to say I don't know, but into the room came the dog. Beti. She trotted over happily, wagging her tail. I sighed. As I reached out to stroke her head, I saw my hands were shaking.

"You scared me," I told her.

She sat beside me. Her company calmed me, though I knew I should have taken it as a warning, a sign I should stop. I was still holding the letter from the hospital. I decided I had no right to read it and no reason to. But as I put it back in the box I noticed the edge of another kind of photo, one I recognised instantly. I pulled it out and stared at the white frame, the black background, the tiny text at the edges and, in the centre, the grainy outline of a foetus, forming in a fluid-filled womb. I glanced at the top, looking for the name that I knew would be there, somewhere, in the margins. *Greta L. Jones*. As I searched for a date, I heard knocking. The front door. I threw the photo back in the box, replaced the lid and neatly stacked the shoeboxes as they were.

NINE

I was thirty-seven weeks pregnant when I painted the nursery. I wanted you to sleep in the room next to ours partly because the cottage walls were too thick for baby monitors and I couldn't bear the thought of you crying in the night and no one hearing. But it was a lot of work. Before I took it on, it was neglected and cold. The radiators had been off for years. The walls were faded, with blue-grey patches that looked suspiciously like mould. Your father assured me there was no damp, though we were keeping the windows open for now, just in case. Even before its transformation I felt affinity with the room, shabby and overlooked, and I spent hours at charity shops and craft fairs and sprawling home stores trying to find the right things to make it comfortable and loved.

As your father got ready for work, I was already dressed in an old pair of joggers, rolled down below my swollen belly, and a baggy T-shirt. You were inside me, which I still found amazing, even as my due date rapidly approached. I didn't want it to end, the togetherness of us, the way I kept you safe so effortlessly, fed you from my blood and bones. I was terrified at the thought of you being out in the world, and I grew more anxious by the day. Everyone told me to rest — "Sleep while you can!" — but instead I was waking earlier and going to bed later, edgy and restless with a constant, faceless worry that told me to stay busy, keep moving, get ready. I had already left it late to paint the nursery — your father had kept saying he would do it but never did. When he came in to say goodbye I was on my hands and knees, preparing to take up the moth-eaten carpet. Your father wanted new carpet, for the sake of insulation. I wanted laminate floor.

"Don't do that," he said, looking down from the doorway.

"What do you mean?"

"Have you ever pulled up carpet? You'll hurt yourself. I'll do it later."

He said this — that he would do it later — but I knew he wouldn't. Something was preventing him from doing anything to help me get ready. That same resistance had prevented him from getting cash for the scan photos. It was hurting me but I didn't want a confrontation. I would not allow myself to be the nagging wife — the nagging, pregnant wife.

"I'll be fine," I said.

"You should wear this, too," he said.

I looked up and saw he was holding out a mask, white with yellow straps. He wore these when he worked with chemicals, dozens of them in the back of his van.

"Why?" I said, looking over at the unopened tins of paint.

"What do you mean 'why'?"

I sighed. Asking a simple question seemed to provoke such irritation. I wondered if he had been like this all along. Or was it the pregnancy, making him distant and tense?

As I stared blankly at him, he said, "The baby."

"Oh," I said. "Should I not be painting?"

"It's fine if you wear this," he said impatiently, pushing the mask further towards me. I took it. As he watched, I placed the hard dome over my nose. It smelled clinical and new. The straps caught in my hair and I had to readjust, aware of your father watching me. When the mask was on, he nodded and disappeared downstairs. I heard the front door close, the sound of his van.

* * *

Your father was right. The carpet was heavier than I expected and I felt the effort in every joint as I ripped it from its grippers. When I had dragged it out to the landing, releasing clouds of dust, I kneeled down and pulled the lid off the paint tin, dipping my brand-new brush in the thick, gleaming liquid.

I painted all morning, not realising until I stepped down from the ladder I had been going for over four hours. It was after noon. My arms were heavy. I knew I should eat. A week or so ago, my ravenous pregnancy appetite had vanished and now I hardly wanted to eat at all.

I looked around at the walls. My application was uneven, some patches blotchy. I sighed. My head felt light. My legs were weak. I looked outside. The sky appeared stark and threatening. The mask, which I had worn the whole morning, felt suddenly constricting. I pulled it off and threw it on the floor. When I looked outside again, the mountains looked darker and closer somehow, as though they might be moving in on the house. A giddy feeling rose through my body.

"What is happening?" I said to myself.

I had a sudden urge to take off my clothes, pulling my paint-stained T-shirt over my head, ripping off my joggers. I unclasped my bra, relieved as its grip loosened. I looked down at my belly, swollen and huge. Suddenly I realised something — you had not moved since the night before. There had been no somersaults in the middle of the night nor the gentle kicking I woke to in the morning.

I was sure, then, that you had died. This was why I felt so strange, so suddenly afraid. There was grief in the air. Unless the baby was dead, how could I explain this emptiness around me and inside me? As I imagined delivering a stillborn child, a hollow sensation overcame me. I heard a loud spattering and looked down to see a puddle between my legs, clear liquid pooling at my feet.

* * *

I didn't ring your father, nor the number for the labour ward Cadi had written on my notes. I didn't contact anyone. But the contractions came quickly and grew worse, and I was frightened not only by the severity of the pain but how it was rooted at my core, erupting from a part of me I hadn't known existed. There was something barbaric about this pain, cruel and unnatural while supposedly ordinary. It made me feel that something must be wrong. People had warned me, of course. Everyone tells you, flippantly, that there's no pain like this. You hear it on television. It doesn't prepare you. Those comments seemed frivolous and disconnected from what I was experiencing now I was finally in the grip of this primitive pain ripping through the fibres of my body.

The contractions came faster until they were almost continuous and with each one I was forced to my knees, gripping anything in reach, and screaming wild, inhuman sounds that rose though the empty house and died in the mountains beyond, no one to hear them but me.

* * *

The midwives were asking questions. Where were the towels? When did my water break? Why didn't I ring sooner? When did I last eat? I didn't remember calling anyone but suddenly there were two of them. Neither was Cadi. I could think of nothing but the pain. A bath was run and I was lowered into the water, holding on to the edge.

"She needs sugar," one of them said. The second one brought me a glass of apple juice that I sipped once before vomiting down her tunic.

She scolded me gently. "You need calories."

I closed my eyes, swaying on my feet. "Leave me alone."

Your father was there. When he first got home he had said, "Why didn't you ring me? Why aren't you in the hospital?"

I didn't answer.

"Elin? Did you hear me?"

"It's too late for a transfer now," said the midwife.

* * *

You came in the night. It was dark. I was on all fours, holding on to the window seat when a bloodied lump, fleshy and hard, slipped into the hands of the midwife. There was a hush of relief after the urgent shouting that had gone before.

"She's here," said a midwife, but her voice was cautious, hesitant. I could see nothing but the black sky and the wide mountains. The room was quiet. For a long time I hadn't heard your father's voice or caught his brooding figure. I did not seem to be located in the same place as him. I was far away, out of myself. The midwives were talking quietly to each other. I turned my head.

"Is she breathing?" I cried.

The midwife kneeling between my legs was rubbing circles into your chest. Your tiny eyes were stamped shut. Your body was still. No one had answered me.

Finally, a bleating cry pierced the air, breaking the silence in half. I closed my eyes. The midwife lifted my leg, turning me onto my back. My legs trembled, my feet sliding through the blood beneath me. Positioning myself seemed too much for my body, like all I could do now was collapse. I could sleep or die, I thought. I didn't care. But my legs shook violently.

"It's the adrenalin," said the midwife.

She placed you, face down, against my chest, the two of us wet and bloody as beaten animals. The size of you shocked me, the weight of your body against my own, and the realness of you, the fact of your emergence into this room, as though from nothing. Your head was covered with thick, white paste, matted into your hair and clumped with blood. Steadily, you cried. With a long pair of steel scissors, the midwife bent forward and snapped the cord connecting us.

* * *

People came, bringing presents and clichés. I was aware of an obligation to smile and look grateful. But something tightly held unravelled, the neat containment of the last nine months dissolving in the fluids of birth. We called you Rhiannon and you were out in the world, helpless yet charging the air with your primal agency. It was my job to protect you, the walls around me seemed to say. I had no other job except this. You would not allow me to drift aimlessly. I watched you in the cot, eyes sealed, nails sharp as a kitten's claws, and even as you slept I felt the overwhelming urgency of your existence. And though I was exhausted, I couldn't sleep, lying awake with my swirling thoughts until your cry drew me up through the darkness like an invisible string.

TEN

As I hurried to replace everything I had moved, the knocking got louder, more insistent. I knew it wasn't a delivery driver or the postman banging on the door like that. I looked around the bedroom, checking I hadn't left anything out of place, then hurried out of the room.

On the landing, the doorbell chimed. Chimed again. Through the letterbox came a voice.

"Elin? Are you there?"

It was your nain. I stared down into the empty hall then ran quickly downstairs. As I opened the front door, a rush of wind swept into the house. I wedged my foot under the door to stop it swinging open, as I had done a thousand times. She stood on the doorstep, buttoned up in a floral blouse, the wind blowing strands of hair across her face. Carrier bags were collapsed at her feet.

"I didn't expect you to be asleep," she said accusingly.

"I wasn't."

She blinked at me, waiting for an explanation as to why I took so long to answer the door. When I said nothing, she turned her head towards the farm as though preparing to say something difficult. Looking back at me, she simply said, "I never forget my key."

"Do you need help with the bags?" I said.

When she didn't answer, I bent down and took the handle of the nearest one, which contained towels. I noticed her looking at it, too, and I wondered if she was remembering, as I was, the time she came round with a new bath towel shortly after you were born. She was always dropping things off for your father and now you were here — her first grandchild — and she began to bring things for you. Who could blame her? She was overjoyed by your arrival. It didn't upset me as it did when she brought things for him. You were a baby. You needed things. And it made me feel a vicarious sense of safety, as though her looking after you meant she was looking after me, too. This wasn't actually true, but that was how it felt.

Anyway, one day she brought round this towel. It was a Saturday morning, too early for visitors. I was feeding you in the kitchen. Breastfeeding wasn't going well. It wasn't your fault. It wasn't mine, either. It's just hard for some women. You should know that. If you ever have a baby, I don't want you to believe, as I did, the lie that it's easy and painless. You will only feel disappointed and blame yourself, as I did every time I couldn't settle or satisfy you or get you to latch, every time I cried and swore and gritted my teeth through the work and pain.

Needless to say, having your nain round was the last thing I needed, particularly given how opinionated she was on the subject. When she had found out while I was pregnant with you that I was considering bottle-feeding, she sent me an email. She had never written to me before and even in her polite, formal manner I could hear the outrage in her voice. *I wondered if you might be worried about breastfeeding for some reason. Perhaps there's something I can do to help? I'm sure you know how important it is to the new baby's development. The doctor will have told you about that. When David was a baby, I was one of the only mothers I knew who breastfed. Formula was still very popular in those days. They didn't know the things they know now. But I didn't trust it a bit!*

The towel was not the only thing she brought round that day, but as she lifted it from its sheer paper bag I was struck by the texture of the luxury cotton in her hands. Baths had become important to me since you were born. Soaking in hot water was the only thing that cleaned up the mess between my legs after another day of post-partum blood matting itself over my healing stitches. But it was more than that. Since you were born, I had lost ownership of my body. The pregnancy, the birth, the midwives and health visitors, the breastfeeding counsellors, your nain, your father — and, yes, you. My body seemed to belong to everyone in the world but me, my inner self becoming split off, getting smaller, disappearing. A bath was not a magic cure but there was something restorative about being in the locked room, late at night, and slipping into the hot water, alone with my sagging belly, sore breasts, torn muscles, stretch-marked thighs. I would trace my fingers over my stitches, remembering how they were threaded at the birth by a trainee midwife learning how to suture, and thinking how strange it was to have been ripped open and sewn back up in this way.

I think all this was why, as your nain pulled out the towel and placed her hand on your father's arm, saying, "I got this for you in the sale," I became quietly enraged. "I made sure I got a bath sheet," she went on, speaking directly to your father. "So it's plenty big enough for you." I stared at her, finding it almost impossible to believe, even knowing her as I did, that she had brought this towel here for him, your father, who wasn't breastfeeding, who hadn't given birth, who wasn't awake all night with a hungry baby.

"Why didn't you get two?" I said, and really it was something of an out-of-body experience, as though the words jumped from my mouth independent of any mechanism in my brain. They turned to me, both of them. In my arms, you suckled furiously. With genuine sincerity, your nain said, "Do you think he needs two?"

I sighed. "For me and David, I meant."

She stared at me. "I didn't think you'd want one."

"Why wouldn't I want one?" I said bitterly. "David isn't a student in a house share, you know. This is our home. If you bring one towel, you should bring two."

* * *

I had always felt this incident had marked a shift in my relationship with your nain. She didn't stop bringing presents — and she still brought nothing for me — but she was less brazen about the whole thing, a little more cautious. More than anything it was her attitude to me that changed. I was no longer inconsequential, a speck of dirt on the windscreen that she could simply ignore. I was a serious obstacle that, without careful navigation, could prove dangerous.

* * *

I was so distracted by the memory of the towel, I wasn't listening to your nain.

"What did you say?" I said.

"I was just saying you look tired," she was saying.

"I suppose I am."

"You always were tired," she said.

She still hadn't come in, though I had picked up two bags and was holding the door open, wind still blowing into the house. Once I let go it would swing wildly on its hinges. She shuffled through, rustling the shopping through the hall and into the kitchen. As I helped her put the shopping away, I thought about the scan photo I had found upstairs. Having not had time to find the date on it, I was disturbed by the possibility that it might be recent. That Greta could be pregnant. But surely that couldn't be the case. With everything that had happened, and only ten months between now and when I left, and your father and I still married, it was absurd to think he had not only met another woman but conceived a child.

But maybe he had.

I considered asking your nain whether Greta had any children. She was young to have a child from a previous relationship. But it might be some comfort, if I could convince myself this was the explanation. I couldn't think how to ask this without sounding odd, though, or somehow revealing I had been going through their things.

Anyway, your nain had something else on her mind.

"Elin," she said, holding a box of cereal. "I'm very concerned about the girls. I don't know what your plans are, but if they get used to you being around and then you leave again — I don't think I could cope with it, quite frankly. You have no idea what the last ten months have been like."

"I have some idea. They're my children."

"But you weren't here! I was here." She jabbed her thumb into her chest. "I saw all of it."

"Look," I said. "I think we can agree you're not going to forgive what I did. And I'm not going to beg for it, either. I also don't think there's any point telling you I'm not going to leave again, because you're not going to believe me either way, are you?"

"So that's it?" she said. "No apology, no assurances."

"I just don't see the point."

She shook her head, disgusted.

"Anyway," I said. "It's not you I owe an apology to."

"You're right. It's David."

"No," I said. "It's my children."

She sighed, opening the fridge and placing a packet of tomatoes on the shelf.

"For the first few weeks," she said, closing the fridge door, "I stayed here every night. It was very early in his relationship with Greta, then. She was still living at home with her mother. David needed help making the girls their tea and putting them to bed, not to mention all the work involved in caring for Catrin after the accident. It's still work now but back then, when her scar was healing and she had the bandages on — it was awful, Elin, you just don't know. Anyway, I slept in the spare room — or what used to be the spare room — and every morning I would be woken by Catrin calling from her cot. 'Mummy! Mummy! Mummy! Mummy!'"

Four times she said it, as though once wasn't enough, and, as she did that horrible impression, I felt a clamour in my mind, a crowding. I abandoned the unpacking, bags still on the counter, and sat down at the table. Your nain watched me intently. She wanted me to feel as wretched as possible. I wanted to leave the room but I stayed, letting her get it out of her system. It was better that way.

"David would go to her," she continued. "He'd get her out of her cot and he'd have to explain, again, that you weren't here, that you were gone. That went on for weeks. Eventually she started crying for David instead. In the end it surprised me, to be honest. How quickly she switched."

ELEVEN

"You know," Ben said to me in our next session, "I have patients who talk too much."

Ben didn't dress particularly smartly — I mean, he didn't wear a jacket or work shirt or anything. It was always jeans and jumpers. That day I thought he looked particularly nice in a navy-and-red flannel shirt. The colours suited him, warming his skin.

"What do you mean?" I said.

He paused. "I mean there are different kinds of talking. The patients I'm referring to tell me every detail of their week. But it's a kind of avoidance. It's like they're painting pictures to distract me from what's really going on."

I was reminded of Cain, a boy Jude had fostered for a few weeks when I was eleven. Just before he came to live with us — he was eight at the time — he had witnessed something awful. Jude wouldn't tell us what it was but she said it was his father who had done this terrible thing. Cain had a habit of running away, though he never went far. One night, he climbed out of his bedroom window and Jude found him in the Wendy house in next door's garden. After a while a counsellor came to the house. She brought huge sheets of blank paper and every colour pencil you can imagine. I remember when she opened the enormous tin with what must have been fifty brand-new pencils inside. I was jealous that Cain would be allowed to use them. At first Cain drew pleasant things, gardens and rainbows. Jude smiled and put them on the wall. The counsellor looked disappointed. After a while, he started to draw angry, indecipherable scrawls of red and black. Jude was alarmed. The counsellor said, "Now we're getting somewhere."

"So what do you do?" I asked Ben. "With these patients, I mean."

"I try to get beneath their stories, find out what was really going on for them. If that doesn't work, I address the problem directly."

"How do you do that?"

"I just say, 'These are your sessions. I can sit here and listen to this but you have friends who would do that for free.'"

I laughed. "Do you really say that?"

He nodded. "If I can't help them, there's no point in them being there."

"What do they say?"

"Some of them are shocked. They thought they were already doing therapy just by being here. Other people know what I'm talking about."

I looked at him. "I don't talk much. In our sessions, I mean."

"That's right," he said.

"Is that bad?"

"No, it's not bad. I just wonder if there's any way I can make you more comfortable. It's important that you feel safe. Does it bother you that I'm a man, do you think?"

I was shocked by this question.

"Of course not," I said.

He nodded. "I wouldn't be offended. A lot of women will only see female therapists, which seems reasonable, especially if their trauma has been inflicted by men."

This was his language — careful, sensitive. I wondered what it would be like if everyone talked to each other like this, how different things would be.

"It worried me after I had children," I said.

"What did?"

"My quietness."

He nodded. "Explain more?"

I thought about it. "After Rhiannon was born, I was around other mums a lot, you know? In cafés or baby groups or whatever. I watched the way they talked to their babies, smiling, doing funny voices. I wasn't like that. Not with either of my girls. Especially not at the beginning, anyway. For the first few months, I was kind of mute. Dazed, I think. Overwhelmed. Especially with Rhiannon. I felt there was something very wrong with me. Then I saw this thing on YouTube, this experiment they did where the mothers look at babies with a blank face."

"The Still Face experiment," said Ben, nodding.

"You've heard of it?"

"I've studied it. It was fairly groundbreaking when it was done."

I didn't say anything else. Neither did Ben. The air in the room shifted. Tentatively, he said, "Elin, those mothers in the experiment — they're under instruction to be entirely unresponsive. No facial expression, no engagement at all. Not only that but they switch to this from a state of warmth. That is what causes such a distressed reaction in the babies."

I nodded. But I felt my skin prickle, thinking about those babies.

TWELVE

When you were born — and it was the same with your sister — the midwives told me not to wash you. "Leave her be for now." It used to be that they took a newborn baby away, cleaned and dressed it before the mother even got a look. We had learned things now, how babies needed instant contact with their mother, that it regulated their heartbeat and temperature after the trauma of birth. Separation only enhanced their distress. Coming out of the birth canal, babies knew the sound of their mother's voice already and even cried at the same pitch. On their foetal journey they listened, her voice echoing outside the walls of the liquid womb. And those unpleasant-looking substances covering newborn skin, the creamy vernix and wispy lanugo — these provided vitamins and moisture and healthy bacteria. Nature knew what she was doing. We had underestimated her. All of it was obvious, really. But everything is obvious once you know.

* * *

I didn't wash you for days, as I was told. But at the health visitor's third visit, a week after the birth, she looked in the folds of your neck to find dried clumps of breastmilk and said, "Haven't you bathed her yet?"

So I washed you.

I was terrified. Terrified the water was too hot — I must have checked the floating thermometer a dozen times — and terrified you might slip under when I wasn't looking, though there was not a second when I wasn't looking. The vernix had gone — it had cleaned itself, as the midwives had said it would — and the lanugo, too, had largely come away from your skin, though traces remained. The bloody stump of your umbilical cord was still there, clinging stubbornly to your belly button, and thick cradle cap was clustered on the top of your head.

When your feet touched the water, you looked stunned, your eyes more open and alive than I had seen in your short eight-day life. I panicked that the water must be scalding you, pulling you out and checking it again, even though the thermometer told me it was thirty-seven degrees, the perfect temperature for newborn bathing. Cool enough that you wouldn't be scalded, hot enough to keep you warm.

When I submerged you a second time, lowering you until the waterline reached your chest, your face was calmer, your eyes more curious than frightened. Lightly, I splashed water on your chest, squeezed the flannel over the creases of your elbows and the pits of your arms. I wet my fingers and ran them through the tight folds of your neck, behind your ears, between your legs.

I was scared to handle you. Your skin was so soft, your bones so supple, everything I did seemed a grave risk. I didn't know if it was normal, to be as afraid as I was. Mothers were meant to know what to do. They were supposed to be smitten and content, a calm infatuation boosted by oxytocin and maternal tenderness. But for me it was wild fear, stained with grief for an unknown loss, waiting for disaster. I felt as though a thousand delicate sensors had been switched on, a bruised excess of sensitivity crackling in the fibres of my skin.

73

I could no longer watch the news. I couldn't tolerate what had previously passed me by — pictures of mothers in war zones, too hungry to produce milk, and dead babies at disgraced hospitals, their parents white-faced and stricken.

I stared at you helplessly, stranded in a thick blanket of shock. I was devoted but impotent, shut down yet alert to the slightest hint of danger, my mind inventing threats with a new intensity. The ground floor of the house became dangerous to me — I didn't want to be down there. I kept you in the bedroom, the door closed, the curtains shut. My breasts were engorged, angry red patches blotting the skin, and my supply refused to adjust to feeds, so milk spilled pointlessly from my nipples, soaking my clothes in dark patches.

* * *

You didn't care about any of this, nor that my hair smelled of sick and my body stank with sweat. You just wanted milk in your mouth and fistfuls of skin. But dread gnawed at me like a tiny animal, transmitting a message I was failing to grasp, embodied in your soft bones and feathery skin, the spongy spot at the crown of your head. Terrifying images flooded my mind. I saw you dropped on the hard kitchen floor, your fragile body hitting the tiles, and slipping from my hands as I descended the stairs. And then there were those visions, flashing like torchlight, in which I did unthinkable things, reaching for the kettle to pour scalding water on your skin, throwing you from the bedroom window. These thoughts intruded from nowhere and devastated me. I pushed them out, despising them and myself.

I had been told that a newborn didn't know where they ended and their mother began, yet to understand their separateness. But it was me losing my grip on the edges of myself.

* * *

The health visitor came and went, scribbling things inside your little red book. She observed me with you, studying the latch, taking in, with all her professional experience, the bond between us. I was sure she would notice something was wrong. During her fourth visit, she said, "You have mastitis."

"What's that?"

She pointed to my breasts. "The red patches — do they feel hard?"

I nodded. She told me she would ring the GP for me. Perhaps she knew I wouldn't have done it myself. When I went to my appointment, the doctor glanced at you, asleep in your car seat on the floor.

"How is she getting on?" he asked absently.

"Fine, I think," I said.

He was not interested in the answer. How strange, I thought, that to him you were only another baby while to me, you were . . . I couldn't even say what you were yet.

* * *

In late July, you caught a cold. You were seven weeks old. The mucus in your nose, which I could not remove, interfered with your feeding so you came off my breast every few seconds, gasping for air, then latched on again in furious hunger only to find you needed more oxygen. Agitated, you grew hungrier, and I felt a new kind of despair.

By the third evening we were both exhausted. At ten thirty, you collapsed into sleep, drained by the effort of eating. I knew your hunger would wake you again soon. Cradling you in my left arm, I walked over to the bedroom window and opened it into the night. The garden below was full of shadows. Your father was downstairs, tidying the kitchen while a football match played on the radio. I could hear the faint jeers of the crowd, the steady stream of commentary.

I lay on the bed, sliding down to let the pillow catch my head. You slipped onto the mattress beside me. You were asleep now, your breath thick with phlegm. I held you loosely against my side. I would rest there for a few minutes, savouring the cool air from the open window while I found the energy to put you down in the cot.

* * *

"Elin! Elin!"

When your father's voice cut through I was dreaming about your cold, imagining the congestion spreading through your body until it paralysed you. My eyes flew open. He was leaning over me, his hand shaking my shoulder. The room was mellow with shut-out light. I sat up, searching for you, and realised you were in the same position, fists clenched at your face, sleep drawn around you. I bent my head to hear your breath.

"Thank God," I whispered. "What time is it?"

"Six thirty. What is going on?"

"Six thirty," I said, repeating the words. I knew there was something important about this but it took a moment to realise. "David," I whispered. "She's been asleep for seven hours!"

In the hazy half-light I could see he was still with rage.

"Elin, what were you thinking? I didn't even know she was there when I got in bed. I could have killed her!"

I closed my eyes and lay back on the pillow. "I must have fallen asleep."

"Jesus."

"I'm sorry," I said. "It won't happen again."

* * *

The next time I let you sleep in our bed you did it again, sleeping contentedly beside me for six hours. Then it was five. Then six again. You never repeated the seven-hour stretch of the first time but slowly I caught up on my sleep. Though I did everything to make it safe — tucked the duvet tightly at the foot of the bed so it reached no higher than our waists, removed my pillows, never drank so much as a sip of wine, while your father drank the same amount he always had — he remained bitterly opposed. He never went so far as to remove you from the bed — he didn't want to get involved in the practical side of caring for you at night — but he played on my fear that I had no idea what I was doing, that I was bound to hurt you.

"It's not safe," he said.

"Yes, it is. I've read all about it."

"Where? Netmums?"

I lied. "No. Proper medical sources."

"Co-sleeping is dangerous. You heard what the midwife said."

"That's because they're worried about parents who drink and take drugs. So they just tell everyone not to do it."

He laughed. "I see you're an expert now."

I sighed. "We'll never agree about this, David."

He was reluctant to express his unspoken belief that it didn't matter what I thought — he saw me as clueless. He preferred to wear me down with moral arguments, to intellectually defeat me, to make me feel incompetent or insane.

"Do you want to be one of those mothers whose three-year-old shares a bed with them?"

"David," I said. "She's two months old."

I thought this might soften him. But his expression hardened. "I'm not going to change my mind about this."

THIRTEEN

You and your sister were home by lunchtime, car doors slamming, a flurry of noise and excitement on the driveway and then in the hall. Greta was shushing you. "Nice and quiet, girls, okay? Inside voices."

When you appeared in the kitchen you had damp hair and fresh faces. I was at the table, drinking tea. After her little outburst, your nain had offered me a hot drink as though nothing had happened. As I drank it, I turned over what she had said, imagining your sister's distress and confusion in those early weeks as she tried to understand my disappearance. Of course, I had imagined it a hundred times. It was not a revelation to me, the pain I had caused you and your sister. And I knew that ruminating in guilt would help none of us. It certainly wouldn't allow me to bond with you again, slipping into self-loathing, becoming paralysed by regret. I knew what I had done. I had punished myself plenty. Ben had taught me that shame was a useless emotion, preventing people from making amends because they believed themselves unworthy of forgiveness. Blame isn't the point, he would say. It's about responsibility. I was trying to hold on to this.

I also couldn't stop thinking about the scan photo. I felt even less able to ask your nain about it now, since she'd told me off. The longer I turned it over in my mind, the more I told myself, *No, it's not possible.* It was an old photo, a child Greta had before she met your father. There were plenty of women round here who had kids when they were younger than her. That was the explanation. I was obsessing needlessly. Still, I was very keen to go back upstairs and find the date on the photo. It wouldn't take long. But it was too risky with everyone back in the house. I would have to wait until everyone was out again.

"Well!" said your nain as you walked in the room. "Did Auntie Greta take you to the pool?"

Auntie Greta, I thought. She was 'auntie', already. Yet I hardly knew who she was.

Catrin ran over and climbed in her lap. "We been in the sea!" she cried.

"No, you haven't!" said your nain, looking at Catrin and then at you. "My goodness, you were brave. And was it cold?"

Catrin chatted away to your nain, trying her best to explain in her repetitive three-year-old talk where you had been and what you had done. Your nain watched intently, responding, "Did you really?" and "Is that right?" She was great with small children, she always had been, animated and engaged and relentlessly interested in your long, rambling stories. She made all the right noises and faces and she answered your stream of questions clearly and willingly. While she and Catrin talked, you were quiet and withdrawn, as you had been the day before. You had never quite recovered, though I didn't know whether it was just because you were near me again that you were acting like this.

Greta hadn't come through the door yet. When she finally did make her way into the kitchen, she was pushing a pram. Not any pram but the one your nain had bought when you were born, the one I'd still been using for Catrin when I'd left, the toddler attachment allowing her to sit upright. Whereas now the carrycot was back on it, retrieved from the garage where I'd put it when Catrin had outgrown it just under three years ago. I knew it was the same pram, not just from the model and colour but the scratches on the wheels, the tear on the hood and the dull squeak it made as it was pushed along. My first thought when I saw it was, *Why has Greta been pushing Catrin around in that carrycot? Is she crazy?* Once again my brain was failing to process the obvious.

As the unmistakable bleat of a newborn rose from beneath the hood of the carrycot, Greta sighed. "I knew I should have left her out the front."

"Well, it's not safe these days," said your nain.

Greta leaned forward, reaching into the cot. Her hair was wet, too, darker and curlier against her pale skin. Her face shone with damp. She wasn't wearing her hair tied back, nor the scarf around her head that she'd had on this morning and last night. Instead her dark wet curls framed her face. Fiddling beneath the hood, she stood up again, bringing to her chest a startlingly small baby, no more than a month old, I would have guessed, wrapped in a thin cotton blanket. Once held, the baby stopped crying, flopping against Greta's bare shoulder as she gently held the back of its tiny head.

"She needs a feed," said Greta.

"Have you had any more luck with breastfeeding?" said your nain.

Greta flashed her an angry look. "I'm not trying to breastfeed. I've told you. She's bottle-feeding."

Your nain pulled a face of innocent shock, one I knew well. "I was only trying to help. Shall I get a bottle ready?"

"Yes, please. Thank you."

Your nain set about boiling the kettle, washing her hands thoroughly and lifting the lid of what I now realised was a steriliser. I hadn't noticed it yesterday though it was plainly obvious now, a dome of white plastic on the black slate counter. She picked up the tongs from inside and used them to lift out a bottle and teat, careful not to touch anything with her fingers. When the kettle finished boiling, she poured hot water into the clear bottle, bending down to measure the level precisely. From the cupboard below she lifted out a box of formula. It was the most expensive brand, I noticed, but your nain treated it with disgust as she levelled the powder and tipped it into the bottle. With each scoop, I watched the water turn milky and thick.

The baby had begun to cry. Greta moved around the kitchen rubbing her back, whispering in her ear.

"The problem with formula," said your nain, "well, one of the problems — is it takes so long to prepare. It's no good having to do all this when they're already hungry and crying. This isn't even cooled yet!"

Greta ignored her, shushing the baby. You and Catrin had taken Beti into the garden, leaving the back door open as you threw the ball, squealing as she chased after it then raced back to drop it at your feet.

"You know, Greta," your nain was saying as she shook the bottle, "it's not safe to take the girls in the sea. Catrin can't even swim and Rhiannon is only just learning."

Greta smiled, resting her cheek against the baby's head. The baby was still crying but only lightly. "There's nowhere like the sea to learn how to swim," she said.

"Oh, Greta!" Your nain turned to look at her. "You don't teach them in the sea! You teach them in the pool. When they're strong in the water, then they can go in the sea."

"Is that ready yet?" Greta nodded towards the bottle.

"It's too hot, of course! Let me just run it under the tap."

As your nain shuffled back over to the sink, I found myself in that same state of shut-down shock as the day before, unable to ask any of the questions flooding my mind. There were so many things I wanted to know — was this really her baby? There didn't seem to be any other explanation. But Greta was so young. I thought of the tunics in the wardrobe and wondered why she would have a baby now, when she must have only just finished her training. And then there was the most important question, the answer to which seemed inevitable and obvious, yet I couldn't believe it any more than I could bring myself to ask the question.

"I think I'll make more tea while the water's hot," said your nain. "Would you like another, Elin?"

I stared at her as she turned to look at me, waiting for a reply. Greta, still moving around the kitchen with the baby, looked over at me, too.

"Are you okay, Elin?" said your nain. "You look very pale."

"I didn't know," I said, too quietly for anyone to hear. I cleared my throat. "I didn't know about the baby."

Greta and your nain glanced at each other, then back at me. "David didn't tell you yesterday?" said Greta.

I shook my head. Greta pursed her lips. Your nain sighed. "What's he like?" she said, smiling indulgently.

"When did you have her?" I said.

"She'll be three weeks tomorrow."

I nodded. "Where was she yesterday?" I knew this was a rude question, technically, but somehow I felt I needed to know.

"With my mother," Greta replied coldly. "I needed a break."

"I understand. Sorry. I was just confused. What's her name?"

"I think this is ready now," said your nain, handing Greta the bottle, dripping with water from the tap. Greta tested the temperature on her wrist, as your nain had just done, then angled the teat into the baby's mouth. The baby latched frantically, sucking with furious newborn hunger.

"Her name's Deryn," said Greta to me.

I stared at her. Your father and I had talked about giving Catrin that name. It was one of his favourites. Your nain was watching us both closely. Suddenly, Catrin burst into the kitchen, Beti charging after her. Catrin shrieked, clutching a tennis ball in her hand.

"Catrin!" your nain shouted. "Your shoes are filthy! Take those off now! Rhiannon? Come in here and take this dog outside."

Obediently, you came to the back door and removed your shoes, leaving them on the mat as you went after Beti and took her by the collar, leading her to the garden and shutting the door.

"We put her in the utility room if she's muddy," said Greta, looking at your nain. "She doesn't like to be shut outside."

Deryn had finished her bottle now and Greta was holding her upright at her shoulder, rubbing her back. Deryn yawned widely then hiccupped.

"Oh, she doesn't mind," said your nain. "She's a dog!"

"No," said Greta. "It makes her very anxious."

"Yesterday Nain put Beti in the cellar," said Catrin.

"What?" said Greta.

"Oh, Catrin!" said your nain. "Don't say such silly things!"

"It's not silly! It's true," said Catrin. "Don't lie!"

"Catrin," said your nain sternly. "You must not accuse people of lying."

"But you are lying," she said.

"Did you?" said Greta, looking at your nain.

"Oh, just for a little while," said your nain, flustered. "She didn't mind at all! You must realise that a dog like that shouldn't be around children? It's not safe."

"Beti is very protective of the children," said Greta. "She would never hurt them."

"Oh, Greta. That's not how dogs operate. They're animals. Not people. It doesn't take much to turn them. Then how will you feel, if she attacks Rhiannon or Catrin or, God forbid, baby Deryn?"

Having taken off her muddy shoes, Catrin walked over to me and grabbed hold of my hand, looking up at me. As though to put an end to any lingering doubt, she pointed at Deryn and said, "That's my baby sister."

* * *

I waited in the driveway for your father. It was the only place I felt I could speak to him privately, without Greta listening or your nain interfering or you girls running around us, interrupting, wanting his attention. There was a humidity in the air — particularly noticeable, I thought, given it was

April. Your nain had been talking about how uncomfortable it was, how much more difficult she found it to breathe, and now I noticed it myself, a suffocating stuffiness, as though there was a lack of oxygen in the air. Finally, I saw your father's van on the road far below, between us green sloping fields, dotted with sheep. From this distance the van seemed to move incredibly slowly as it turned onto the track and moved towards the house. I could not hear the engine or the crunch of the tyres, only the warm wind rustling the trees.

I was sitting on the wall between the house and the farm, the sheep behind me sheltering beneath the large oak in the corner of the field. When he eventually reached the driveway, the van's tyres crunched the gravel and he slowed to a stop in front of me. He glanced at me through the glass before opening the driver's door and hopping down. He wore a brown corduroy shirt, his sleeves rolled to his elbows. There were mud stains on his hands and forearms, his fingernails black with dirt.

"What now?" he said, as though I'd been pestering him constantly since I got home. In reality, I hadn't seen him at all since the night before, when our only conversation had been about the lack of availability at Tŷ Gwyn. I got down from the wall and walked towards him. I could tell from his face that he knew exactly what I was going to stay. But he feigned ignorance. "What is it, Elin? I've been at work since eight. I would like to get inside and have a shower."

"What do you think, David? The baby."

"What about her?"

"Don't do this. Don't act like I'm making a fuss over nothing. You've made me feel crazy about a lot of things but you can't do it with this."

"What is it you're asking?"

"I'm asking how it is you've had a baby in the time I've been gone. Were you with Greta before I left?"

He looked at me. "No. I met her at the hospital. While Catrin was ill. After you'd left us."

"She's a midwife, isn't she?"

"Yeah," he said. "So?" Thankfully, he didn't ask me how I knew this.

"So how did you meet her at the hospital?" I said. "Midwives don't work on paediatric wards."

He sighed. "We met at the café."

"And you instantly decided to have a baby with her?"

"We didn't decide anything. It just happened. Like it happened with us."

I looked at him. "We were together a year before we had Rhiannon."

He shrugged. "We didn't make a decision, though, did we?"

It was true. I was surprised he would make this point, though, given he was the one who had taken my pills.

"It's not the same," I said. "It's not the point at all. Greta must have got pregnant literally as soon as I left."

"It was a few weeks later. And, yes, it was fast. I know. I wasn't exactly thrilled at the time. But like I said, it happened. She didn't want to get rid of it and I wasn't going to ask her to. What do you want me to say? You were gone, Elin!"

"It can't have been a few weeks after I left," I said.

"What?"

"It doesn't add up."

He nodded, understanding what I meant. "Deryn came early," he said.

"How early?"

He laughed. "It's really none of your business, but about four weeks."

We were silent for a minute. Then I said, "I don't think I should stay here. It was one thing before but it's not right with Greta and now the baby." I felt strangely sad saying this. Even though there was nothing between your father and I anymore, at least not in the way of love or affection, part of me wanted to stay.

"Greta doesn't care," he said. "She's very easy-going."

"No new mother is easy-going, David. There must be somewhere else. I just need something temporary while I look for a place of my own."

85

He eyed me carefully. He knew what I was asking. He knew everyone round here. If anyone could find me somewhere, it was him. My circle was small. Smaller than ever now that no one wanted to talk to me. But he was strangely reluctant. Having not wanted me here at all when I showed up on the doorstep the day before, I was now getting the sense that he wanted me in the house. Which made no sense at all, not with Greta and Deryn living here now.

"I told you," he said. "There's nothing. I've already asked. You know what it's like round here in the holidays, Elin."

"You can't have asked everyone. And half-term will be finished in a few days."

"I've asked everyone we know. Look, Elin, I'm knackered. I need a shower. Is there anything else?"

He moved over to the front door. I followed him.

"Why are you talking to me like this?" I said.

"Jesus, you never stop. Like what?"

"I don't know," I said. I really didn't want to do this with him. He bent down and began to loosen the long laces on his boots, groaning as he pulled off one then the other, wincing as he stood up. Taking a step towards me, I could smell the afternoon coffee on his breath and the fresh sweat on his skin.

"What did you expect?"

FOURTEEN

It was winter when you caught bronchiolitis. There was snow on the ground. The car was dead, the engine or battery frozen, and your father was working away from home. I had been alone for two nights and I will always remember how I walked — it was more like trudging — through the deep snow, along the mountain road, holding you in my arms. You were six months old and there was a rattle in your chest, lethal sounding, and a rasping as you breathed. Your lips had turned blue. That was when I decided to take you in. As time went on, I learned more about infant illness, and if I'd known then what I know now I would have taken you sooner. But I doubted myself incessantly, every instinct untrustworthy. I didn't ring your father because I knew he would only make me question myself more.

There was no point calling an ambulance. By the time they got to us — and they might not have made it at all — I could have walked into the village. I wanted to see the GP before going to the hospital. What if I was overreacting? What if I was imagining the colour around your lips? What if you just had a cold?

The village was clearer, snow swept into high ridges on the sides of the road, and in front of the surgery — a tiny hut, pebble-dashed, with black windows — the path had been gritted, mounds of dirty snow piled on the grass. The doctor took one look at your bare tummy, where the skin was folding beneath your ribs every time you took a breath, and said, "You need to take her to the hospital."

"I don't have a car," I told him.

An ambulance came. Paramedics took you from me, strapping you onto the stretcher with a complicated attachment for babies that took an eternity to assemble. You began to cry. You didn't like being taken from me. You were hungry, too. I had stopped breastfeeding you by then and in my hurry I had not brought any milk. It didn't matter. You were admitted to the high-dependency unit where a doctor — who came and went within minutes — decided you would be tube fed.

"You don't have to stay," the nurse said, looking at me over her shoulder as she prepared to insert the tube. "Lots of parents don't."

I was confused before I realised she meant while she inserted the tube.

"I'll stay," I said.

It probably made no difference to you — your view of me was obscured by the nurses — but abandoning you to this ordeal when I was the one who brought you here was unthinkable to me. Enduring everything you went through, staying as close as I could to your experience, was the least I could do. I made myself watch, holding on to the frame of the cot as one of the nurses pushed a tube up into your tiny nostril. As it threaded its way through your nasal cavity, your eyes widened in an intense shock I had never seen on anyone. Your little body stiffened like wood. You began to thrash your head wildly. The second nurse held you down, placing a hand across your chest, the other over your head, and instead of thrashing you simply gasped, your eyes wide in terror, too stunned to even cry, as the tube wound its way down into your oesophagus.

When they were done, you let out a loud wail. It was a relief compared with the look of terror, the helpless thrashing.

As you sobbed, you jerked your arm towards the tube, trying to pull it out with helpless, grasping baby hands. The nurse moved your hand away.

"You can hold her now," she informed me.

I moved round the bed and slid my hands beneath your back, trying not to tug the tube as I lifted you towards me. When I placed you against my shoulder, I felt your tiny heart pounding against my chest. Normally, when I picked you up, you would calm almost instantly. But you continued to scream, arching your back and snatching at the tube lodged invasively inside you. I held you tighter, disturbed by the depth of your distress and my inability to comfort you.

"We need to keep her as calm as possible," the nurse said. "When she's upset, it's harder for her to breathe."

Her tone was accusing, and a sudden fury rose inside me. *You're the one who stuck a tube down her neck*, I wanted to say. I wanted to shout at her, hurt or frighten this nurse in some way that might make her feel the pain and fear that I was feeling. But I said nothing.

* * *

The night was long and there was no escape. On a flimsy rolling bed I lay beside you. But I didn't sleep. The nurses, in deference to hospital policy, allowed you three ounces of milk every three hours. This was half what you drank from bottles at home. The rationale, the nurse explained, was that a full stomach put pressure on your lungs. It was better for you to be hungry than unable to breathe. Why these were the only options, when doctors could practically work miracles, I didn't know, but keeping you hungry seemed sadistic to me and I wondered if the nurses could stand to do it to their own children. And in this hungry state, you cried. My God, you cried, and the crying went on through the night, filling the air of the mechanical room as wires encircled your body.

On the bedside table, a white machine with a black screen showed a fluorescent green number that rolled higher and lower slowly, then would dip, flashing red as the machine beeped catastrophically.

But no one came. We were alone.

As the night wore on, I thought about the woman on the news the winter before who, the day after giving birth, had left the hospital with her newborn wrapped in sheets and wandered the cold streets. The next morning, the mother and her baby were found beneath a bridge, frozen to death. I looked at you and thought about removing the feeding tube and the high-flow oxygen, unclamping the needle in your hand. The ward was quiet. I could walk through the lanes back to the house, feed you until you were sleepy and full. I wanted this helplessness to end, for me and for you, and I knew then why that mother went wandering in the cold, and I knew why there were people who kept their children away from hospitals, and I knew that parents might do anything for their children but that when they could do nothing, that was another thing altogether.

FIFTEEN

By the time you're reading this, you'll probably know the story of your nain. She came from a religious family in the north of England — her parents were extremely strict — and she had an affair with a married man, becoming pregnant with his child at the age of sixteen. That child was your father. When they found out she was pregnant, her parents, unable to condone an abortion, wanted to raise your father as their own. Your nain wouldn't agree to that. She wanted the baby and she wanted to raise it as her own. So she came here, from inner-city Liverpool to rural north Wales, young and pregnant, in defiance of her parents — and to let them live without the stigma of an illegitimate grandchild. Your father's father — the married man — stayed in Liverpool, wanting very little to do with them, though he did send money and occasional birthday presents.

All this your father told me early in our relationship, when I asked him what had happened to his father. Though he never said so, I understood this history as central to not only the relationship between your father and your nain, but how they lived in the world. They were two people touched by shame, and for a long time they had only each other. They worked hard to prove they belonged to the rural middle class of which they were uneasy members.

Your nain, in particular, was constantly worried about the slightest disgrace, believing it would expose her as an imposter. Your father had inherited this preoccupation, interpreting it in his own way and imposing it just as exactingly. It was only after I left that I realised the toll it had taken on me, this constant pressure to conform to their expectations, which were rigid and high and reverberated powerfully between the walls of this house.

I was thinking about this a lot as I watched Greta play the role of new mother, looking after her newborn under their scrupulous gaze. I realised how stressful it was to have those closest to you standing in judgement when the pressure to mother correctly was already so immense. With every criticism levelled against her by your nain — your father was more subtle, administering his disapproval with silence and neglect — I was taken back to what it had been like for me, and my sympathy for Greta grew.

The most contentious issue was feeding. Although the baby was three weeks old and Greta had made it unambiguously clear she was choosing to bottle-feed, they couldn't let it go. It wasn't helping that Deryn was a sickly newborn, similar to how your sister had been in the early months — straining with reflux, crying with every feed, hard to settle. Vividly I remembered how demoralising it had been to care for a baby I couldn't soothe. It makes you feel all kinds of unworthy. Greta was struggling along, as new mothers did, striving for solutions.

One evening she came through the front door, leaving Deryn asleep in the pram in the hall, and breezed into the kitchen, placing a tub of formula and a small box of colic drops on the counter.

"Where have you been?" said your father.

I was with Catrin at the kitchen table, helping her colour in a butterfly. She was very particular about which colours I was allowed to use and which parts of the butterfly I should colour. In the few days I had been home, your sister had quickly accepted me as another adult in her life, someone else to play with and ask for drinks and snacks. She wasn't holding a grudge, I suspected, because she didn't actually remember me, not in the same way you did. She accepted, in theory, that I was her mother, and perhaps she had vague memories — the way she looked at me sometimes, I felt there was a recognition there — but, essentially, in the transition from toddler to preschooler, she had lost her grasp on concrete recollections. It might have been only ten months but that was over a quarter of her life.

"I was in town with Deryn," Greta was saying. "I told you that."

"I rang you," he said. "It went to voicemail."

"My phone died. I forgot to charge it last night. Sorry. Anyway, I went to the pharmacy and found this, look. It's for babies with colic. It's easier for them to digest. The pharmacist told me about it. He was really nice. He also gave me this." She pointed to the colic drops. "You just put a couple of drops in her bottle."

She touched her fingers to the new products tenderly. Your father was barely listening. He had picked up the receipt from the shopping bag.

"Is this right?" he said.

"Is what right?" said Greta.

"Thirty quid?"

Greta glanced at the receipt. "For the formula and the drops, yeah."

Your father picked up the drops, holding the small box between his thumb and index finger. I had tried these drops with Catrin. They hadn't worked. I hoped he wouldn't tell Greta this. She seemed so happy and hopeful.

"Ten pounds for this?" he was saying.

"But you only use one or two drops at a time. It's actually quite good value."

"Is that what the pharmacist told you?"

"I think it's worth it if it's going to help her," said Greta, snatching the bottle from him. "Don't you want her to be able to feed without crying and being in pain? Don't you think it's worth the money?" Her eyes filled with tears. She glanced over at me indignantly, as though I was the one criticising her purchases.

I looked down at the butterfly, pretending I wasn't listening.

"Do you know what would allow her to feed without being in pain?" said your father. "Breastfeeding. Do you know how much that costs?" He turned his thumb and forefinger into the shape of a zero. "Nothing."

Greta looked at him in shock. "David!" she cried. "Why are you bringing that up again? I thought we agreed to stop talking about it?"

"I didn't know you were going to start spending my money on crap like this."

"It's not crap! And it wasn't your money. I used my own." She looked over at me again. I thought about leaving the room but trying to drag Catrin away from her colouring would only create another scene.

"What money?" said your father. "You don't have any."

"I have my maternity pay," she said. "You know that."

He laughed. "Greta," he said. "This stuff isn't going to help. It's a con. They take advantage of desperate mothers who are feeding their kids formula. But it's the formula that's the problem."

She was crying now. I looked down at Catrin, who had glanced up from her colouring, looking at Greta and your father with mild alarm. Greta picked up the formula and drops, shoving them back in their carrier bag, and ran out of the room.

"Greta!" your father shouted. He sighed, shaking his head.

"Catrin had reflux," I said, looking over at him.

At the mention of her name, Catrin looked up at me for a second before returning to her colouring.

"Yes, Elin. I remember," said your father.

"So why are you telling her it's because she's bottle-feeding?"

He sighed. "You always were simple-minded, weren't you?"

"I'm just saying, it seems a bit unfair."

"Just because Catrin had reflux when she was breastfed doesn't mean Deryn's reflux isn't because she's bottle-fed, does it?"

I shrugged. "I guess not."

"Anyway," he said. "You gave her bottles."

"What?" I said. "No, I didn't."

"Yes, you did, Elin."

"I gave her formula once. She had a terrible reaction because she was allergic. She had to go to hospital, remember?"

"No, I don't remember. But I do remember you giving her bottles. Regularly."

"Why are you saying that? It isn't true."

"I'm just telling you what I remember."

* * *

I started spending time with you and Catrin alone, just the three of us. Getting your father to agree wasn't easy, but after some persuasion he said it was okay as long as I told him exactly where we would be and when we would be back. I didn't argue. I needed to be with you away from the house, no one monitoring how I behaved. I took you to the swings, the beach, the leisure centre, the rabbit farm. Anything you wanted to do, we did it, and out in the world I felt a stronger sense of my right to be with you. I was less of an intruder, more able to relax.

You didn't trust me, though. That was obvious. And why should you? When I left, you were five, young enough to suffer terribly but old enough to carry the abandonment with you as fully-formed memory as the days and weeks passed and I didn't come home. You had lived with this betrayal for ten months. During that time another woman had come into your life, replaced me. A baby had grown in her belly — your sister, your blood, but not your mother's child. How had that made you feel? And how had your father handled it all? Had he given you the comfort you needed? Or had he deferred to Greta and your nain, assumed they would fill the void?

I turned all this over as I watched you pushing Catrin on the swing, reading the flavours to her in the ice cream parlour, passing her the cuddly toy she dropped in the back of the car. You were more protective of her than ever. You told her off now and then, but just as quickly as your voices rose — you scolding, Catrin wailing — you were on her side again, defending her fiercely. You were the first to get her inhaler if her breathing concerned you, and to rush over and comfort her when she fell. I guessed it was the accident — and her consequent illness — that had made you so loyal, the fact that her scar wasn't the only damage. I understood now that the acid had got into her lungs and caused a lasting respiratory illness, like a severe form of asthma. She had chest pain and trouble breathing and she coughed a lot, especially at night, when the weather was cold or if she was anxious or stressed. Apparently she was sensitive to everyday viruses, the coughs and colds that were a routine part of children's lives. And according to your nain, she couldn't cope with too much exercise, either. I had heard your nain make this point to Greta, telling her we must stop letting Catrin play for long periods with Beti as it was causing her to overexert herself.

"What does overexert mean?" you asked her.

"Nothing, darling," said your nain. "I just mean she shouldn't exercise too much, in case it makes her even more poorly."

"The doctor said it's good for Catrin to exercise," you said.

"Oh, darling," said your nain. "It's nothing for you to worry about."

* * *

I needed to get away from the house, find a place of my own. But the scope of the task was overwhelming. For one thing, I needed a job. I had very little savings, only enough for a deposit on a modest rental. I didn't know where to begin finding work here when, for one thing, I didn't speak the language, and for another, I had no qualifications or experience. I was also frightened of what would happen when I tried to leave. I couldn't escape the feeling that your father wanted me to stay. He wasn't going to say it out loud — it would sound too strange — but even with half-term coming to an end, he was maintaining that there was nowhere else to stay. I knew that wasn't true. So did he.

I knew him well enough to know that if he didn't get his way then there was no way I would have mine. I feared that, if I left, he would stop me seeing you, using the courts if he needed to. Unlike me, he had the money for a fight. He also had plenty of history to use against me — my abandonment of you, my carelessness in the months before I left, the accident that had left our daughter permanently damaged. There were witnesses to all of it. Whereas your father had nothing tangible against him, not a single thing. Why would a court decide anything in my favour? I might end up in a situation worse than the one I was in now — supervised visits, watched by a stranger.

I couldn't afford a solicitor. And I no longer had any friends who could support me through a custody battle, if I'd ever really had any at all. The school mums had been allies of sorts, but always with the understanding that the relationships were transactional and cooperative. I had been friendly with Sioned — the woman who owned Tŷ Gwyn — but never spent time with her outside of school events. She had four kids — all boys — on top of everything else she did, rushing between PTA meetings, football and swimming, running a bed and breakfast. When Rhiannon started school, Sioned made a point of bringing me into the fold, more than anything because I was an unknown entity and she wanted to slot me in. She added me to the messenger group and gave me her mobile number, telling me to ring her if I needed anything. I never asked her for a thing.

I no longer had her number, having thrown away my phone the day I left. If I wanted to check if there was any loyalty between us, I would have to go to her house — and what would showing up unannounced look like after all this time, except confirming any suspicion that I might be mentally unstable? It all seemed impossible. And it wasn't just the practical aspects. Being back here, in the physical vicinity of your father, I was beginning to feel as small and powerless as I had in the past.

Still, I began looking for somewhere to rent. There was very little available. When I mentioned to your nain that I might need to rent my own place, careful to make it sound like a future endeavour, she explained that local landlords had been selling their properties, creating a supply problem in the rental market.

"You'll never find anything," she said. "There's nothing out there."

SIXTEEN

Your sister was born in December. There was no snow that winter but there were storms. More than once, the power cut out in the middle of the night. I wouldn't have noticed if I wasn't feeding Catrin through the night, finding myself in total darkness as I nursed her in a blacked-out room. I felt like a cavewoman. As your father slept, I went looking for candles and torches, Catrin in my arms while the weak light from my phone lit the way. When the power came back, the radio burst to life and woke you and I sang you back to sleep as the sun rose.

You were three when Catrin was born and you were frightened by the power cuts and you were frightened by the wind that moved outside the window, day and night, whistling in the trees as I paced the floor with Catrin at my shoulder. "Shh, shh," I said, just like the wind.

Catrin was an unhappy newborn, often crying, hard to console. It is strange to think of this now, given what a happy, carefree child she became. But it was a physical thing, like she had an undiagnosed illness or she was allergic to my milk.

"It's wind," said the midwife. "Give her gripe water."

"Reflux," said the health visitor. "Have you tried a dummy?"

"I don't want her having a dummy," said your father. "She'll be fine."

"Let's hope you have enough milk," said your nain. "If she's anything like her father, she has a big appetite."

I expected you to be jealous but instead you claimed ownership. "Where's our baby, Mummy?" you would say to me. "Is she sleeping?" When the wind was extreme, trembling the glass, you crept over to the window, hiding against the frame as though it might see you.

"Who's there, Mummy?" you whispered. "Who is it?"

You were never satisfied when I said, "It's the wind. It's just the wind."

* * *

I was a mother. This was who I was. And when people gazed at you and Catrin with doting eyes, their approval moved through me and filled in some of the hollowness at my centre. When you threw your arms around me and said, "I love you, Mummy," I was wanted in a way that was pure. Yet somehow I was disappearing, too, unravelling like the thread you took from the sewing box and unspooled across the living room floor. You were so fiercely demanding, so self-centred, that my needs were invisible to you. That was how you were meant to be. Young children do not care what their mother wants or feels. "Don't do that, Mummy," you would say if I looked at my phone or began tidying away toys. "Look at me!" "Play with me." "I want more juice."

Your sister was, like all newborns, consuming and infinite in her needs. But I could not be cross with her the way I sometimes felt angry with you. When this anger rose, I suppressed it, but quickly it would rise again until it was hot and ready, a volcanic pressure at the surface of my skin. A tiny provocation unleashed it — you knocked over the nappies or spilled your juice — and I snapped at you like the mothers I hated, and then I hated myself.

* * *

One day in March when Catrin was three months old, I noticed a metallic taste on my tongue. My heart was beating very fast. Your father was at work. I was breastfeeding Catrin on our bed. You were next to me, watching CBeebies. Certain physical sensations had been constant since Catrin was born — a squirming in my tummy, a breathlessness that stayed with me all day. But the metallic taste was new and it scared me, as did the palpitations. *Something is wrong*, I thought.

Catrin began to writhe, as she often did during feeds; she seemed uncomfortable in a way you had never been, even when nursing you was at its most difficult. Suddenly Catrin bit down hard on my nipple, making me cry out in pain as her face turned red and she kicked her legs. I pulled her away and held her upright. The beating of my heart quickened. *I'm having a heart attack*, I thought. *I will die and the girls will be alone and crying out for me and what will happen to them?*

Suddenly, you jumped into the air, squealing in excitement as you bounced back down and rocked the mattress. Reaching towards me, you knocked Catrin's head against my own. Catrin wailed.

"Rhiannon!" I shouted, pushing you.

With a look of shock, you tumbled backwards, falling off the bed and hitting your head against the radiator before you collapsed on the floor. After a second of shock, you let out a devastated wail. "Why did you do that, Mummy?"

* * *

That evening I told your father I wanted to send you to Cylch.

"Just a couple of days a week," I said.

I tried not to make it sound like I was pleading. Conversations like this — about money, housework, childcare — were necessary, but they felt forced and tense now that the children took up all our time. They had to be planned, like work meetings, and they made us focus on each other in a way we rarely did anymore.

"Why?" he said.

He looked tired, which irritated me. He wasn't doing the night feeds, although, since Catrin was born, you had begun getting into bed with us every night, lying sideways, kicking your father in your sleep. He said it was driving him mad and threatened to go and sleep in the spare room. I wished he would.

"I think it would be good for her," I said.

I couldn't tell him I wasn't coping. He would find it laughable. Given he took care of you after he got home from work, and got up with you at six while I stayed in bed nursing Catrin, he felt I had plenty of support. In some ways, he was right. But he didn't know what it was like in between, alone all day with the two of you, no other adult in the house. He didn't understand the loneliness and the crushing responsibility.

"Good for her, how?"

"I just don't think it's a good idea for her to start school with no experience of other kids. The only people she spends time with are me and Catrin. And you."

"How much does it cost?"

Money, I thought. It always came back to money. But I was prepared, explaining to him that it was half the cost of the private nurseries. Although this appealed to his financial prudence, it also, as I had worried, made him suspicious that Cylch was full of poor children whose parents received benefits, the kind of people he didn't want our children to have anything to do with.

"Ceri's kids go there," I told him to reassure him. Ceri owned one of the most upmarket restaurants in the area. He raised his eyebrows, nodding, weighing it all up.

"I think she's bored," I said. "There's only so much I can do when Catrin is feeding so often. At Cylch they follow a syllabus to help them prepare for school. I don't want her to fall behind."

Education was everything to your father. He hated the idea of his children being disadvantaged in any way. When he read to you in the evenings, he talked to you about the

102

stories afterwards, as you were supposed to do, like a teacher would do at school, and as I was sure your nain had done with him. Meanwhile, I would shut myself in the bedroom with your sister, able to feed her without you climbing on top of us, tugging my arm, shouting, "Mummy, look at me!" By the time your father had got you to sleep it was eight or later and there was just enough time for us to eat dinner in front of the television. If I managed to keep my eyes open, we didn't talk. I didn't ask your father about his day and he didn't ask about mine. We just let the sounds ripple over us.

* * *

The morning you started Cylch, a woman called Gwyneth came out to greet us. She wore a bright-pink hoody with her name printed on the chest. I had met her at the introduction a week before, when you had chatted with staff — the 'aunties' — and played happily with the other children. When I explained to you that we were going back, you were delighted. But as we approached Gwyneth at the gate, your mood changed. You stopped dead in the middle of the car park.

I looked over at Gwyneth, beaming from behind the gate. Your eyes turned dark. Suddenly, you let go of my hand and sprinted in the opposite direction. Gwyneth gasped and I stood motionless, holding Catrin, as a small truck pulling into the car park swerved to narrowly miss you.

Gwyneth pushed open the gate, clanging it shut behind her, and hurried after you as you disappeared behind the parked cars. "She can't get out that way. I'll get her, don't worry."

I was paralysed, holding your sister tight against my body, as I watched Gwyneth moving among the cars.

"I've found her!"

Slowly, I walked towards them. You were huddled in the shadow of a parked car, your back against the wall. As Gwyneth tried to coax you away, crouching down and describing the painting the children were doing inside, I moved back to our car, realising I would be more useful if I wasn't carrying a small baby. Buckling Catrin in her seat, I returned to you. Gwyneth stood up.

"You know, it's better if I just pick her up and take her in. She'll cry, but prolonging it doesn't help anyone. Especially not her."

I knew she was right. I looked at you, glancing suspiciously between Gwyneth and me. Suddenly, you stood up and ran over to me, grabbing hold of my leg. I picked you up, your legs swinging at my hips.

"I want to stay with you," you said, starting to cry.

As I moved towards Gwyneth to hand you over, your grip around my neck tightened. Gwyneth held out her arms, nodding encouragingly. "She'll be absolutely fine when we get inside. They always are. If you hesitate she'll think there's something to worry about. It's got to be a clean drop."

I stared at her. "What did you say?"

"This isn't helping her," she said.

I watched Gwyneth for a moment. Then I walked back to the car, still holding you. When I opened the back door, I expected Catrin to be crying. But she was silent. I put you in your car seat. As I buckled you in, you stared at me, unable to believe I had given in. Even as I did it, I knew it was a mistake. But I couldn't stop myself.

Gwyneth walked over. I turned to face her.

"She's not ready," I said.

She pursed her lips. "It's your choice," she said. "You just have to—"

"Clean drop, I know. Sorry for wasting your time."

"Let us know if you change your mind."

"She's not ready," I said again.

She smiled, a mixture of pity and disapproval. "You both have to be ready."

* * *

That night, I put your sister down in her cot and had a bath. I peeled off my clothes, stained with vomit and milk, and threw them on the mounting pile of washing. Steam rose as the tub filled. The water was too hot, but I sat on the edge of the bath for a while, letting the steam encircle me. As I soaked in the hot water, I thought about what had happened and I was filled with shame. I had done exactly what you were never supposed to, what mothers never did, however much their child cried and however distressing they themselves found the separation. I had given mixed messages, encouraging you to feel positive about starting Cylch then confirming your unfounded belief that it was something to be frightened of. I didn't know what the repercussions would be, whether you would now believe you never had to go there or, worse, that you could refuse to attend school and I would give in to that, too.

But there was something else. Separating from you for the first time — I had not expected it to feel like that. It wasn't the weepy sadness I knew other mothers felt when their children started nursery or school, but a deep and dark fear. I had been terrified. Why? What was wrong with me? Nothing bad was going to happen to you and I would have seen you a few hours later. I wondered if you had sensed it, this disproportionate fear, communicated in the tension of my body. You couldn't hide fear from children. They learned it, absorbed it, made it their own.

Getting out of the bath, I wrapped my hair in a towel, stood at the sink and rubbed moisturiser on my cheeks. I was tired. It was dark outside, nothing lighting the fields but the moon, the mountains looming black shadows in the distance. Behind me, I heard a murmur, like a person speaking quietly, and I turned, assuming I would find your father there, having not heard him come in. Lately, I found myself startled often by him seeming to appear from nowhere, as though my ability to process the sounds and movements around me was shutting down. But when I turned the bathroom was still empty. I switched off the radio. The room was quiet. Beyond the closed door I could hear Catrin stirring. Water dripped from the tap into the emptied bath.

I turned back to the sink, picking up my toothbrush. Out of the corner of my eye, I saw a fast movement like a small animal scurrying along the wall. I turned, searching the floor, and walked over to the edge of the bathroom, looking behind the bin and the caddy full of bubble bath and shampoo. I moved back to the sink again, facing the darkness through the window. The murmur came again, more loudly now. Faintly, in the window, I could see the reflection of the bathroom. No one was there but me.

SEVENTEEN

When I found a post online for a converted outbuilding on a farm ten minutes from the house, I messaged straight away. The outbuilding was small, only two bedrooms with a combined living room and kitchen, but it was affordable, if I could get a job paying just minimum wage, and it would be easy to manage. The setting appealed to me — private but not completely isolated, with the farm only next door. As I messaged, I felt a flutter of excitement that I might have a chance to live in a place of my own, somewhere I could be your mother without anyone watching.

It was Saturday. I was in the garden, Beti lying beside me, panting in the heat. It was a warm day. Sunshine bathed the garden and streamed through the windows. The air was warm and sweet. Near where I lay, a bee, spellbound by petals and buoyed by the heat, droned loudly. There were gunshots in the air — your father out with his shotgun, shooting rabbits for the farm next door. Greta had taken Catrin and Deryn to the park. You had wanted to stay at home. The last time I had seen you, you were watching television in the living room, but you wandered out to the garden so quietly I didn't notice when you walked up behind me.

"What's that?" you said.

Startled, I turned off my phone screen. "Nothing."

You frowned. "Tell me."

You wore fleecy pyjama bottoms and a soft hooded blanket draped over your arms. I was worried you might tell your father. I wasn't ready for that. I needed more certainty. But I also didn't want to lie to you. It was hard enough getting you to trust me again.

"It was a house. Well, an outbuilding that's been turned into a flat."

"Why were you looking at it?"

"Because I'm thinking about renting it."

"What does renting mean?" you asked.

I explained.

"So you're leaving again?" you said.

"No," I said. "It's close to here. You'll be able to come and stay."

You looked sceptical. "Why can't you just live here?"

I sighed. "Greta and your dad need their space."

"Why?"

"You know how sometimes you don't like Catrin playing with your toys?"

You nodded.

"Well, this is your dad and Greta's home. I need a place that's mine. Does that make sense?"

"So I'll come and stay over?"

"Definitely. You and Catrin might have to share a room. Would that be okay?"

"That's a good idea," you said. "Then I can help with her inhaler in the night-time."

"Good thinking," I said. "You can help me look after her."

"And you'll look after me?"

"Yes," I said. "I'll look after you."

You watched me carefully. "Can I show you something?"

"Of course," I said. But I was alarmed by the dark expression on your face. I stood up, brushing grass off my trousers.

"I'm just going to get my trainers," you called as you ran into the house. You were gone a long time. When you came back, you had changed into clothes, your trainers on and tied perfectly. You led me along the track behind the house that circled the farm then sloped down towards the woods.

"Rhiannon, where are we going?" I said, looking back at the house.

The back door was unlocked, the windows open. Beti was still loose in the garden, watching us as we moved past the wall. Your father was close by. I could still hear the gunshots in the air.

"I need to shut Beti away, don't I?" I said.

You ignored me, rushing ahead. I shouted for you to be careful, running downhill towards the road. Once we were past the farm, you led us across the lane, which was deadly quiet, and onto the wooden bridge over the stream. The water below glimmered in the light, punctured by rocks. Insects hung in the air, the thousand midges drawn to the water when the weather turned warm. On the other side of the bridge were the woods, a stretch of trees clustered at the foot of the mountain.

Moving deep among the trees, the wood smelled of ripening fern. Bluebells bloomed in thick patches. The ground was dry. Birds chirped in the high branches. You were far ahead, running over inclines then disappearing for a second before the ground rose again. Trying to catch you, I tripped over the root of a tree and fell to the ground.

Finally, you stopped in a clearing. When I caught up I was breathless. Your father would be furious to know I had taken you out of the house without telling him where we were going. But I hadn't taken you. You had taken me. *But who is the adult, Elin?* he would say. *Are you a child?*

I looked around. The clearing was an intersection of footpaths, shadowed by trees, with bare ground in the middle. You were standing next to something on the far side. I walked over to find a piece of broken slate pushed into the mud. Scratched into the surface was *MUM* in capital letters, and next to the slate, a glass jar with dead bluebells and grey feathers, a wild and scant bouquet.

Somewhere behind me, a bird fluttered from the trees. You sat down on the ground, sighing, and began pushing a stick through the dry mud.

"Who did this?" I said.

You looked at me. "I did."

"On your own?"

You didn't answer. I was chilled by the thought that you might have been coming down here alone. I was even more chilled by this strange memorial. Abruptly I remembered how, when you were four, you had asked me about death. We were watching television, Catrin in my lap and you beside me, when you turned to me and said, "Mummy, is it true that all people will die, even if no one kills them?" There was no fear in your voice, only curiosity. Still, I could hardly bear to tell you the truth. But you waited, blinking. "Mummy?" you said. "Are you listening to me?" Finally I nodded.

"Yes," I said. "All people will die. Even if no one kills them." You stared at me for a few seconds before turning back to the television. You never brought it up again.

You were staring at me now, still sitting on the bare ground. "Did you leave because I was so so bad?" you said.

"What? No. God, no. Is that what you think?"

"I did bad things," you said.

I sat down in front of you. I wanted to hug you but I was afraid it would frighten you. I didn't want you running off in the middle of the woods. Instead I leaned forward and said, "Rhiannon, you didn't do bad things. It wasn't your fault. None of it." You stared at me. I knew you wanted to ask why I did leave, then. But you said nothing. "It was nothing to do with you," I said. "It's hard to explain when you're so little."

"I'm not little. I'm nearly six."

"I know. But it's still hard for you to understand grown-up things. But one day I'll explain everything. I promise."

* * *

We walked home in silence. The sun was still high. There were a hundred things I wanted to say but none of them felt right.

You were not even six — how could you understand? I had always felt you understood more than I gave you credit for. At the same time there were moments when you would ask something and I was reminded of your innocence, how children came into the world knowing so little compared to what they needed to learn. I had never been sure how to talk to you then. And I wasn't now. I would look at you, feeling that you were both transparent — telling obvious lies, plainly declaring the basest feelings — and at the same time complex and inscrutable, driven by emotions that neither of us understood.

Now you were a marginal age, drifting into childhood, the coddled preschool years behind you. You no longer wanted stories at bedtime, choosing instead to watch your tablet alone in bed until your father came in to kiss you goodnight. Who did you talk to in quiet moments, like you used to talk to me? When I considered the fragments of a mother you were carrying — my picture in the living room, a piece of slate in the woods, your memories of me from before, me here now — I could feel the hazardous confusion of it. It was hard to believe I had inflicted such precariousness on my own child, just as my parents had done to me.

* * *

The rest of the walk home you held my hand. When we reached the track, you said, "Did you go away because Catrin got hurt, is that why?"

I stopped and looked at you. "In a way, yes. But it was more complicated than that. I wouldn't have left her when she was poorly unless I felt I had to."

"I didn't do it," you said.

I looked at you. "Didn't do what?"

You didn't reply. You were distracted, tracing a woodlouse along the top of the wall with your finger.

"Rhiannon?" I said. "You didn't do what?"

"Hurt Catrin," you said, your back still turned as you studied the insect.

"Of course you didn't," I said. "It wasn't your fault."

I nearly said it was mine. But I stopped myself.

"You know woodlice?" you said, turning to face me. "When you turn them over at this time in the year, the mummies have eggs under them."

I nodded. "I know."

"And then they hatch and the babies come out."

"That's right."

"And the mummy stays with them."

"Yes."

"But not with moths, no? Moth babies don't see their mummy anymore."

* * *

As we approached the house I was thinking about the accident, what I could remember of it. The phone call from your nain, who had fallen downstairs after getting home from your party. She had had too much to drink, which wasn't like her. She fractured her leg, dragged herself to the landline. I was clearing up when it rang, walking around dumbly with an open bin bag, stuffing deflated balloons and wrapping paper inside. Catrin was asleep in the nursery. You were still up, shattered but overexcited, playing with your new toys. Your father was outside, furious with me because of how I had behaved at the party. He had gone out to work on the patio, cleaning the concrete slabs with diluted brick acid, the steel bucket at his side. Through the glass he clenched a hard brush in his gloved hand, a mask over his face.

I stared at the phone as though knowing, in that second, that it signalled the start of everything. When I picked it up I heard your nain's hysterical whine.

"David? Is that you?"

"It's Elin," I said.

"Oh!" she cried. "Get David! Please!"

I hesitated. "He's outside. He's—"

"Get him now! Quickly!"

I glanced at the patio again. As I moved towards the glass, the world seemed slow and surreal. It was the party, I had thought at the time. All those people in our house — talking, laughing, drinking — had done something to my brain. I was still absorbing it all. Walking towards the doors, your father on his knees with the bucket at his side, was the last thing I remembered. My next memory was being in the hospital, your sister bandaged in a rolling cot, tubes pumping oxygen into her lungs, and your father at her bedside, refusing to speak to me. There was a terrible sense of his anger in the air. I knew he hadn't spoken to me for hours, not since before the accident. Then finally, he said, coldly, staring at Catrin's unconscious body, "I told you how dangerous it was to let her outside. You did it anyway. You're not fit to be a mother."

The hours in between were lost to me, coiled in the recesses of my brain like a caterpillar dead in its cocoon.

* * *

That evening I told your nain that I was worried you had been going to the woods alone.

"What on earth makes you say that?" she said.

I didn't tell her about our excursion that afternoon. I just said, "It was something she said."

"Oh, I'm sure she was just confused. You know what they're like."

"I don't think so," I said. "I think she goes down there."

"That's ridiculous," she said. "David would never allow it. Neither would I."

EIGHTEEN

The next time I was on my way to see Ben it was a Wednesday evening. I waited for my train, as I always did, at a small station near my flat. It was November, winter closing around us. The weather was getting colder, the days shorter, and I knew it would be dark when I came back. The platform was raised above the houses, with black roofs and bare trees below and a white sky overhead, and it was empty except for myself and a man, getting on the same train.

This man I had seen before at this station, more than once. He was medium height and thin with an olive-green raincoat that he wore with the hood raised, even when it wasn't raining. I never saw his hair, only his face, framed by the hood. His nose was large and his lips were thin. He carried a satchel. It was hard to know his age.

While we waited for the train, I imagined all the places he might be going. I wondered about his family and friends, whether he lived alone or with children, and although we never spoke to each other, and I knew nothing about him, not even his name, I thought of him as my friend, my old, good friend.

* * *

His office was cold. The window behind him was open, as it had been every session since we started. The sky was white, the tree outside the window dwindled and bare.

"Do you want me to close the window?" he said.

"I don't mind," I said.

But I was cold. He waited, watching me.

"Yes," I said. "I'd like you to close the window."

He got up immediately and moved behind his chair, reaching out for the white handle, pulling the window closed, lifting the handle to lock it in place.

* * *

Since he'd brought up the issue of avoidance, I hadn't been able to stop myself from telling him any random story that came into my head. I found myself doing it more each session. I wasn't trying to dodge therapy, at least not knowingly. It was just that, since starting, I was remembering things I had forgotten, and I felt the urge to tell Ben everything, all of it.

"When I was living with Jude, a boy came to stay for a while," I told him one day. "His name was Luke."

"This was another foster child?" he said.

I nodded. "I remember him very clearly. He had skinny legs and thick eyelashes — you know, like little kids have sometimes? Especially boys. Well, maybe they're just more noticeable on boys. Anyway, he couldn't talk."

"Couldn't or wouldn't?"

"I don't know. Jude told us that his mum — she was in police custody — said he'd never said a word."

"How old was he?"

"Two. The only sound he made was this high-pitched squeal. I had never heard a child make a sound like that before. The first couple of times he did it, all the kids stopped playing and stared at him. It was shocking, the sound."

I paused. Ben took a breath and I wondered, fleetingly, if he was annoyed with me.

"I don't know why I'm telling you this," I said.

"It's fine," he said. "Carry on."

I thought back to what I was saying. "There was another thing he did. Whenever he saw an adult — I mean, any adult, like the postman or the agency woman — he would walk up to them and grab hold of their leg."

Ben nodded, unsurprised.

"Don't you think that's strange?" I said.

"It's not normal behaviour in that age group, no. Or in any age group, come to think of it."

"It made Jude really upset. She would have to go over and pull him away. And then he would make that squealing sound."

Ben cleared his throat. "It sounds like an attachment disorder."

I nodded. "What's that?"

"As you say, children don't usually approach strangers. But that's provided they've formed a secure attachment to a caregiver."

"And if not they grab onto any adult they see?"

"Not always. But they're less likely to discriminate between safe and unsafe if they've never known safe."

"Jude asked his key worker what she should do. It was making people uncomfortable."

"What did the key worker say?"

"She said, 'Let them be uncomfortable. It's nothing compared to what he's been through.'"

Ben smiled. "She had a point."

There was silence. Then Ben said, "What made you think about that?"

"I don't know. He just came into my head the other day. He was only with us for a few weeks. I never saw him again. I'd forgotten all about him until recently. After he'd gone, I asked Jude if . . ."

I paused. There was a whooshing in my mind, like the crashing of a wave.

"If what?"

116

"If I was like that when I arrived. I was the same age as him, so . . ."

"What did she say?"

I looked at him. "She said I wasn't like that at all. I had a few medical problems but, emotionally, I was normal."

He looked at me. "Why do you think that was?"

"At the time I thought it meant that whatever happened to me couldn't have been very bad, compared with whatever happened to Luke."

"Do you have any evidence for that?"

"No. Just the fact I wasn't so messed-up."

"Children respond differently to trauma," said Ben.

"Jude said I was always okay, more or less. 'You're so good, Elin,' she used to say to me. 'How are you so good?'"

NINETEEN

By the time your sister was six months old, I did not recognise myself. The world was tilted and blurred. My mind was chaos. I never felt fully awake. I was often unwell, which didn't help. Given neither of you were in childcare, I didn't know how you picked up the stream of viruses and infections that plagued us. But the illnesses could not explain my state of mind, the way I lost chunks of time, unsure, when your father asked, what had taken place in the hours since I'd seen him last, making things up so as not to make him think I was losing my mind. The illnesses couldn't explain the noises in my head, the sudden movements in the corners of my eyes, nor how my body turned cold and I would shiver so violently I had to turn up the radiators and climb under the duvet, telling you and your sister we were hiding from a monster as they shrieked with excitement and clung on.

    I became convinced I was causing the illnesses. As your sister's reflux continued and she developed eczema on her face and legs, I believed that my breastmilk was poisoning her. I tried formula instead, which made her vomit so violently I had to take her to the hospital, waiting for over an hour in the waiting room as she lay floppily in my arms, vomiting green bile down her sleepsuit once her stomach had emptied of milk.

Then there were the accidents. You fell down, bumped your heads, trapped your fingers. The second time Catrin tumbled down the steps to the utility room, your father lost his temper.

"Why was the stairgate open again?" he shouted. "After last time?"

"Rhiannon opens it!" I cried, shamefully blaming you for my own negligence. You were three.

"Then you should be watching her, shouldn't you?" he hissed.

"I can't watch the two of them every second! It's impossible! I'm trying, David, I am."

"Try harder."

A month later, your big toe was crushed by a falling rock on the garden wall. You had lifted it to look for bugs. We waited in A & E for five hours. The next day, you had surgery, struggling against the general anaesthetic as three men held you down until your body became floppy and lifeless. A week later, the stitches got infected. Three times a day I force-fed you antibiotics, closing your mouth until you swallowed, just as the surgeon and technicians had forced the mask on. You hated the taste and you hated me for forcing the medicine on you, crying bitterly when it was over. These were the things we did to children when we were trying to make them better.

* * *

The car incident happened during a heatwave in August. Catrin was eight months old. You were three. I had taken you to soft play. The heat was impossible to escape. Anywhere air-conditioned was swarming with people. As it was the summer holidays, the area was packed with schoolchildren and their parents, not to mention the millions of tourists who flooded to north Wales in the holidays.

We left the soft play at two. The sun was hot and high. A long afternoon stretched ahead. I planned to take you home and fill the paddling pool or give you cool baths to bring your temperatures down. You were red-faced, your hair sopping with sweat, and giddy from the stimulation and mayhem of the soft play. When we reached the car you ran to the front and hid, your eyes peeking above the rim of the hood. When I moved towards you, you dashed to the back, giggling. I was irritated and thirsty, holding Catrin in my arms, wanting to get home and drink something. During those years I didn't look after myself. I didn't drink when I needed to. I missed meals and medical appointments. All those things seemed trivial and impossible.

I opened Catrin's door, the heat from the car hitting me like an oven. Her car seat buckle was scalding hot. I wrapped a muslin around the metal to protect her skin, aware of you still loose near the road. I was parked on a side road off the high street but cars sometimes turned in, less than a hundred yards away.

After strapping your sister in, I knew I would have to force you into the car. You were in one of those moods. You would not be coerced. I threw my handbag and keys on the driver's seat. As I moved round to where you were hiding, you giggled, ducking away from me and crouching behind the wheel. My anger sharpened. Eventually, I got hold of you from behind. You let out an indignant cry, squirming and kicking, your sandals banging against my thighs. With your elbow you delivered a sharp blow to my stomach.

"Rhiannon!" I said through gritted teeth, squeezing you tighter against me than I should have. You began to sob. I moved to your door. The sweat between us — so much I didn't know if it was yours or mine — was loosening my grip. I felt you slipping as I reached for the handle. When the door didn't open, I assumed I hadn't gripped the handle properly. I tried again. You were still wailing in my arms. This time I wrapped my hand firmly around the handle.

The door was locked. Through the darkened window, I saw your sister, on the far side of the back seat, blinking over at me. I moved round to her door and found it also locked. I tried the driver's door. None of them opened.

How could the car be locked? I had unlocked it. No one had touched the keys, which were on the driver's seat where I had thrown them. My bag was on the seat with them, containing my phone. I looked at Catrin again. For a moment, I couldn't get my head round any of it — the keys on the driver's seat, the locked doors, the heat and Catrin in there, alone.

Then I snapped into action, like a zap of energy injected into my blood, and ran to the high street, you bouncing against my thigh.

"Mummy, where are we going?"

I looked around, taking in the people on the pavement, milling between the shops, holding ice cream cones. I spotted a woman pushing a double pram, her skin lightly wrinkled and sunburned. As she approached, I stepped out in front of her. She stopped, pulling back like I might be crazy. As I began to tell her my situation, she softened, bending down to find her phone at the bottom of the buggy. "The battery's low," she said.

She was right. The little bar in the top corner had only a slither of red. Holding the phone, I hesitated, struck again by that self-doubt, the fear of wasting the time and resources of essential public services. What if I had made a mistake, Catrin wasn't really trapped, I was making a fuss over nothing?

Then I dialled 999. A fire engine came, sirens blaring. Turning into the side street, parked cars obstructed its way, forcing it to reverse and manoeuvre. This took an unbearably long time. *Crash into them*, I thought. *Knock off their wing mirrors — who cares?* Your sister was crying now, wondering why you and I were on the wrong side of the window while she was inside a hot car. I pressed my face to the glass, talking soothingly to her. But the wail of the sirens drowned me out.

A fire officer jumped down from the cab. "How long's she been in there?"

Two other officers emerged behind him. They wore full uniform — yellow helmets, black boots, heavy shirts. I had no sense of time, which had slowed down.

"Maybe half an hour," I said. "But I'm not sure."

"Do you have the child lock on?"

I hardly wanted to admit that I'd never got round to it, but I sighed and said, "No."

He nodded. "We'll break the glass."

I nodded, thinking I could have done that myself.

"Right," he said, puffing out his cheeks. "Try getting her to look your way through that other window. We don't want glass in her eyes."

Your sister was hysterical now, screaming as she watched helmeted men in buckled shirts gathering at the window. Their method was gentle and slow. No shards flew in Catrin's direction at all. Instead, fissures appeared gradually in the glass until the whole window cracked like a trodden slab of ice, a thousand fragments collapsing. As the glass shattered, Catrin's screams pierced the open air. She squirmed in her chair, turning her body away from the officer towards her window, frantic to escape. One of them reached through the broken window and opened the door. He stretched over Catrin, who was wailing in terror, to unlock her door. I ran round the car, yanked it open and unbuckled Catrin, her skin hot and slippery with sweat.

"Get her in the shade," said the first fire officer, walking round the car and studying your sister, who cried in my arms, her face rash-red, her hair wet with sweat. "Plenty of fluids. If she's sick or doesn't seem right in any way, take her to A & E."

* * *

When we got home, Catrin was still alarmingly hot. Putting the television on for you, I ran a cool bath and lowered her in, sprinkling tepid water on her head. I dressed her in a clean nappy, took her downstairs and placed her in front of the electric fan in the living room. She babbled gently. I went to the kitchen and made her some water and apple juice. Back in the living room, she had toddled over to the fan, reaching up to poke her fingers dangerously close to the slats.

"No," I said, picking her up.

She took a few gulps of the apple juice before vomiting down my top. Wearily, she flopped against my shoulder, her forehead hot against my neck.

I looked at you, engrossed in the television.

"I don't know what to do," I muttered.

You looked at me. "Mummy," you said, "that fire officer said, if Catrin is sick, we have to take her to the hospital."

I nodded. "You're right. He did."

But I couldn't bring myself to go back out, to take either of you near doctors or fire officers or anyone else. They frightened me, their disapproval and judgement and power. I lay on the couch, holding Catrin against me in the stifling heat.

* * *

Your father was home by five.

"Where's the car?" he said, walking into the living room.

"I thought it would stay cooler in the garage."

Really, I had parked it in there so he wouldn't see the window. I wasn't sure I wanted to tell him what had happened, though I doubted I could get it fixed before he found out.

"What's wrong with her?" he said, looking down at Catrin, floppy and red-faced in my arms.

"She's just hot," I said.

"Why is that window open?" he said, tutting as he crossed the room. "You're letting heat in, Elin, not out." He shut the window and drew the curtains.

"Daddy," said Rhiannon, looking up from the television, "we saw a fire engine."

"Did you?" he said absently. After he had left the room, I considered telling you not to tell him what had happened.

123

But I couldn't bring myself to involve you in my deceit. Besides, if you knew it was a secret, you were more likely to blurt it out.

I heard a car on the drive. The front door opened, your nain's voice in the hall. Your father had given her a key, though I had asked him not to, and she now came round whenever she felt like it.

"Nain!" you squealed, jumping off the couch.

"There's my little angel! And how is poor little Catrin?"

My heart stopped.

Your father's voice came back in reply. "Catrin? She's fine. Why?"

"After what happened earlier!" cried your nain. "Janet told me all about it. She was in Lyndsey's having her nails done. She saw the fire engine across the street."

There were footsteps in the hall, slow and deliberate. Your father appeared in the living room doorway.

"I was going to tell you," I said quickly.

"When, exactly?" he said.

You appeared beside him, taking hold of his hand. Looking up, you said, "Daddy — the fire officer said, if Catrin is sick, we have to take her to the hospital."

TWENTY

While I waited for a reply about the rental, I wondered how I would get round the problem of your father. I thought about talking to Greta. She must have wanted me out of the house as much as I wanted to leave. What kind of future did she have with your father if his ex-wife — his wife — was in the spare room? I wondered if together we could make him see that it was in everyone's interest, including his, for me to leave. Perhaps we could make him think it was his idea. But I couldn't trust her not to talk to him, make him feel I was conspiring behind his back.

I decided to try talking to him directly, at least once, to reassure him I was no threat. I didn't want to take you away. I just wanted a life. He must have known this was reasonable. Besides, I knew he would prefer to settle things privately, if we could. He distrusted lawyers as much as he did doctors and nurses.

I felt it was safer to mention work first, telling him one morning that I wanted to find a job. I tried to make it sound like I wanted his help, rather than his permission. It was a fine line, making him feel he was important — indispensable — but not going along with the idea that he was in charge.

"You know everyone round here," I said. "I was thinking you could ask around? Text a few of your friends? Ceri, maybe? I wouldn't mind waitressing. Or even housekeeping, if he needs anyone to clean the rooms."

"Why do you want a job?" he said, banging his cafetière against the rim of the bin to dispense with the wet coffee inside. He sighed as some of it spilled on the floor, and he took the kitchen roll from the counter.

"I'd like to contribute," I said. "Get clothes for the girls. Toys. I haven't been able to buy them anything since I got back." This was dangerous territory, though, letting him know how financially weak I was.

"The girls don't need clothes. They get plenty from their nain. And you are contributing." He was kneeling on the ground, cleaning up the spilled coffee. "You're helping with the girls. That's more important than money. Greta is relieved she can just focus on Deryn now. And Mam was really in need of a break."

"I want to contribute financially, though."

He stood up, putting the dirty piece of kitchen roll in the bin and snapping the lid closed. "You've never worried about contributing financially before."

"It was different then," I said.

"Why?"

I looked around the room, exasperated to have to explain. He was being facetious. "We were a couple. You were working and I was looking after the house and the children. We're not together anymore. I have to support myself now, don't I?"

I didn't mean to make this a question. It was a fact. But your father was dubious. Saying nothing, he moved back over to where he had been making his coffee before the spill had distracted him.

"And there are six of us under this roof now," I added.

With his back turned he said, "It's not a problem. I've got no mortgage. The business is doing better than ever. There's no issue with money."

126

"Okay," I said. "But I need money of my own. I can't ask you to buy things for me if I need something."

"What do you need?"

I sighed. "That's not the point."

"What is the point?"

"David." What was I supposed to say? *I'm a grown woman? I need a job, a house, a life of my own?* All this was obvious. But he was doing his best version of brushing me off as an irrelevance, a minor obstacle in his morning routine. This was his most frequently employed tactic, even more than ridicule, and it was worse, in a way — the light, casual dismissal making you feel you weren't even worth the effort of bullying.

"I can't stay here for ever," I said.

"You don't have a choice," he said.

"What?"

He turned around, looking at me. "How are you going to support yourself, Elin? You've never had a real job. No one is going to employ you."

"That isn't true. People with no experience get jobs all the time."

"The worst kinds of jobs. Do you really want to work long hours on minimum wage cleaning dirty caravans like a Romanian? Just so you can have some independence?"

He said *independence* mockingly, like it was an absurd objective. I knew I was getting to him, otherwise he wouldn't have switched tactics. But he couldn't bring himself to say aloud that he wanted things to be left as they were. He knew how crazy it would sound. If there was one thing your father distanced himself from, defined himself in opposition to, it was craziness.

"You're right," I said. "You're completely right."

* * *

I gave up any attempt to negotiate. I would have to prepare for a fight, make as strong a case as I could for my own competence by finding a job and somewhere to live. I made a list of all the incidents he could use against me. I would need to get in touch with Ben, my only witness. I would keep your father in the dark, give him as little time as possible. His belittling view of me was an advantage, in this respect. He took it at face value when I said he was right, assuming I wasn't capable of doing anything without his help.

It was also to my advantage that he was distracted, stressed by his job and arguing with Greta almost any time they were both home. Deryn was becoming more unwell, more uncomfortable after her feeds, bringing up greater quantities of milk than ever. It was supposed to go in the other direction, colic and reflux settling as babies got older and their digestive systems matured. That was what happened with your sister. She had just needed time. But Deryn didn't just have reflux. She was picking up every cold and cough circulating. It was worse now that half-term was over and you had gone back to school, picking up viruses and bringing them home. This wasn't at all surprising. Yet your nain was convinced there was a terrible crisis, saying Deryn needed to see a doctor urgently. This was causing Greta a great deal of anxiety.

"Catrin was like this," I told her. "She picked up everything going in her first year. It was worse at the beginning. I wasn't even taking her anywhere, really. She just seemed to get ill at the drop of a hat. I blamed myself, too. But I think some babies are just like this."

We were in the living room. Your father was at the pub with some friends, leaving Greta alone with her escalating worry. It was not like him, I thought. You and your sister were upstairs, playing. Deryn was asleep in the Moses basket by the bay window. Greta and I were whispering, making sure not to wake her. One of the many things Greta and your father argued about was her tendency to keep Deryn in whichever room she was in, moving the Moses basket around the house with her. Your father complained that this only disturbed Deryn's sleep, made her wake when she otherwise wouldn't, and forced the rest of us to be quiet. "Why not put her down in her crib?" he would say. But Greta didn't like her shut away upstairs when baby monitors didn't work in the house. It frightened her. I understood that fear. As much as anyone made you feel you were being overprotective and paranoid, it was just how you felt.

"Do you think she needs to see a doctor?" Greta whispered to me. We were on the couch, facing each other as we leaned against the armrests at either end.

"You could take her to the GP, if it'll make you feel better," I said. "But they'll probably say the same."

Greta nodded, sipping her wine. She drank a lot, I had noticed, especially when your father wasn't around. She opened a bottle of wine early — at five if he wasn't home — and drank through the evening, finishing the bottle, sometimes opening another. Of course your father knew she had been drinking and rarely failed to remind her that it was irresponsible when looking after a baby. This didn't stop her. It was her only mechanism for coping with her anxiety, which was getting worse by the day. I wondered if it was the reason she hadn't wanted to breastfeed. It would have entailed giving up this level of drinking. I remembered how I had wanted to drink when you were little, to take the edge off the crushing pressures and relentless routines. But I restrained myself, wanting to get things right, be the best mother I could. And knowing how ashamed your father would make me feel if I did. He only drank in moderation himself — a lager or two when he got home from work — and he saw it as a failing when people around him drank to excess, particularly parents. Particularly mothers. Breastfeeding mothers, in his view, shouldn't drink at all.

"Agatha says I should keep her in the house, stop taking her into town and stuff."

"That's crazy," I said. "It's Rhiannon bringing stuff home from school. Schools are full of coughs and colds."

"They also say it's because I'm not breastfeeding."

"I don't really believe that, either," I said. "I breastfed Catrin and she was the same. Maybe it's David's genes. He was a sick baby, from what Agatha has told me."

She looked at me in surprise. "He's never told me that."

* * *

When she woke up, Deryn had a temperature.

"She needs Calpol but she won't take it," Greta was saying, close to tears. "She keeps spitting it out!" The rest of us were at the kitchen table, eating. Greta had abandoned her food to console Deryn, holding her near the open back door to try to cool her down.

"You're making it worse doing that," said your nain, who had cooked the dinner and stayed to eat it.

"She's so hot," said Greta, ignoring her. "I think I should take her in."

Your nain nodded. "Maybe you should."

"Don't be ridiculous," said your father. "She's just got a cold. She'll be fine."

"But how am I going to bring her temperature down if she won't take the syringe?"

"You can put Calpol in her bottle," I said.

She looked at me. "Are you allowed to do that?" she said. She was sweaty from the humidity and the cooking heat. Outside, birds trilled happily in the trees, Beti lifting her head to stare through the glass.

"Yes," I said. "Well, maybe not officially. But I don't see why it's any different to them having it through the syringe. I did it with the girls all the time."

"And look how well that turned out," said your father.

"I'm not sure she should be having Calpol at her age at all?" said your nain. "But if you take her to the hospital, a doctor can decide."

Looking at Greta, your father said, "She doesn't need to go to the hospital. Check online later about putting it in the milk. For now, why don't you sit down and eat?"

"I'm not hungry," she said.

"You need to eat," said your father.

"She'll cry if I put her down again."

"I'll take her in a minute," said your father, cutting his meat.

"I can have her," I said. "I've finished."

Your father looked at me. I stood up and walked over to Greta, reaching out to take the baby.

"Are you sure?" she said.

"Of course. You sit down."

Greta took her place at the table, picking up her knife and fork and staring at the food on her plate. I believed her that she wasn't hungry.

"You really must eat," said your nain to Greta.

"Can I have a drink, please?" you said, looking at your nain. This was the first time you'd spoken since we'd sat down.

There was tension in the house, more because of your father and Greta's fighting than anything. He was losing his grip on her. That was how he felt. I could see it in his mood, how he was behaving. When they met, she had probably been more susceptible to his influence. But having children changed a person.

"Eat your food first, Rhiannon," said your father.

"I'll get her a drink," said your nain. "I don't mind at all." She winked at you as she got up.

"*Diod!*" said Catrin.

While your nain prepared juice for you and your sister, she broke the tension in the room with a rambling account of her conversation with a woman she had bumped into at the supermarket. This woman apparently used to cut your nain's hair and they'd got into a long conversation about the mother of a baby that had gone missing from the hospital. I had heard all about this baby — your nain talked about her a lot — but the new information she had acquired was that the missing baby's mother had been sectioned.

"I won't go into detail," said your nain, nodding towards you and your sister. "Suffice it to say she is very unwell."

"I'm not surprised," said Greta. "The whole thing is just horrible. I keep thinking how—"

"Greta!" said your nain. "You mustn't think about that."

"I know, I know," said Greta.

"About what?" I said.

I was pacing the floor with Deryn. She was hot, as Greta had said.

Greta shook her head. She still hadn't touched her food. "It's just that this baby was taken the night I had Deryn," she said.

I looked at Greta and then down at Deryn. "Were you on the same ward?"

Greta nodded. "It could have been her. I think about it all the time."

"You mustn't think about it," said your nain. "It's morbid. You'll drive yourself mad. It wasn't Deryn. It was some poor other woman's child."

"I don't understand how this kind of thing can happen," I said. "You can't get in and out of those wards without a fob or something. I remember constantly having to be let in and out when the girls were in the paediatric unit. The maternity wards are the same."

"Well," said your nain conspiratorially, "this is why the police think it's someone who knew someone who works there. Maybe a boyfriend or a friend who was let in, or even borrowed a fob, and now the staff member isn't coming forward because they don't want to get sacked. Who knows? There must be ways. It does happen, after all."

"This is the first time I've known anything like this to happen since I qualified," said Greta. She sighed, walking over and touching Deryn's cheek affectionately. "What I really hate about it all is that I'll never be able to think about that night without thinking about the stolen baby. It's not really fair, is it? And with David missing the birth, too, the whole thing was not how it was meant to be at all!"

She looked like she might cry.

"Why weren't you there?" I said, looking at your father.

"I was on a stag weekend in Prague. Which I only went on because Greta was barely thirty-six weeks at the time. I took a chance — and of course she came early, just to spite me."

"Oh, David!" said Greta, smiling. "Don't talk about her like that."

"So you gave birth alone?" I said, looking at Greta.

"Not exactly. The other midwives looked after me."

"Oh, of course," I said.

I felt sorry for Greta. From the type of person she clearly was, I knew she must have found it hard to go through childbirth without your father there. I looked down at Deryn, imagining if she had been the baby who'd been taken instead of the one that was missing, thinking what that would have done to Greta and your father, how they would have explained it to you, not to mention Catrin, who was so in love with her baby sister. And then I imagined if it had been you, taken from me after the birth. Your nain was right. It didn't bear thinking about.

* * *

After dinner, Greta took Deryn for a walk along the track.

"I'll put the girls to bed," I said. Your father nodded at me from where he was bent forward, stacking the dishwasher. I left your father and your nain in the kitchen and took you into the living room, agreeing to let your sister watch an episode of her programme before bed. From next door I could hear your nain talking loudly to your father over the running tap.

"It can't be helping that she keeps taking her off for these long walks."

"Greta says it calms her down," your father replied. "What do you want me to say?"

Your nain sighed. "Well, poor Deryn wouldn't be nearly this poorly if Greta was breastfeeding. Breastmilk is full of antibodies."

To my surprise, your father said, "Catrin was breastfed. She was ill constantly, remember?"

He was tired, I could tell, wanting to clear the dishes and go to bed, wishing your nain would just go home. It was late for her to still be here. But through the open doorway, while you and Catrin fixed your gaze on the television, I could see her watching him intently, wanting him to pay the attention she felt the subject deserved. For her, your father was the vehicle through which life happened. Important things could only be done vicariously, through him. She observed, commented, complained, but it was he who had the power to transform her wishes into reality — if he was willing to take any notice.

"Not like Deryn," said your nain. "It's getting out of hand. And, David, I do worry terribly about Catrin catching something, too. You know how vulnerable she is. It only takes a harmless virus and it could be catastrophic. David — are you listening?"

Your father sighed. Frowning, he squeezed the bridge of his nose between his thumb and forefinger.

"Mam," he said. "You're not making sense. Do you really think it's Deryn who's bringing home illnesses? Greta hardly takes her anywhere."

"She certainly does!"

"Not really. It's Rhiannon," he said, lowering his voice so you and your sister wouldn't hear. "She's bringing things home from school. There's nothing we can do about that. Catrin herself will be starting school in a few months. In the meantime, she has to build up some resistance. You know what the doctors have said about this."

"That last specialist we saw didn't have a clue what he was talking about. He hardly knew Catrin's history."

"They all say the same thing. Anyway, if Catrin gets ill, it'll be something she gets from Rhiannon. Or from being with you — you take her out, too."

"Oh, hardly ever, David! I have my coffee morning on Tuesdays, which I don't always go to. Apart from that I keep her home, where she should be."

"She can't stay at home the rest of her life."

"Don't get upset, darling. It's not really Catrin I'm worried about, anyway — I was just saying that's an extra concern. It's Deryn I'm worried about. Wherever she's getting these illnesses, she'd be much better equipped to fight them off if she was being breastfed. Can't you talk to Greta again?"

Your father sighed. "I think that ship has sailed, Mam. Greta's mind is made up. And don't you think it's a bit late now? Greta hasn't tried to breastfeed since they were in the hospital."

"Oh, new mothers can resume breastfeeding any time, David. She's five weeks postnatal. Her body is chock-a-block with hormones."

At this point it was more like they were talking about a farm animal than a woman. Through the doorway I watched your nain move over to your father and put her hand on his arm.

"Don't you want her to have the best start in life?"

"What do you want me to do? I can't force her!"

"You have tremendous influence. I can see how much she looks up to you. Please try again. It's not natural, all this formula. It breaks my heart, the poor thing trying to digest milk that her body is too little to tolerate! I can hardly bear it."

He sighed. "I'll talk to her again."

TWENTY-ONE

There was a hum in my brain, a pulsing that energised me during daylight hours in my half-awake state, but then kept me awake at night, my mind swirling with trivialities — where had I put the yellow bottle? It was in my hand when I came through the front door but what had I done with it? And where were my keys? Did I give you too much Calpol at bedtime? I had been getting my doses confused. As my mind deteriorated, my need for control increased and I felt myself becoming obsessive. Every day, I took you out, and the outings were getting further from home. I drove for hours, pushing your sister's pram around a country park thirty miles from the house, surprised to realise, an hour or two after we had arrived, that we needed to leave, scrambling back to the car to be home in time for your father.

I didn't tell him anything now, if I could help it. I found myself lying all the time, even about little things, as though concealing minor details protected me from his judgement. He always found ways to belittle me, though — the state of the house, the front door left open, keys hanging in the lock, or the hob left on, slowly burning last night's bolognese.

* * *

When you were almost four, Catrin eighteen months, I took you to a fair. As always, I waited for your father to leave. As soon as I heard his van pull away, I rushed around, restocking the nappy bag, finding the girls' clothes. The world outside was big and open. So many places to go where no one knew us. As I struggled to get you both ready, I was gripped by panic, as though the difficulty meant we would never leave. But when you were strapped in your seats and the car flew down the motorway, I was free, fizzing with reckless abandonment, like running away from school.

When we arrived, stewards in hi-vis vests guided us in, the car bumping along the grass. Rows of cars filled the huge field. I got you out, moving Catrin's pram among the crowds while you walked beside us, the big sky above us. We wandered between stalls mounted with glinting mirrors, handmade soap and second-hand toys. Now and then, you broke free and I called you back, repeating my instruction to hold the pram. Though it made me furious when you ran off, I found your compliance almost as upsetting. As you walked along, sullen and chastened, I wanted to tell you, "Don't worry. It won't always be like this." But it would have been a lie.

By mid-afternoon it was time to leave. Apart from needing to be home before your father, you were becoming giddy with tiredness and overstimulation, reaching your limit. As we walked towards the car, I noticed a small tent with an open front. A girl in her early teens sat on a plastic chair, her bare legs crossed. She wore white trainers and a rebellious smile as a man with spiky hair assembled equipment. He was getting ready, I realised, to pierce her tongue. In the corner was a woman, knitting.

"Why we stopping, Mummy?"

I looked down at you. "Let's go in," I said, pushing the pram into the tent. The spiky-haired man glanced at me, then at you. I looked at the girl, remembering when Jude had taken me to get my ears pierced. I was eight or nine. I crouched down to face you.

"Shall we get your ears pierced?" I said.

You stared at me. "What is it, Mummy?"

I pointed to my earrings. "Like this."

You beamed, nodding. I was impatient as I waited for the girl to leave. When she finally did, I parked Catrin, asleep, in the corner of the tent.

"I'd like to have her ears pierced, please," I said. The man exchanged a look with the woman in the corner, who glanced up from her knitting.

"How old is she?" he said.

"Four," I said, hoping you wouldn't contradict me. It was almost true.

He nodded. "I'm fine to do it. I just have to make sure you know the risks, which are the same as for adults. Infection, swelling, bleeding."

You stared blankly at the man. I was sure you didn't understand those words, but a dark expression moved over your face, before you pulled your hand out of mine and ran out of the tent. Leaving Catrin, I sprinted after you, spotting the flash of your dress disappearing behind another tent. I ran across the walkway, knocking the arm of an old man, who looked at me in shock. By the time I reached the back of the tent, you were ahead again, running past the Portaloos.

When I finally caught up with you, I yanked you towards me, breathless and enraged.

"What are you doing?" I shouted.

You, too, were panting and red-faced, a defiant smirk on your face. But you were afraid, too.

"I want sweeties," you said.

I stared at her. "What are you talking about? You had sweeties."

You frowned. "I didn't."

I thought back over the day. You were right. I had promised them but we never went back to get them.

"We'll get them after you've had your ears pierced."

"I don't want to, Mummy."

"You don't want to what?"

138

"Ears."

"You just said you did! That man put you off. Come on. Let's get it over with."

I took your hand and pulled you back to the tent. You resisted, tugging your hand away. But I held on tight. I didn't know what I was doing and yet I was compelled by some mania. I was desperate to regain control yet I was out of control, out of my mind. My mind was going a hundred miles an hour. By the time we reached the tent, you were crying. I knelt down and held your arms against your sides. Tears rolled down your cheeks.

"Rhiannon," I said, "it will only hurt for a second. And when it's finished, you'll have your ears pierced like Mummy's. And then you'll be happy."

You watched me carefully, as did the man, who was sterilising his equipment with a browbeaten look, as though being forced to perform the service against his will. I sat on the chair, taking you in my lap.

"You'll have to hold her still," the man said, snapping on fresh gloves. I nodded. You took shaky breaths but slowly I felt your body soften. The man held out a tray of earrings. You chose butterfly studs. As he reached towards your right ear with cotton wool, you flinched.

"I'm just cleaning it, my love," he said.

"It's cold," you said.

Your voice was small. I felt awful. But I was gripped by a belief that I had to see this through. When your lobe had been cleaned the man reached for the needle gun. You stiffened. I held you, wrapping my arm around your front, stilling your head.

You gasped. "Mummy."

"Nice and still for me, okay?" said the man.

He bowed his head and closed his eyes briefly before placing the gun against your tiny lobe. You went still, an insect playing dead as the gentle click of the gun belied the pain of its needle. After a second's delay, you let out a stunned wail and pounded my legs with your fists in retaliation.

The man sighed. "I won't be able to do the other if she's like this."

"Just do it quickly!"

He gave me a look of disgust before moving round to her other ear. I turned your head the other way. She scrunched against me. When the second shot went in, you let out a fresh cry.

"All done now," I said, kissing your head. "You were very brave."

You sobbed. I looked over at the woman in the corner, who had put down her knitting and was watching me with contempt.

* * *

As we drove home a heavy feeling fell over me, like a bad hangover. You sat in the back, kicking your feet against my seat and chattering away about our odd experience. You couldn't believe your ears were pierced and you repeatedly touched them while I warned you to leave them alone.

"Still hurt, Mummy."

"It will hurt less all the time," I told you. "The main thing is to make sure they don't get infected."

"Special medicine," you said. "Can I hold it, please?"

You had requested to hold the saline solution several times, proud that the magical-looking blue bottle was yours.

"I'll keep it for now," I said.

As we drove up the track, I could see your father's van. It turned my stomach.

"Show Daddy," you said.

After I stopped the car, I turned and looked at you. With your little butterfly studs, you looked much older. "Show Daddy," I said.

Catrin was awake now and began to babble. I unbuckled you first. You scrambled from your chair and ran to the front door. I went round and lifted Catrin out. She had taken off her shoes but she clambered over the gravel in her socks as

I collected up coats and dropped food wrappers from the back seat.

You rushed upstairs, calling your father. You ran back down and found him in the kitchen.

"Daddy, look!"

"Hello, my angel," I heard him say. "Where have you been? I was starting to worry."

I stood in the living room. Catrin toddled over to her blocks and tipped them on the floor. The kitchen door was open but I couldn't see you or your father.

"Daddy, look," I heard you say.

There was a silence. I waited. Finally, your father walked into the living room.

"Are those real?" he said.

"Of course!" I said. "We got your ears pierced, didn't we, Rhiannon?"

You reached up and held your father's hand. "Do you like them, Daddy?"

"Rhiannon?" he said, slowly. "Can you go to your room, please? I need to speak with Mummy. I'll be up in a few minutes to get you ready for bed."

You stared at him. Then you looked at me. You didn't move.

"I stay with Mummy," you said.

Your father looked down at you. "Choose a story, Rhiannon. I'll be up soon."

You looked back at me again.

"Go on," I said.

You complied. Noticing you leave the room, Catrin followed you. Your father and I watched as you both disappeared upstairs.

He looked at me. "What did you do, Elin?"

"I pierced her ears," I said. "What's the problem?"

"What's the problem? Are you insane?"

Looking at his face, I was certain he would hit me. Part of me felt it would be a relief. Perhaps that was why I started blabbering on. "You need to stop making me feel like this,

141

David. I know how to look after my own children. I know what they need. You're not even with them most of the time!"

He wasn't listening. He walked into the kitchen. I heard him opening a drawer, rummaging inside. The sky outside the window had grown grey. From upstairs, I heard you talking to yourself, and Catrin babbling incoherently. When your father came back into the room I began to plead.

"It's not as bad as you think," I said. "It was just a spur-of-the-moment thing. It's not a big deal."

He walked straight towards me and put his hand on the back of my neck, guiding me to the coffee table. At first I didn't struggle. I didn't know what he was doing. But when he said nothing, I panicked.

"David," I said, pushing back. "What are you doing?"

He kicked my feet from under me. I fell to the floor. He took hold of my neck and pinned my head against the table, spreading his hand over the side of my face. He moved his body over mine. I was aware of how easily you or Catrin could slip downstairs and see us. For a moment, I saw myself as you would, subdued under the weight of your father, and I was ashamed. I closed my eyes and felt a stab of pain. At first, I couldn't place it. It didn't feel located anywhere, pulsing through my whole body. But as he lifted his weight, I realised, reaching up to feel the light metallic object hanging from my ear. A safety pin, pushed through my lobe, its sharp point scratching the skin of my neck on the other side. I felt the light trickle of blood. Taking a deep breath, I yanked the pin from my ear, lifted myself up. Dizzy, I looked around the room. Your father was at the door, preparing to go up and read you your story.

"David," I said.

"I don't want to hear it."

TWENTY-TWO

I didn't have to wonder how your father's conversation with Greta went. The next afternoon I had just put your sister down for her nap. I was feeling happy about this. Having put you both to bed the night before, Catrin had now allowed me to oversee her daytime nap for the first time. I had tried to do it a few days before but she had told me, politely, that she wanted your nain. But after playing together in the garden this afternoon — throwing the ball for Beti, watering the plants, looking at the flowers — she was exhausted and didn't mind when I picked her up and carried her upstairs. I gave her a dummy from the table beside her cot. When I lowered her over the rail she flopped on the mattress, a dead weight, turning her back to me. This was a good sign. She would be asleep very soon.

I stayed with her a while, letting her drift into heavier sleep, looking out of her window at the sloping fields and the sweeping patches of slate on the mountains. When I stepped onto the landing, closing the door quietly behind me, I heard the rumblings of the argument from their bedroom. The door was closed so it was unclear, at first, what they were arguing about. But then Greta shouted, "I've told you this so many times! I don't understand why you're saying it again!"

Then the door opened. She was on the landing.

"I can't cope with this," she said, more to herself than to him as she hurried towards the stairs.

Your father followed. "You're overreacting, as usual."

When he saw me there, in front of Catrin's closed door, his expression darkened.

"I just put her down," I whispered. "She's asleep. She's really tired."

I was worried they would wake her, the way they were acting. Greta paused at the top of the stairs, your father close behind, and stared at me for a few seconds before she fled downstairs, him hurrying after. Slowly, I followed them. You were at school — your nain was at her own house, so there was no one else around. Your father followed Greta into the kitchen. I sat down on the stairs, midway down, listening like the child of fighting parents.

"Just calm down for one second," your father was saying.

"I can't cope with this," Greta said again. "I need to get out of this house. I can't bear it. It's too much." She was taking deep breaths then exhaling them loudly like she was in the early stages of labour. "I can't cope with this," she said again. "I just can't do it."

"Jesus Christ," said your father. "You are so bloody melodramatic. I knew I shouldn't have talked to you. You are incapable of having an adult conversation."

They fell quiet, Greta continuing to take her long yoga breaths. I couldn't see what she was doing, whether she was sitting or standing, looking at your father or turned away, but when she spoke again she was calmer. "David, I can't keep going through this. I've explained why I can't breastfeed. You don't have to understand it. But you have to accept it. You have to accept it, David."

Your father came back gentler. "Greta, I'm not saying it's easy for you. But that first time you tried, after the birth — when you had those memories—"

"Not memories, David. Flashbacks."

"Whatever we're calling them," he said. "You were alone at the hospital. You had no support. Don't you think it would be different now, at home, with me here?"

She began to cry softly. "Please don't make me."

* * *

When the woman from the farm finally replied about the rental, I went to see it straight away. I went alone and told no one, not even you. The woman who owned the farm was called Margaret. She had told me in the message she had had a lot of interest and I would need to decide quickly if I wanted it. I knew the minute I got out of the car that I did, just from how it looked from the outside, the low stone building with ivy and flowers covering the walls, the stretch of farmland behind it and the backdrop of the mountains beyond. So often these things were not as you had hoped, but this was better. I moved through the rooms behind Margaret, pretending to listen as she explained about the boiler and the heating and the water. But I just wanted to pay the deposit there and then.

As she walked me back to my car, she asked me a few questions, explaining that she needed proof of employment and that she wouldn't accept anyone on benefits.

"I can't cope with any fuss," she said. "I'm too old."

I told her I was looking for work and had savings to cover the deposit. She looked uncertain and I rushed to reassure her.

"It's only because I've just moved back here. It's not that I don't want to work or lost my job or anything like that. I'll find something quickly."

I could have told her I was working but she would have asked where, and the likelihood was, round here, she would know the owners or someone who worked there.

"Let me know when you find work," she said. "In the meantime, I'll send through the contract for you to have a look."

* * *

145

I signed the tenancy agreement anyway and sent it back to her, just so she would know I was serious. I reassured her again in the email that I was looking for work and would let her know as soon as I found something. I began looking the next day, printing out my CV, bare as it was, and handing it in everywhere I could think of. I was down at the ice cream parlour, having just given my CV to the man at the till, when I saw Sioned. Tŷ Gwyn was right next to the shop so it wasn't surprising that she was there, though I was a little stunned to see her. She looked exactly the same, tall and stooping, her frizzy red hair tied back with a wide band.

"Elin?" she said, moving towards me. I was near the back of the shop, looking at the toys. The ice cream parlour was also a shop for the tourists. They had a selection of toys and I wanted to bring a couple of small presents home for you and Catrin, though I couldn't really afford it. My money was running out, that was the truth. Sioned was blinking at me like she had come across a wild animal. "I had heard you were home. I didn't really believe it, I don't think. Are you okay? We've been worried about you."

I nodded but I was surprised. It hadn't occurred to me anyone had been worried. I also remembered what your father had said to me when I got home — that no one wanted to see me. I looked at Sioned, who was watching me, waiting for an explanation.

"It's good to be back," I said, just for something to say.

"Where are you staying?" she said.

I looked at her. "At the house."

She stared at me. "With David and Greta? And the baby?"

I nodded.

When I didn't say anything else, she said, "It was just before you came back that this baby went missing. Did you know about that?"

I didn't know why she linked the two events in this way, but it felt as though she was accusing me somehow.

"I heard," I said. "It's terrible."

146

She nodded and looked away. "It's horrible. I don't know the mother except that she worked at the nursery for a while. As far as I understand it, she became pregnant by mistake. She wasn't sure she wanted it, you know?" She lowered her voice. "She'd been taking drugs during the pregnancy. It's not clear she would have been allowed to keep it. But now it's been taken, she's gone out of her mind."

I nodded. I was only half listening, wanting to get on with handing out my CV. But I was also aware that Sioned was being kind by talking to me about this missing baby and its distraught mother. My story — the bad mother who left her kids — had been replaced by a new local drama. By talking to me about it, I felt she was in some way offering me my old status as a basically acceptable mother.

Looking at her, I realised how strange it was that she had asked where I was staying. "Didn't David message you about a room?" I said. "I was looking for somewhere to stay when I got back."

She shook her head. "He didn't mention anything. I haven't spoken to him for a while, actually."

I wanted to ask if she was sure. But of course she was.

"I've got rooms if you need one," she said. "And I have a couple of caravans free."

"I think I've found somewhere longer-term. Although she won't take me until I've found a job. I just handed my CV in." I pointed to the man behind the desk.

"You won't get anything here," she said. "They've just had their intake for the summer season. I've got something for you, though, if you don't mind cleaning caravans?"

I looked at her. "I don't mind at all!" I said. I wanted to cry.

"Have you got a new number?" she said.

I nodded, reciting it as she keyed it into her phone.

"Shall I add you to the group again?" she said. "It's not really changed since you left!"

I thought about this. It was understood, round here, that mothers were in charge of everything when it came to the kids. I would have been amazed if your father had been added while I was away. More likely it had been assumed that, as long as there was no mother in the house, he was out of the loop and could be excused for not knowing what was going on. Still, I wondered if I should ask his permission before rejoining the group, feeling perhaps I had lost my right to this. But then I remembered he hadn't messaged Sioned at all about the rooms, and lied when he told me he had.

"That would be great," I said.

* * *

When I got home, your father's van was parked out the front. You were still at school. As far as I knew, Catrin was with your nain. I went upstairs and shut myself in the bathroom, ringing Margaret straight away to tell her I had a job. She listened quietly while I talked. When I finished she said, with genuine remorse, "I'm so sorry, love. I've had to go with someone else."

"What?" I said. "I don't understand."

It was only the day before that I had seen it. At the time Margaret had made it seem that if I found work quickly, it was mine. I knew she didn't owe me anything, but I was devastated.

"I really am sorry about it," she said.

"You told me to keep you updated about work. I got a job the next day." I knew I sounded like a child. But there was something maternal about this woman that made me feel I could express my disappointment.

"It's not that, love," she said. There was a silence as I waited for an explanation, trying not to cry. "You seemed lovely when we met. I just don't want any fuss. I'm not up to it."

"What do you mean?" I said. "What fuss?"

"I'm really sorry," she said again. "I have to go now. Good luck, love."

She hung up. I stared at my phone, trying to understand what had just happened. Downstairs, your father was in the kitchen. All the cupboards were open for some reason.

"What are you doing?" I said.

He didn't answer. He seemed to be looking for something, rummaging between tins and packets of pasta. On the counter were three bottles of wine, two unopened, one half empty.

"Where's Greta?" I said, looking at the wine.

"At her mam's."

He began to close the cupboards, one by one. Then he picked up the half-empty wine bottle and walked over to the sink. As he unscrewed the cap, I realised what he was doing. I knew this wasn't a good time to talk to him. But I didn't care. I was so angry.

As he poured the wine down the sink, I said, "Do you know a woman called Margaret Roberts? She owns a farmhouse out by the copper mine. She's renting the outbuilding."

He didn't say anything, shaking the upturned wine bottle to thoroughly empty its contents. The kitchen suddenly smelled of wine. He ran the tap and refilled the bottle with water, swilled it out then threw it in the recycling where it clinked loudly against the other glass.

"David?" I said.

"Mam knows her," he said finally.

"Right," I said. "So she told her I'm mental or something?"

"What are you talking about?" he said.

"Don't bother lying, David," I said. "I know it was you."

"Elin," he said, "I don't know what you're talking about, but if this woman thinks you're not a reliable tenant it's probably just because she asked around a bit. Plenty of people know you round here."

"I don't believe you," I said, though I wondered if that could be true.

"I'll talk to your mum instead," I said. "She's not as good a liar as you."

He sighed. "Fine," he said. "Mam did talk to her. But she didn't tell her anything that isn't true."

I stared at him. "Why did she do that?"

"I asked her to."

"I don't understand this," I said. "Do you expect me to stay here for ever? I need a life, David. I can't live here with you — and your girlfriend. It's crazy! And why are you pouring her wine away? Does she know you're doing that?"

He had moved over to the unopened bottles, putting them in a bag he had put on the counter then placing the bag by the door. At first, I thought it was pointless, getting rid of her booze, more an expression of his anger than anything else. She would just buy more. But of course that wasn't the point. The point was to show her that he could.

"Elin," he said, "I don't know what you expected. But I'm not going to let the girls come and stay with you in some shed in the middle of nowhere. That was never going to happen."

"Why didn't you talk to me about it instead of going behind my back? I'm not a child, David!"

"Because I can't trust you," he said simply.

"David, we can't go on like this."

He shook his head. "You can leave any time you want."

"But if I do you won't let me see the girls? That's what it comes down to, doesn't it?"

He didn't answer for a moment. "If I thought they were safe with you, it would be different."

"But it's okay for me to take them to the swings and the beach, as long as I'm living here? How does that make sense? This isn't about the girls at all. You're just punishing me."

He shrugged. "Tell yourself whatever you like."

* * *

That evening, Catrin had a temperature. She had seemed withdrawn at teatime. By bedtime, her forehead was hot. Your father took her up to bed while I made her some warm milk in her sippy cup.

"Get her some Calpol, too," he said to me as he carried her upstairs.

I found the medicine in the cupboard above the microwave, where it had always been. I turned the Calpol bottle upside down, as I had done a thousand times, extracting the fluorescent pink syrup with the syringe. When I went into your sister's bedroom, she was on your father's lap. Her face was red, her brow damp, and she was writhing from the heat in her body, trying to make herself comfortable then sobbing with the effort.

"I'm bad poorly, Daddy."

"I know, darling," he said.

Your father gave her the Calpol, pushing the syringe between her lips. She took it with no fuss. I handed her the cup, which she took weakly in her hands, closing her eyes as she sipped slowly from the spout. By the time she had finished it she was asleep, her head tilting back over your father's arm. I lifted her from his lap and placed her in her bed.

* * *

That night I couldn't sleep. It was partly Catrin, that haunting fear that came when your child was ill and you didn't know the cause or outcome. But mostly it was your father, what had happened with the cottage. I was starting to feel like a prisoner, unable to escape his malicious control. But how could I beat him? I had done everything wrong. And as always, I wasn't sure what was true. I couldn't explain all the things that had happened. That was what distressed me most of all.

When the coughing began, rising through the quiet dark, I was wide awake. From the kitchen, Beti began to bark. I got out of bed. When I stepped onto the landing, your father moved past, knocking into me as he hurried to your sister's room. I moved after him, standing in the doorway to watch him bend down and lift her from her bed.

"Jesus," he said.

"What?" I said.

"Feel her."

As he helped Catrin take her inhaler, I walked over to feel her forehead. But I only had to brush my hand close to her skin to feel the immense heat coming from her body.

"She needs to go to the hospital," I said.

Your father looked at me. "Not yet," he said.

"David," I said.

Even after drawing on her inhaler several times, there was a thick rattle in her chest that hadn't been there a few hours before, and she grunted with each breath.

"We can get her temperature down at home," he said.

"What about her breathing?" I said. "It sounds bad."

"She'll be fine."

"How do you know?"

I knew what he would say next. We had been through this so many times. I was overreacting. He was being calm. I shouldn't give in to my irrational fears. Meanwhile, all the official advice was the opposite: *If you're worried, take your child to the hospital. Trust your instincts. You know best.*

"So what's your plan?" I said.

"I'll stay in here. Keep an eye on her."

At the other end of the landing, I heard Deryn stirring.

TWENTY-THREE

"I was wondering," said Ben at our next session. "Did you ever want to call Jude something else?"

I looked at him. "Like Mum, you mean?"

"Along those lines."

"She always told me I could. She wanted me to. She actually wanted to adopt me. But she couldn't afford it."

"What do you mean?"

"I mean she would have lost the money she got for fostering me. She couldn't afford that."

He watched me for a moment. "How did you feel about that?"

"It was fine. It's not like I was treated differently. I remember I was in Aldi with Chris once. He was Jude's biological son. She had him when she was really young, before she started fostering. He had just passed his driving test and his dad had bought him a car. Jude was furious about it — you know, because his dad didn't see him for months and then he'd suddenly get him an expensive present. Anyway, Chris drove me into town to get a McDonald's. We stopped at Aldi and there were these Mother's Day cards. Chris picked one up — I remember he didn't even look at the card, he just picked it up because he had to get one — and when he put it on the belt, I was looking at it and he said, 'That's from both of us.'"

"That was important to you," Ben said. "To be included with him?"

"Yeah. I think I remember that day because of the new car and how Chris seemed different, grown-up. He had his keys in his hands. That was how I thought of grown-ups, always holding their keys."

"How old were you?"

"I don't know. Seven or eight."

"Did you ever feel angry?"

"Angry?" I said. "With who?"

"Jude? Chris?"

"Why would I be angry with them?"

He shrugged. "For being a family. For choosing not to adopt you."

"It wasn't a choice," I said. "She couldn't afford it."

"But she could afford to look after Chris. Why not you?"

"That's not really fair. She had Chris first, way before she fostered me."

"I know," he said. "I still think you'd be entitled to feel angry."

"I never felt angry with them," I said, though I felt angry now. Angry with Ben for saying these things. "Is that the point of therapy, making you angry about things you don't even care about? Making you think you're a victim?" I was surprised when I said this, how aggressive I sounded. I never talked to anyone that way, especially not Ben, who was so kind to me.

"No. That's not the point of therapy."

"It was Abi who was angry."

"Abi?"

"My foster sister. She was with us for years, almost as long as me. Jude wanted to adopt her, too, but Abi said she wouldn't want that anyway."

"Why didn't she want that?"

"Because she was obsessed with her mum. She was always going back to her, trying to get her to like her. I think she thought that if she was adopted, then, I don't know—"

"Her mother would have an excuse to stop seeing her."

"Exactly. Stupid."

"Stupid why?"

"I mean, if your mum is like that, why cling on? Just give up."

"So it was Abi you were angry with?"

"Sometimes."

"For wanting her mother to like her?"

I sighed. "You don't understand. Abi's mum hated Abi," I said. "She couldn't care less about her. But Abi kept trying to make her like her."

Ben nodded. "That's sad for Abi, isn't it?"

I shrugged. "You have to accept things as they are. Otherwise you spend your life wanting stuff that will never happen. Even when I left home, Abi was still going after her mum, saying she had changed. 'She's not drinking now.' 'She's been doing loads of mindfulness.'" As I imitated Abi's voice, I could see how childish I sounded and I wondered exactly what Ben was probably wondering — why was I so angry with Abi? I noticed Ben looking down at my lap. I looked down, too, realising I was opening and closing my fists.

"I don't know why I'm doing that," I said.

"It's okay."

"I just mean that Jude was there for her and Abi was ungrateful. She would refuse to speak to her for days, for no reason. And she said the most horrible things, things she would never say to her mum. Jude didn't deserve it."

Ben nodded, looking, as usual, like I was telling him things he already knew. "It's funny how people do that, isn't it?"

"Do what?"

"Direct their anger at people who don't deserve it. Jude was a safe person for Abi. Her mother wasn't. Her mother would use any excuse to reject her. Children behave all day in school then throw a tantrum the minute they get home. Anger is directed at those who can tolerate it."

"It just seemed like she wasn't protecting her own interests."

"Maybe she was, in a way. But what interests me is your attitude, not Abi's."

"What do you mean?"

"Well, as far as I can tell, you showed enormous good-naturedness towards your foster home, in a way children from your background often don't."

"I just don't think you should throw it back in people's faces when they're trying to look after you."

Ben watched me for a minute. Then he said, "Sometimes, in my job, I go into schools. I have to meet with teachers to discuss a particular child. A child like Abi, perhaps."

"What do they want you to do?"

"They just want advice on how to manage them. Once, there was a boy who set fire to a bin on school property. He threw a chair at a classmate. They didn't want to expel him, if they could help it. I asked about his background and they told me he slept in a multi-storey car park. Yet every morning, he got up, got himself dressed and went to school."

I stared at Ben. "Is that true?"

"Yes."

"What happened to him?"

"I don't know. But something the headteacher said stayed with me. One of the other teachers was condemning the boy's behaviour, saying how disruptive it was, not fair on the other kids, and how any other child would be expelled. What the headteacher said I have never forgotten."

"What did he say?"

"He said, 'The only normal thing about this boy is that he's angry.'"

TWENTY-FOUR

While your father stayed with Catrin, dozing in the wide armchair beside her bed, I found my phone and went downstairs. It was dark outside, the fields black, the sky above the land faintly infused with the light of the moon. When I walked into the kitchen, Beti barked, rising from her bed. Seeing that it was me, she relaxed and padded over, pushing her wet snout into my hand. I sat by the window, the garden full of shadows beyond the glass, and dialled the NHS helpline. I had been through this many times — in the dead of night, delirious with sleep and worry, I would scroll through web pages with medical advice, often contradictory, usually unhelpful, and eventually ring this number, knowing I would get no more reassurance but doing it anyway, because there was nothing else.

The woman asked a series of questions, trying to rule out specific illnesses. Yes, she was drowsier than usual. Yes, she seemed disorientated. Yes, she had a high temperature and trouble breathing. So was I right to be worried? Or was I losing my mind? It was never clear. It was both. It was neither.

Keep an eye out for red flags, said the woman, and she went on to list them: blue lips, very pale skin, cold hands, unresponsiveness. Some of them I had already told her Catrin was experiencing but this seemed not to have registered. Or did it not matter? And what did drowsiness look like in a three-and-a-half-year-old in the middle of the night? What qualified as severe difficulty breathing? Wasn't all breathing difficulty severe? And wouldn't I be the one blamed if something went wrong? They said mothers knew best but only when it suited them.

* * *

I lingered in the kitchen, turning everything over, trying to make sense of my thoughts in a familiar state of paralysis.

I made a decision.

Upstairs your father was snoring lightly in the chair, his head tipped forward, his chin flat against his chest. I crept to the bed and touched Catrin's head. Naked, the bed covers kicked to her feet, she was still extremely hot. Her body was limp with exhaustion, clinging to sleep, but every few breaths she twisted her body with the effort of breathing. With each gasp for air, her tummy folded in and she grunted lightly.

Silently, I collected wet wipes, spare clothing, a soft toy, a dummy, placing it all on the futon in the nursery, where I had not slept at all that night. I emptied my rucksack and filled it with Catrin's things. Then I found my handbag and emptied its contents into the rucksack. When everything was ready, I went back into Catrin's room. I looked at your father, still asleep, then reached down and dug my hands behind her back, lifting her towards me. She hardly responded, not even opening her eyes as she slumped against my chest. I carried her out of the room.

In the nursery, I laid her on the futon and dressed her in a onesie, moving her onto where I had laid it, slipping her arms and feet through the holes, zipping it up. Through all this she stayed asleep. *Unresponsive*, I thought. *Or is it?* I didn't turn on any lights and made hardly a sound but soon Greta was awake, passing the nursery door to get Deryn's milk from the kitchen. Behind her, I could hear Deryn crying lightly in her cot.

"What are you doing?" she whispered, walking into the room as I put the rucksack on my back then lifted Catrin into my arms.

"I'm taking her to the hospital."

"Is David okay with that?"

I looked at her through the darkness, only vaguely able to make out her expression.

"Yes," I said.

You were asleep in your bed through all of this, your door closed.

I realised, as I carried your sister outside, that I would have to move her seat from Greta's car, having switched it back earlier that day. I laid Catrin on the back seat of mine while I went over to Greta's and fiddled with the seat, pushing the button and trying to wriggle it out. My heart was beating faster all the time. Every second, I dreaded your father waking up and finding out what I was doing. For a moment I considered strapping Catrin into the seat belt, but it was a forty-minute drive to the hospital and she wasn't breathing well. I couldn't risk it. Finally, I released the seat. I lifted it out of the car and carried it to mine, my arms hugging its bulky shape. When I got there, Catrin remained asleep, listless on the back seat. I placed the car seat beside her, threading the seat belt through the hole at the back and clicking it into the buckle. Then I picked her up and placed her in the seat, rooting around beneath her for the straps. I felt sick, my mouth ripe with that metallic taste that came with acute fear. I reminded myself of what Ben had told me: *It's just adrenalin. It can't hurt you.*

As I closed the rear door, I heard voices from the house. The front door opened, letting light from the hall into the black night of the drive. I climbed into the driver's seat and slammed the door, turning on the engine to flood the driveway in bright light as your father ran out of the house, shouting. Frantically, I reversed, stones flying to hit the windows of the car before I sped away down the track.

* * *

The lanes were empty and black, my headlights cutting through the darkness. The moon was bright, lighting the fields but not the lanes, which were shadowed by tall trees and overgrown hedges. The mountains were black shadows slicing the moonlit sky. Slumped in the child seat, your sister was wheezing hard, each breath grating the quiet. Aside from that it was still, the dark world outside eerily devoid of life.

The hospital was a black figure against the sky, wide and silent as the mountains behind it. But there were tall windows, glowing with light, breaking up the building's dark frame. The car park was half-empty — it was the middle of the night — and I pulled into a space close to the entrance to A & E. Fifty or so yards away, ambulances were lined up, waiting. I turned the key, shut down the engine. The car park wasn't lit — it had never been lit at night in the years I had been bringing my children here — and darkness stretched ahead of us as I took Catrin from her car seat and carried her towards the doors.

* * *

One thing I had learned through years of arriving at A & E with small and sick children was that whatever panic I felt, I was likely to be met with indifference. The receptionists and nurses who operated as gatekeepers for the paediatricians and emergency doctors you were desperate to see were clinically calm and institutionally fatigued, hardly able to summon the will to ask the routine questions let alone feel human concern. It was a stark and confusing contrast with your own urgency and panic.

Then you waited. An hour, if you were lucky. But there were times it was four or five. The waiting room became a prison, the posters turning oppressive and maddening as you read the same words again and again and you saw your own delirious frustration in the faces of those with you. When a nurse stepped through the swinging doors, calling a name that wasn't yours, your brief hope was quickly crushed. I remembered so well how, as the hours went on and I tried to remain composed and keep you or Catrin (or both of you) happy, showing you the same toys again and again, I became enraged by a deep and dark despair, the unique pain of being ignored by those meant to help.

None of this happened tonight. As I was getting ready to explain Catrin's situation — the accident, her respiratory condition, her temperature and sluggishness — the woman behind the desk looked at her evenly then picked up a phone. As she spoke into the receiver, lips moving but words swallowed by the din behind me, she kept her eyes on your sister. When I looked down in the bright light of the reception, her head flopped against my shoulder, I saw that her lips had turned blue at the edges and the skin on her face was so pale it was almost luminous.

* * *

She was admitted to the paediatric high-dependency unit. The room we were led to was almost identical to the one she was in after the accident, unwelcoming and mechanical, full of wires and monitors and switches. The walls were pale blue, a television perched high on the wall beside a door that opened to a toilet. Two bright bins stood side by side, labelled with complicated instructions. I waited, holding Catrin, while the nurse who had come with us, guiding us along corridors and through swinging doors, rolled a cot out of the room and replaced it with a bed, lowering the rail so I could place Catrin on the clean white sheets.

The nurse told me to undress her, handing me a gown. As I unzipped her sleepsuit, Catrin became more wakeful, looking at me in groggy confusion.

"Why am I in the hospital, Mummy?"

I tried not to show any reaction; it was the first time she had called me that since I had come home. As I pulled the sleepsuit from under her and draped the gown over her arms, she was weak-limbed, still struggling to breathe, and her hands were cold and clammy, while her forehead still burned.

"When is she going to get some help with her breathing?" I said to the nurse.

She was arranging needles on a tray, preparing to take blood. "The doctor will be here soon."

* * *

When a doctor did come, frowning in concentration as she moved the stethoscope around Catrin's back and chest, she gave no diagnosis but instructed the nurse that Catrin should be placed on high-flow oxygen. This was what she was supported with after the accident, as were you when you had bronchiolitis. Placing the cannula in her nostrils and taping the wire to her cheek was an ordeal, as it always had been — she resisted, she argued, she pushed the tubes away then screamed as we pinned her down and forced them on her anyway. But once it was done, the clear tubes strapped to her soft cheeks with silver tape, the high-flow machine whooshing like the noise of the sea and oxygen drifting steadily to her lungs, she went back to sleep.

Below the window, the car park stretched towards the mountains. The sun was rising now, an intrusive orange leaking through the morning sky. Outside the door, the ward was quiet, only the hiss of ventilators and bleep of monitors. I hadn't contacted your father or even looked at my phone to check for his outraged messages. I couldn't face it. Not yet.

I walked over to the window and looked down at the car park. In the mechanical quiet of the room, I heard a noise, heavy and thundering like a loud engine outside the open window. It went as quickly as it came but I was startled by it. I opened the window wider and looked down at the car park, scanning the ground below for a motorbike or souped-up car. Everything outside was quiet and still.

* * *

The nurse who came on shift at the morning changeover was called Anest. She was tall and broad-shouldered with thick brunette hair and she was the first staff member — the first anyone — who didn't come fleetingly then disappear back into the hospital abyss. Her attitude made clear she was available and cared, not just about Catrin but about me.

"It's awful when they're ill, isn't it?" she said.

I nodded. Glancing at the breakfast tray at the foot of Catrin's cot, she said, "She didn't want anything?"

"She's been asleep," I said. "Should I wake her?"

Anest watched Catrin for a moment, her eyes soft with empathy.

"We'll let her sleep for now."

* * *

The doctor woke her anyway, bustling in with a posse of trainees behind him. Earnestly, he explained that he needed to give Catrin another exam, asking if I could remove her gown and sit her up. When I woke her she was red-faced, panicked by the tubes in her nostrils, the tape over her face, the unfamiliar room and strange people. When she saw Anest she smiled, opening out her hand.

"*Helo Catrin fach!*" said Anest. "*Ti'n sâl, cyw?*"

Catrin shook her head, apparently offended by the insinuation that she might be unwell. Her lower lip trembled. I moved over to the bed and she reached for me, clinging to my top. She began to cry. Her breathing worsened rapidly with the effort of moving around.

"Do you know Anest?" I said to Catrin.

She didn't answer.

"I've seen Catrin in clinic," said Anest. "I know her mam, too. I mean — sorry — I mean Greta, her stepmam."

Her face flushed and she moved to the table at the foot of Catrin's bed and began tidying up the mess there. Looking at the doctor, I remembered he was waiting for me to take off Catrin's gown. I reached behind her back to unfasten it.

Anest moved over and lifted the tube for me. As I pulled the gown from beneath her, I noticed the bed was wet. Catrin looked at me, embarrassed. "I had an accident," she said quietly. "I didn't do it on purpose."

"I know, sweetheart," I said.

I glanced at the doctor, sensing some impatience as he moved away and talked quietly to his trainees. I had a sudden fear he might leave, abandon us for patients more available, and I was clumsy and flustered as I rummaged through my bag for the clean underwear I knew I had packed. Or maybe I hadn't?

Anest had lowered Catrin onto the floor so she could strip the bed, looking over at me as I tipped the contents of my rucksack on the floor.

"I know I packed clean ones. I'm sure I did. It was the middle of the night, though." I felt like I would cry, too, and told myself to get a grip.

"I'm sure we can find something here, you know," said Anest. "It's not a problem."

My hands were trembling. And with no warning the strange thundering came back, exploding through my head, and as I instinctively looked around the room I knew for sure now that it was coming from inside me. A wave of dizziness crashed through my body like a breaking wave. My legs gave way and I fell back on the floor, closing my eyes and touching my forehead. There was that pain in my skull again. Anest was beside me suddenly, touching my back. "Take a deep breath, okay?"

* * *

I fell asleep in the chair next to Catrin's cot and dreamed about a helicopter. It landed in Jude's back garden. There were children there, running around, excited but afraid as the vehicle hovered over the grass like a gigantic insect. The children's mouths were open, their eyes wide as they circled the grass where it prepared to land. I was there. Perhaps I was a child, too. I couldn't see myself in the dream and I wasn't running and circling like the other children. I was standing still, watching the helicopter, thinking that I had been waiting for a long time for this.

When the rotors stilled, I walked calmly across the grass and mounted the steps. Looking behind, I saw Jude and the children. There were children I had lived with, like Abi and Chris, and the ones who came fleetingly, like Luke and Cain, and my own children were there, too, all of them lined up together next to Jude, who stood tall in the centre. As I climbed into the helicopter, none of them waved.

* * *

I was woken by the lunch trolley. A woman in forest-green scrubs lifted a tray and placed it at the foot of the cot. I looked over at Catrin, who was asleep again. She had slept almost constantly since teatime the day before, her exhausted little body fighting off whatever was inside it. Vaguely, I remembered the doctor leaving, having examined Catrin but being unable or unwilling to diagnose her. All they knew was she needed oxygen and rest.

Anest had gone, too.

I got up from the chair and walked to the window. The room felt humid, even with the window open. But with the sun now high in the sky, the mountains looked greener. I went into the toilet, splashing cold water on my face. The lights in the main room were off but here in the cubicle it was piercingly bright. In the mirror above the sink, I looked ghostly pale. Except for the short nap in the chair just now, I had been awake for twenty-four hours. An image of your sister flashed in my mind: she was here after the accident, lying in a cot bed with high blue rails around her like a little prison. The same machine, with its stark black screen, recorded her oxygen level, big green numbers rolling higher then falling. Out of nowhere I pictured the same machine in the nursery, positioned on the changing table, and Catrin in her old cot, eyes shut, clutching her wide-eyed bunny. I was in the room, folding sleepsuits and tucking them into an open drawer. The monitor next to Catrin's cot flashed and beeped as it did in the hospital. But we had never had one of those in our home, my mind was making this up. In the same vision I stood up, leaving the drawer open, and walked over to the cot, the mobile above it turning slowly, a lullaby playing on Catrin's dream sheep. When I reached the cot, leaning over the rail to check on her, it was empty. She was gone.

Was this a distorted memory of the day of the accident? Maybe I was remembering things I had buried, now that I was back in the same hospital? Or was it entirely made up, being in that nursery and finding the cot empty like that? It didn't make sense. I'd been alone with you and your sister that evening. Your father had gone to help your nain after her fall, rushed her to the hospital. Perhaps this was what my mind wanted, to create new memories, imagining it hadn't been me who had removed her from the cot that evening and let her into the garden?

My mind snapped back to the hospital now, Catrin asleep beneath the woven blanket. But even as I walked back to the bed I pictured your father there, his back to me, turning his head to say those words that had stayed with me all this time. "I told you how dangerous it was to let her outside. You did it anyway. You're not fit to be a mother."

* * *

When Catrin woke again she was very hot. She began to cry. I rang the bell. After a short wait Anest came.

"Oh, she's burning," she said, touching her back. "*Bechod.* Let me find a doctor to sign off on some Calpol. Has she had any?"

I thought back over the twelve hours behind us. "Not since yesterday," I said. "At about six. Sorry, I should have thought."

"Don't worry," said Anest. "I'll sort it out."

She was gone a long time. I tried to get Catrin to eat her lunch — lasagne and potatoes, now cold — but she would only take the yoghurt, which I spoon-fed her, and the oat biscuit, crumbled in its plastic wrapping. She chewed on it slowly, coughing and crying out from the pain in her throat as she tried to swallow.

"Bad poorly," she said.

Anest came back into the room carrying a tray with a single dose of Calpol inside a syringe. Carefully, she fed it to Catrin, pushing the tip gently through her lips, pressing down on the plunger. Catrin pulled a face but swallowed.

"*Hogan dda!*" said Anest, smiling at her.

"How do you know Greta?" I said to Anest.

"Oh, I've known her for years. We were in school together. And then through work a bit, though we're in different departments. I haven't seen her at all since she went on maternity leave. Is she okay?"

I thought about Greta, a first-time mother at such a young age, all the tensions in the house, and I didn't feel qualified to answer the question. But I said, "She's fine," in case Greta didn't want colleagues and old school friends to know she was struggling.

Anest nodded. "Weird that she didn't come into hospital."

* * *

I began checking my phone, expecting missed calls and texts from your father. There was nothing. I thought it must be the signal and went outside, leaving Catrin with Anest. But I didn't have a single message or missed call. It was more unsettling this way, not hearing anything. That was why he was doing it. I should have known. When it was clear Catrin would be staying another night, I sent him a message, if only so I couldn't be accused of not letting him know what was going on. As I sat down to write it, I concentrated hard, trying to remember what the young doctor had told me after the examination, when I was dizzy with stress and tiredness and whatever was going on in my head since I'd got to the hospital. *Her chest is infected. She's on high-flow oxygen. She's eating a bit. No need for feeding tubes at the moment. They're keeping her here another night at least. She's okay.*

Then I wrote, *I'm sorry for bringing her in behind your back. I didn't have a choice.*

Then I deleted the last two lines and pressed send.

* * *

He didn't reply. Silence was his most effective weapon. I found it unbearable and he knew that. The stress of it weakened me. Your father thought himself an expert in many things, but what he excelled at most was wrecking people while seeming to be doing nothing at all. True to form, I began to look at my phone constantly, desperate to hear something — anything — from him. I couldn't sleep, sick from his silence. I felt I would die from it, that was how it made me feel. It had always made me feel that way. I closed my eyes on the low rolling bed beside your sister and played Ben's voice in my head like a familiar song. *It isn't him you fear, Elin. He's a symbol of what they did to you. That's the terror you feel. But no one can hurt you like that now. You have more power than you realise.*

* * *

Early the next morning I received a text from your father. It didn't mention Catrin. It was about you, three words that chilled my blood. *Rhiannon is missing.*

168

TWENTY-FIVE

When you finally started school, you had never experienced anyone's care but mine. You never did go back to Cylch. I'd left you with your nain or your father for a couple of hours here and there, but even that I hadn't done often. It had become disturbing and unnatural to be out in the world without you. A relief in some ways, yes. But wrong, too. I knew you had to go to school. I didn't want to prevent it. But as the summer narrowed to a close, dread settled inside me.

"It does seem young, doesn't it?" I said to your father the evening before.

We were in the kitchen. He glanced at you, playing with Catrin on the rug. This was only two months after the ear-piercing. The holes in your lobes had closed since your father had removed the earrings, explaining to you that Mummy made a mistake, that you could have your ears pierced when you were older. You never brought it up with me. You were embarrassed on my behalf, I felt, to see me overruled in this way.

"It seems about time to me," your father replied.

"I don't mean young. I just mean, I don't know — can you really imagine her as a schoolchild?"

"Yes," he said, walking over to you. He bent down and kissed your head. "She's going to be great."

You beamed up at him. He walked back to me, saying quietly, "And I don't think we should be making her feel otherwise."

* * *

The next morning, I helped you dress in your new uniform. As I put the polo shirt on, you stood stiller than you ever had during the thousand times I had dressed you. I put your jumper over your head, waiting while you threaded your hands through the arms. As I tucked the collar over the neckline, you watched me carefully.

"Okay?" I said.

"Mummy, will the teacher make me sit on a chair the whole day?"

"Who told you that?"

"No one."

"I don't think so," I said. "I think you'll mostly sit on the carpet and run around playing. Maybe you'll sit on a chair sometimes."

You nodded. When we were finished you wore black leggings, having firmly chosen them over a skirt and tights, and black shoes with white socks, as well as your smart jumper and polo shirt. All of this we had bought together. You looked so grown-up. I was devastated. But I did everything not to show it, trying instead to appear happy and proud.

"Aren't you a big girl?" I said. "Are you excited?"

"You already asked me that," you said.

I nodded. "Shall we get in the car? It's a bit early but that's okay, isn't it?"

Your face was serene with only the slightest edge of disturbance. I wondered what you were thinking, whether you sensed the turmoil inside me.

* * *

The trees enclosing the school seemed very tall, cutting into the blue sky. It was a warm September day. As I walked you

170

to your classroom behind the other parents and children, tiny birds fluttered in the hedges lining the path. We had been here for the transition afternoon in May. It felt like a long time ago. I looked down at you, staring ahead at the other children. Mrs Williams was smiling in the classroom doorway, greeting the children by name.

"*Bore da*, Rhiannon!" she said brightly.

You clung to my hand. When you glanced up at me, I felt that it was me you were worried about and I hated myself for burdening you this way. I crouched down and opened my arms. "You're going to have a lovely day," I said.

Mrs Williams was smiling but glancing at the children behind us, impatient for me to get out of their way. When I stood up, you looked up at me one last time then skipped past Mrs Williams and disappeared into the classroom. I stared after you. Mrs Williams pushed her face towards me, drawing my attention away from the empty doorway. "One o'clock," she said, nodding for me to move out of the way.

* * *

My car was blocked in, the narrow road rammed with school traffic. I sat in the driver's seat and waited for it to clear. I wished Catrin was with me. Your father and I had decided she would stay home that morning, allowing me to focus on you. But sitting in the empty car, the street slowly emptying, there was a quietness that took my breath away. For a moment, I couldn't get my head round what was happening. Catrin was not with me. You were in a classroom, surrounded by people who knew nothing about you.

I stared through the windscreen. The street was almost empty now. I needed to move, too. But I was compelled to sit and stare at the road and the trees. Suddenly, a feeling came over me of total bereavement, like I had been severed from not only you but the world and everyone in it. In my mind, I saw a woman moving away from me through an open doorway, disappearing into the shadows of a dark

171

landing. I didn't recognise the house. It wasn't Jude's, or ours. All I knew was I had been left alone and afraid. The image vanished as quickly as it had appeared and I was left with nothing but the castaway feeling. A shiver flushed over my skin. My insides felt hollow. My hands began to shake, a soft tremble at first then a violent convulsion that moved down through my body, into my legs. I held one over the other, trying to still them. But the tremble spread until I was shaking all over, and all I could do was wait for it to pass, hoping nobody was watching.

TWENTY-SIX

I waited for your father in a distant state of dread. I tried to make sense of his first message and the vague follow-ups he sent after my stream of questions. It wasn't clear what was going on — *he* had not been clear. I tried ringing him but he didn't answer. Even in a situation like this, he relished the power of knowing more than me. Perhaps especially in a situation like this. I was surprised when he agreed to swap places — to come to the hospital and be with Catrin so I could be involved in whatever was happening at home.

As I waited, my mind flashed with memories. Most of them I had forgotten or suppressed, but they rushed back now, cruel in their lucidity, pulling me into scattered moments when you had left my side in the supermarket, your eye caught by the gleam of a toy, or vanished in the park, lost in a wild imagined game. I remembered the agony of those slow minutes, the fear that rose as I teetered on a parent's most abject nightmare — a missing child, not just out of reach for a minute but truly gone. I had seen the edge of it many times.

Now we were inside it. Supposedly. I couldn't accept it. Not until I had spoken to your father. Seen the look on his face. Clarified exactly what had happened and when. Been back to the house and checked every room myself, searched the garden and shed and the track behind the house. In the meantime, my mind flitted in and out of denial. *This is a mistake. It is not true.*

* * *

"I still don't understand," I said when he finally met me at the door to the ward. "What exactly happened?"

The nurse who had come on shift earlier that morning held the door open, waiting for him to come through. Your father folded his arms and leaned against the frame. The nurse, who apparently hadn't anticipated that we might want to talk to one another, became annoyed.

"Can we have some privacy?" said your father.

The nurse stared at him. "I'm waiting to let you in."

"I'm capable of holding the door open," he replied.

She pursed her lips. "I'm not allowed to do that. I need to make sure the door is locked behind you. This is a children's ward."

So we were forced to have this discussion with her there, listening. Your father looked at me. He looked pale, his eyes betraying the fear in his body. His effort at control gave him an even more severe appearance than usual, his face taut, jaw tight.

"Look," he said, "I've told you everything I know. I put her to bed last night. I thought she was sleeping late this morning, that maybe she was ill with whatever Catrin's got. I let her sleep. By eight I was worried. I went in to check on her. She was gone."

I watched him. "Did she take anything?"

"Her backpack."

"Her schoolbag?"

"No. The other one. And I think her brown bear is missing."

"So she did run away," I said.

"What do you mean?"

"She wasn't taken."

"Of course she wasn't taken," he said, as though I was a lunatic for suggesting it. The nurse, too, was watching me now, having previously been pretending not to listen.

"It's not beyond the realms of possibility," I said, trying to ignore the nurse. "A baby was snatched from this hospital a few weeks ago."

The nurse looked reproachful when I mentioned the baby, as though it was distasteful to bring it up.

"She's run away, Elin," said your father. "Something like this was bound to happen, don't you think?"

"Why?"

He leaned towards me, lowering his voice to a snarling whisper. "You went missing for months and came back with no warning. You brought her sister into hospital in the middle of the night without telling anyone. It's all pretty confusing for a five-year-old, don't you think?"

The nurse looked away — embarrassed, I felt, on my behalf. I ignored him.

"Was her window open?" I said.

"No. She couldn't have got out that way. She'd have got stuck on the lower roof or hurt herself jumping down. She must have gone out the front door."

"And what?" I said. "Wandered into the mountains? Where is she?"

"I don't know, Elin. Obviously."

I thought about how you had been going to the woods, the broken piece of slate you had put in the ground. I needed to tell the police about that. I couldn't face telling your father.

"And you didn't hear anything? In the night? Or this morning?"

"No, Elin."

"What about Greta?"

He sighed. "No."

I frowned. "Was she asleep when you left her?"

"What?"

"Last night — did you leave Rhiannon asleep or awake?"

175

"Awake."

"And did you check on her?"

"When?"

"Any time! Did you go in to check on her after you left her awake in bed?"

He looked at me. "What is it you're trying to say, Elin? Because if you're going to even think about blaming me for this, after everything you've done—"

"Then what?" I said. "You'll do what?"

* * *

Back at the house your nain was on the phone. Greta was lying on the couch, her trainers kicked off on the floor. With Deryn asleep on her chest, she scrolled lazily through her phone, stroking the screen with her thumb. Deryn didn't have a blanket round her for once, just a white sleepsuit with a clean collar and frills on the sleeves. The window was open. Beyond it the mountains looked less real than ever, like a beautiful and sad painting. The humidity was worse today, a sense of pressure all around.

Hearing me come through the front door, Beti barked and ran out from the kitchen, wagging her tail and pushing her wet nose into my hand. Greta glanced over, watching the dog but saying nothing.

Your nain put down the phone and walked over to me. "Elin. Thank God you're back. We're all worried to death."

Her habit of pronouncing on the events around her seemed even more absurd in this context. She watched me, waiting for me to say something. I got the unsettling feeling she was looking for leadership of some kind. I had nothing to offer. I had slipped into a marginal space between reality and the unknown blackness of losing you. I did not know how to function.

"Elin?" she said, watching me closely. She didn't tell me I was acting strangely but I knew she wanted to. I was struck that she did not, as a mother herself, understand the

176

impossibility of behaving normally in these circumstances, that she was persisting in making me feel my reaction was off-kilter.

Greta watched me, too. But she looked detached. I expected this was all too much for her when she had a six-week-old baby.

"I'll be back in a minute," I said.

"Where are you going?" said your nain.

I went back into the hall. Your nain followed me upstairs and into your bedroom, where I got down on my knees and looked under the bed, then got up and walked across the room, opening the doors of your wardrobe.

"For goodness' sake, Elin," she said. "Don't you think we've checked? Thoroughly?"

"Just give me a minute, please," I said.

I pulled the duvet off your bed, as though I might find you hiding there, and sat on the blue-carpeted floor, bundling the duvet in my arms. It smelled of you. The room felt heavy — the quietness, your absence. I looked at your nain. "Why is this happening?"

* * *

Your nain wanted me to stay there, saying the police had made it clear we should wait — by the landline, at the house, in case you came back or someone contacted us with information. But this was impossible. You were not yet six years old and you had been missing for at least four hours, possibly much longer. To me it seemed much more likely that you had run away at bedtime than either first thing this morning or in the middle of the night. I couldn't explain why. But the fact was, we didn't know. No one had checked on you since your father tucked you in the night before. Twelve hours he had left you in your room, assuming you were safely in bed. Though I had done the same countless times, I was furious with him for this. Either way, I wasn't going to stay in the house.

All kinds of people were out looking for you. Most of them I knew. Teachers, parents, neighbours, the woman who owned the ice cream parlour. I passed Sioned on the side of the road, walking with the two eldest of her four kids, boys nearing the end of high school. She raised her arm, waving, and turned her head to watch as my car shot past.

Some people had brought dogs, giving the disturbing impression we were looking for a body. I wouldn't allow myself to believe that. Children ran away. I knew this. They ran away for attention or because they were upset or frightened. They ran away because they were bored or because they didn't get their own way. They came home. They were found. Abi, my foster sister, ran away from school once. There was a big fuss. I remember how out of proportion it had seemed to me at the time, a child myself, though I understood it now. She was nine. I was ten. There were police officers at the school, their conspicuous cars blocking the gates. Jude was crying in the headteacher's office. The police questioned me, though I had no idea where she was. We didn't talk to each other in school. Later that day, she was found shoplifting trainers Jude had refused to buy her.

I thought about Cain, too, how he would go out of the window at night and hide in the Wendy house next door. There had been others. They had always come back.

All this I told myself.

But as I drove around the lanes, people staring when they saw me, many of them seeing me for the first time since I'd come home, I felt untethered from myself and my surroundings, the landscape surreal and disconnected.

After a while I decided the car was getting in my way. I needed to be on foot, feel the ground beneath my shoes. That would bring me closer to you. I parked by the church and walked into the fields. Quickly, I felt more rooted, my boots squelching in the wet mud. It had rained overnight. Did you have a coat? You were five. You never wanted to wear your coat.

I could hear the search all around, people shouting your name into the mountain air. I pictured you out here alone and thought of the mother who had fled the hospital in winter with her baby wrapped in sheets. It was late April now. You weren't going to freeze. But images churned through my mind, visions of you washed up on the beach, limp in the shallows of the river, buried among fallen leaves on the forest floor. What if you had tripped and hit your head? What if you'd fallen in the river, been pulled under by the current? Could you swim? You couldn't when I'd left, not without armbands. Your nain said you'd been learning, but for how long?

I didn't have the answers. I hardly knew the questions.

I had never believed in a mother's intuition. But suddenly it seemed possible that I would gain some knowledge of where you were if I paid close enough attention. Perhaps this was my way of coping. Perhaps I was going mad. But eventually certain instincts did arise, and the less I fought them — the more passive and receptive I made myself — the clearer they became. I felt that you had been here, covered the ground I was walking. I didn't know if it was true or not but I wanted to get down on my knees and sniff the earth like a dog. My feet were taking me to the woods before my mind knew what we were doing.

When I got there, I was tired, my legs heavy. A smell of vegetation hung in the air. Overhead the sky was grey, dark clouds circling the high trees. The woods were strangely quiet, no birds calling, none of the search party here except me. When I reached the clearing you had brought me to, the slate was gone, pulled from the wet ground. Only the pasta jar remained, brimming with dirty rainwater and floating flowers.

Walking back, I saw Sioned. She was muddy and wet, like me. I was so grateful, I wanted to hug her. She didn't have to do this. When I got close, she looked stricken.

"What is it?" I said.

"I haven't said anything to the police. I wanted to tell you first."

I had a sensation of falling, like the muddy ground had been pulled from beneath me.

"What?" I said.

"I need to show you something."

She took me to the river. There were people there, Sioned's boys and a middle-aged man I vaguely recognised. The man was crouching at the edge of the water, using a stick to poke an object I recognised immediately as your backpack. It was blue with a red lining. The straps were red. I had bought it for you. I moved closer and got down on my knees on the wet stones. The bag was soaking, water surging from the bottom as I lifted it. I unzipped it. The dark bottom shimmered with water, a browning apple core abandoned inside. I pulled out your drenched brown teddy, the one your father had noticed was missing. Then a small spotted dog that technically belonged to Catrin, though ownership of soft toys seemed to be negotiable between the two of you. Everyone was watching me, nobody speaking. The woods themselves remained unnervingly quiet, your absence suspended in the spaces between the trees and the white mist over the mountains.

* * *

Rain came down fast as I walked back to my car. I needed to go home and change. I left your backpack where it was, asking Sioned to tell the police. I couldn't face doing it myself. I didn't want anything to do with the police, in all honesty. I hadn't known it until then, but I had the same feeling about them that your father had about doctors and hospitals. I wasn't sure why. Perhaps I had seen too much of them in my childhood, reminding me too much of the children they rescued. Reminding me of myself.

I didn't want to tell your nain about the bag. I knew she would reach the worst conclusion, even though a lost backpack didn't actually mean anything. You had been in the woods. That was clear. You had unearthed the slate, though you might have done this before. Technically, anyone could have done it. It might have been the rain. You had lost your bag. So what? Contrary to what your nain believed, I was doing everything in my power to control my thoughts and stay calm. It was the most tiring part of the whole thing. As the hours dragged on, it was getting harder. By now I longed to scream and throw things. I wanted to hurt someone, most of all myself.

Before I had the chance to tell your nain anything, she walked into the hall and said, "An officer just rang."

I was taking off my shoes. "And?"

"Someone's seen her."

"Oh my God!" I said, looking at her. "Thank God. Where?"

"In the woods."

"Really? I've just been there. Where is she now?"

"They haven't got her yet."

"What? You just said someone found her."

"Someone saw her. He didn't bring her in."

I stared at her. "Why the hell not?"

She sighed. "Apparently he didn't want to approach her. A strange man in the woods. You can understand it."

"So he just left her there? For God's sake — she's five years old!"

"Stay calm, Elin. At least we know she's safe."

"We don't know that though, do we? Not if she's still out there. I can't believe this."

"Look, the police are all over the woods now. She'll be home in no time, mark my words. They probably have her already."

I gritted my teeth. "If they had her, we would know, wouldn't we? I need to go back."

"Elin, do you really think you can do better than the police?"

"Yes."

She looked me up and down. "What on earth has happened to you, anyway? You look feral."

Glancing in the mirror, I saw she had a point. As well as the mud spattering my trousers, the hems soaked and filthy, there were splashes of it on my face. Wet hair clung to my cheeks. Somehow, my lip was bleeding. There was a wildness in my eyes, my dread turning manic as time stormed on and you weren't found.

"Why don't you have a bath?" said your nain.

I looked at her. "A bath?"

She pursed her lips. "You're not doing anyone any good behaving like this."

"Like what? A mother looking for her daughter?"

"It's the way you're going about it, Elin. We're supposed to stay at home. I told you what the police said."

I took off my trousers and dumped them on the floor.

"What are you doing?" she said, staring at me like I'd gone insane. I pulled off my wet socks, putting them with the trousers. I walked into the living room barefoot. Through the bay window, the sun was setting, plunging the mountains into shadow, stranding you in the darkness. I didn't trust the police to find you. I didn't trust anyone.

Deryn began to cry. Almost instantaneously, the phone rang, as though she had caused it. Your nain rushed to answer it. Putting the phone to her ear, she spoke rapidly, relaying every detail of the situation to whoever was at the other end. When she put down the receiver, she sighed. She was beginning to look worn out herself, I thought.

"Who was that?" I said.

"Oh," she said. "It was just Maggie checking to see if we've heard anything."

"Useful," I said.

She gave me a disapproving look. Greta, who had been giving Deryn a bottle on the couch, got up and left the room. It occurred to me later — after everything else that happened — that she had behaved strangely during this episode. Given she had been living with you for ten months, effectively a stepmother to you by this point, she was oddly removed, as though it had nothing to do with her. Later I understood why, recognising her behaviour as another overlooked sign of what was going on.

"Now listen, Elin," your nain was saying. "I'm going home now. I know there will be people ringing my house, too. I need to be there, in case anything important comes up. David is at the hospital. Greta can't deal with all this alone. She has Deryn to think about. You need to listen to me, for once, and stay here."

"What is there to deal with?"

"Oh, Elin! People are ringing all the time. What if we miss a call from the police?"

"We will if people keep ringing."

"Elin, please! We know she's been spotted now. I'm certain they'll ring any minute and say they've found her. Do you really want to not be here when they ask you to come and collect her?"

"They have my mobile number, I'm assuming?"

"You know very well how poor the signal is."

I sighed. "I'll stay for a bit."

Satisfied, she nodded her head.

* * *

Rain came again, as the skies had promised. The day behind me was unfathomably long, a gaping hole of time since I had left your father at the hospital. Your nain went home. I changed my clothes and went back down to the living room. Greta was on the couch, kissing Deryn's sleeping head.

"I can't stay here," I said.

"I know," she said.

"Will you be okay?"

Looking at her through the half-light, I had the strangest feeling I shouldn't leave her alone, though not for any of the reasons your nain had given.

"I'll be fine," she said.

As I watched her, I thought about what Anest, the nurse, had said at the hospital, how Greta hadn't come in to give birth, and wondered fleetingly why Greta had lied, or how Anest could be so mistaken, while seeming to be sure of the fact. I didn't have time to think about it. Somewhere near the house, I heard the whir of a helicopter. I remembered your nain saying that the mountain rescue was out, as well as the police on the ground. But this was the first time I'd heard one of their helicopters. I went upstairs, looked through the bedroom window and saw it hovering directly ahead, its lights flashing in the descending darkness. As I watched its rotors turning through the rain-soaked glass, carrying it away from the house, an image flared in my head like a flame in the dark, forming itself with shocking clarity.

I closed my eyes, trying to focus on the memory taking shape in my mind. Concentrating, I saw a helicopter on the patio in daylight, rotors spinning. The sun was setting, the sky blue at the top, swollen clouds below, streaks of pink at the horizon. I knew I was seeing the accident. I had forgotten about the helicopter — this entire scene had been a black hole in my memory for the last ten months — but I remembered it now. Paramedics, jumping out of the helicopter with their cases, the bleached sky behind them. Your sister on the ground. They rushed around her unmoving body, talking to me, asking questions. I was mute, speechless. They lifted her onto a stretcher, carried her into the dark pit of the helicopter. I almost left you behind. Shell-shocked and unthinking, I followed them up the skids, holding on to the frame of the doors. Before I could climb inside, one of the paramedics touched my arm, nodding towards you.

I looked back. You were on the patio, staring up at me.

"Is there someone here?" said the paramedic. I looked at the house. Where was your father? I had forgotten.

"I don't know," I said. "I don't think anyone is there. I don't know."

He nodded, accustomed to this level of dysfunction. "She'll have to come with us."

I stared at him, then back at you.

"You need to bring her," he said loudly. "We don't have much time."

I hurried back to you. You thought I wanted to leave you deliberately, as punishment. You began to cry. As I took you in my arms, carrying you back to the helicopter doors, you said something I had heard before, though never in a context like this. "It was an accident, Mummy. I didn't do it on purpose."

TWENTY-SEVEN

It was your birthday. You were five. I couldn't get past the flies. Fast-moving black dots, throwing themselves against windows, scurrying along the glass. They were lethargic, drunk on the heat. As I watched them, I felt them on me, moving over my skin. Guests were arriving at three. It was eleven. I was aware of time in the most literal sense but I had fallen out of it. Your father was working. You and your sister were playing in the living room. There were things to be done. The mess was overwhelming. I didn't know where to begin. Toys all over the floor, dirty dishes in the sink from the night before, a dishwasher to be emptied. I needed to sweep the kitchen floor, polish and vacuum the living room. That was just the cleaning. Was four hours plenty of time or hardly enough?

"It's my party, not yours," you were telling Catrin. "You won't get any presents. Only me."

"Rhiannon," I said sharply. You looked at me in shock. "That's not nice."

"But it *is* my party," you said.

"But why are you trying to upset your sister?"

"She thinks it's *her* party."

I looked at Catrin, who was lining up pieces of Duplo, oblivious. She was two and a half, barely aware what birthdays were.

"No, she doesn't," I said. "Leave her alone."

Birthdays were terrible for children, I had come to believe. Making them the centre of attention was no good, it made them nuts. They became greedy and self-centred. They couldn't tolerate the pressure. Neither could the parent organising it all.

I went to find my phone, which was pinging somewhere among the mess. It was probably your nain, fussing about what she should bring, people asking the start time instead of checking my email. It was too much.

I began blowing up balloons. *This is the wrong order*, I thought. *Balloons come after cleaning.*

Catrin walked over to me, watching a balloon fill with air.

"Balloon!"

"Balloon," I said, nodding.

When I had blown up several, you and she began running after them, kicking them, squealing as they sailed through the air and floated back to the ground. I hung a birthday banner over the mantelpiece. Behind a picture frame, I noticed another fly, scuttling its dirty feet over the wood. I went into the kitchen and looked at the cake, sitting on the counter in its packaging. It was a vanilla sponge with rainbow sprinkles. I had bought it from the supermarket. I had wanted to get you one specially made from the bakery in the village, a proper one with your name and age in colourful icing. But every time I had considered the task — picking up the phone to ring them or walking through the door to discuss it face to face, it defeated me. I could accomplish less than ever. Everything was too much.

In the end I had got this, last-minute, while picking up the snacks and decorations. I didn't know why I had chosen it. It wasn't even a birthday cake. The box simply said *Celebration Cake.*

From the living room I heard you say, "These are my balloons, Catrin. You can only play if I let you."

"That's enough!" I shouted, marching back into the living room. "Just stop it, Rhiannon."

You both stared at me, Catrin holding a balloon in her hands.

"When is it time for my party?" you said.

I looked at you. You were still wearing your pyjamas. Catrin was naked except for her pull-up. Nothing was ready. It was nearly twelve now. How had that happened? Time was being snatched from me like an unfunny trick. I grabbed my keys from the pot by the door. "Come on," I said. "We need to go out."

"Out where, Mummy?" you said.

"Just get your shoes on."

* * *

It was after one when we got home, three bottles of insect killer on the passenger seat.

At two o'clock, your father walked through the door.

"Elin?" he said, hanging up his jacket.

We were on the couch, watching television.

"Have you seen the state of this house? We've got guests arriving soon, haven't we?"

I looked at him. These days he faked indignation to shame me. But this time he was genuinely astonished — appalled — by my negligence. He could hardly believe it. Even by my standards, this was disgraceful. I blinked around at the living room. There were still toys all over the floor. Strewn among them was a half-eaten apple, a dirty plate, a sippy cup and the remains of a piece of toast. Abruptly, I remembered him walking into Jude's house that afternoon, when I had expected the house to be filthy but she had made it immaculate. She had done that for me, I suddenly thought. I had repaid her by never seeing her again.

"I haven't had time," I said to your father.

"What time did you get out of bed?"

I ignored him.

"Are you going to clean up this mess?"

I picked up your sister and carried her towards the hall. As I passed him, I said, "Do it yourself, if it's important to you."

* * *

I took your sister into the nursery, shutting the door behind us. My hands were shaking. I put her in the cot. She was too old for it now. She could climb over the rail if she wanted to.

"Do you need the toilet?" I said.

She shook her head.

"Are you sure?"

Catrin was potty-training. Most days, she had at least one accident. I took off her pull-up and put her on the potty anyway. She sat there staring at me while I waited.

"Try again later," she said.

I knelt down, lifting her off the potty, and began to dress her in the outfit your nain had sent. I put her in pants for the party. When she was ready, I stood back and looked at her in her absurd dress, the top half sequined, the skirt poofy like a ballerina. She smiled at me then wandered over to her book display and picked up a story, bringing it to me. I sighed. She climbed into my lap. I heard your father coming upstairs. You were with him, chattering brightly.

I looked down at the book, the page open to the block colours of a blue sky, green grass and a brown flap.

"Where's the giraffe?" I said, trying to animate my voice like the brightness of the pages. But I sounded dull and flat, my voice faraway.

She pulled the flap open to reveal the cartoon animal. "There it is!"

* * *

Six of your classmates came. Their mothers stayed, too. I knew them vaguely from the school run — and the Facebook messenger group with late-night questions about donations and parents' evenings and uniforms. The messages were almost always in Welsh, and I tended to ignore them rather than googling or asking your father to translate. When I first moved here with him I had planned to learn the language, take classes, speak Welsh in the supermarket. That seemed laughable now, when translating a simple message on Google felt like too much. At the party, the mums spoke Welsh to your father and to each other — and to you — and I didn't try to follow. I focused on practical things, putting out food, getting drinks, clearing up spills. I wanted everyone to leave. But I smiled and smiled.

Standing at the fridge, I noticed a fly on the windowsill. As I walked back out of the room, I heard your father calling me. I pretended not to hear, searching the living room for the spray. There were too many people in the way.

"Mummy! Mummy!"

I looked down and found Catrin clinging to my leg. Her face was red from running around in the heat.

"I need potty," she said.

"Just a minute, sweetheart," I said. I went upstairs and searched frantically for the spray. I must have put it away, though I had no memory of that. In fact, I had no memory of using it. Maybe I hadn't? I wondered if the spray was actually in the car. I went back downstairs.

"Elin!"

I turned around. It was your nain. She was a little red-faced, too, wearing a frilly-necked top with billowing sleeves.

"Elin, the children are getting a little out of hand. I think Rhiannon might have done something to one of the others. I'm not sure."

"I need to find Catrin," I said. "She told me she needed the toilet."

I turned to walk away but she put her hand on my arm.

"There was another thing, Elin. Some of the adults seem bored. Hadn't you better do something about that, too?"

I ignored her and went to find your sister, who was in the bathroom upstairs, standing near the toilet, her tights and shoes soaked. When she saw me in the doorway, she began to cry. "I had accident, Mummy! I didn't mean to."

* * *

A late-afternoon sun came out. The party spilled into the garden. Through the window I watched the children running in circles and the adults huddled together, laughing. Your father found me in the kitchen, filling a plastic cup with wine from a box of red. I jumped when he spoke.

"How many of those have you had?" he said.

"This is my first," I lied.

He eyed me. "We need to do the cake."

"What time is it?"

"Ten past five."

"Are you sure?"

"Yes, Elin. I'm sure."

I put down the cup and went into the living room. The presents were on the coffee table. Your nain was in the armchair.

"Elin," she said, "where have you been?"

Your father walked out of the kitchen.

"I was just saying to Elin I've hardly seen her," said your nain. "But you have been taking such good care of me." She reached out and patted the back of your father's thigh. As I watched her, I felt a wave of nausea. I wondered if I had always been afraid of her, as it became clear to me, in that moment, that I was, almost as much as I was afraid of your father. Yet somehow these were now the only two people in my life, apart from you and Catrin.

"Shall we do these presents, then?" said your father.

I nodded, walking dumbly to the back door. I called for everyone to come inside. As my voice carried into the garden, it seemed to belong to someone else. The children zoomed in, followed by the adults.

"Open mine first," said your nain. "It's this one."

Her present, beautifully wrapped in white paper and tied with a bow, was the biggest. You tore off the paper, revealing a box with a bright picture of a scooter. You gasped, looking round at your father and me. As you tried to open it, your father said, "Open a different one now, darling. You can play with that later."

You would have gone crazy if it had been me who'd told you you couldn't play with it now, but as it was your father you complied. The next present was a doll, dressed in pink, with a dummy and bottle. You looked at it blankly then put it back on the table. You had never been interested in dolls, though your sister loved them.

"Elin, which of these cakes are we having?" called your father from the kitchen.

"What?" I said, walking in after him.

"There are two," he said.

"One of them is mine!" called your nain. "I told Elin I was bringing the cake but she got one anyway!"

"I forgot," I said. "Let's just have your mum's. Hers is nicer."

I walked over and threw the celebration cake in the bin.

"Jesus!" said your father. "There's no need to waste it."

I ignored him and began putting candles on your nain's cake. My mind was racing. My hands didn't look like mine, I thought. I struggled with the simple task of the candles, pushing them too far in, then realising I had put on too many. For a while, I couldn't remember how old you were. Suddenly, you came bursting through the doorway, dragging your scooter, which your nain had clearly opened for you while we weren't looking.

"No, Rhiannon," I said. "You need to open the rest of your presents."

"I don't want to!" you said, moving towards the back door.

I went over and tried to take the scooter from you.

"No!" you cried, holding on to it. Furious, I tugged it out of your hands, knocking you backwards. You hit your elbow on the wall and began to scream.

192

"Elin!" said your father, rushing over to you. I stared at the two of you then walked over to the back door and threw the scooter into the garden. You looked over at the open door in shock then wailed even louder. In the living room, the guests had gone quiet. Your father talked consolingly to you then stood up and walked over to me. "Get a grip of yourself," he said, through gritted teeth. "We have guests here."

"I didn't ask you to invite all these people," I spat.

Your father held your hand and walked you back into the living room, where you began to open another present. In the kitchen, I poured myself another cup of wine and drank it in a few gulps, feeling myself sway as I held on to the counter. *I could drown myself in this wine*, I thought. *I could walk down the track and drown myself in the river.*

"Elin?" your father was shouting. "She's opening our present now!"

* * *

After everyone had left, the house quiet and covered in party debris, your father was furious. He went out to the garden to work on the patio. Guilt was far away from me, like a hangover that would come eventually but wasn't yet there. You were no longer sulking but clingy, wanting me to stay with you as you tore new toys from their packaging. You whined as I told you I needed to put your sister to bed, scowling as I lifted her to carry her upstairs.

The nursery was quiet, the mountains small and far away through the window. I was too tired to read Catrin a story and she was rubbing her eyes, squeezing them open and shut in her own quiet exhaustion. I lifted my top and let her feed until she drifted to sleep, her body limp against me as the evening sunlight streamed into the room. I was vaguely conscious I had been drinking, and not even the prescribed single drink two hours before breastfeeding but far more than I ever allowed myself. I didn't care. I had reached the end of my tolerance for expectation imposed from outside — all the rules and limitations, your nain's judgements, your father's simmering rage. As I lowered her into her cot, I couldn't remember what it felt like to be her mother. I had drifted far away from both of you and I was astray, now, out at sea, alone. I pulled down the blind and walked back to the cot. As I watched her falling asleep, her breath growing deeper, I noticed there were tears sliding down my cheeks. But I felt no connection to them, nor to anything at all.

TWENTY-EIGHT

By the time I went back out, it was completely dark. I had stayed at the house, as your nain had requested, for as long as I could tolerate, pacing the rooms, answering pointless phone calls from friends and neighbours and distant relatives of your nain. It was unbearable. I found your father's torch, which I knew had a strong light, and went back to the woods. Others had joined the search. Dozens of people were now out in the dark and rain, shining torches, moving in groups. Police dogs were out, sniffing the ground. The helicopters were overhead, breaking up the blackness with their flashing lights.

I lost myself in the search, pulled up my hood and worked alone. I was afraid that if I spoke to someone, I would say or do something awful. I was becoming hopeless, despairing, in spite of the sighting. It had almost made it worse, to have come so close to finding you but you still not being home. It had been at least an hour since your nain had told me about it, longer since it had actually happened.

When I got back to the house for the third time that day, your nain was there again. I was not at all surprised to see her car on the drive. When she saw me, even muddier and more dishevelled than last time, she refrained from lecturing me again.

"Were you out looking again?" she said.

"Yes," I said.

She started to cry, bringing her hand to her face. "Elin, I can't bear the thought of her down there on her own in the dark. I can't bear it."

"I know," I said. "It's making me sick. She'll be frightened by now."

I sat down on the couch and looked out at the dark sky. I felt utterly useless. I had achieved nothing. You were nowhere. That was how it felt. Looking back at the carpet, I realised I had forgotten to take off my boots, traipsing wet mud into the living room. Your nain didn't mention it, a testament to her own state of mind. She came and sat next to me instead. To my surprise, she placed her hand on mine.

"We will find her," she said. "We will."

I looked at her. Her lower lip was trembling.

"How is it that someone saw her, but when half the police force swarmed the woods they couldn't find her?" I asked her. "I don't understand."

She stared at me. "Haven't you heard?"

"What?"

She closed her eyes. "I can't believe no one told you. You were out, I suppose, when the police rang. Still—"

"What is it?" I said. "Tell me!"

"The girl in the woods — it wasn't Rhiannon."

"What?"

She sighed. "It was just a girl on holiday in one of Elwyn's cottages. I don't know why this man thought it was Rhiannon. This girl was ten."

"Wait — but how do they know she was the one the man saw? And not Rhiannon?"

"I asked the same. Apparently, the more he described the girl, the more they realised he was talking about someone else."

"They didn't think to check these details in the first place?"

"Apparently not."

"I don't believe this. What is wrong with people?"

I strongly wanted to kill this person, whoever he was, calling in useless information, pointlessly raising our hopes.

"It was an unfortunate mistake. I'm sure he really did think it might have been Rhiannon."

"A ten-year-old?"

"Well, he probably saw her from a distance. A little girl in the woods. Better to say something, isn't it? He was trying to be helpful. And nothing has changed, if you think about it. We're in the same position we were in before."

"Nothing has changed?" I said, staring at her. "First I thought she'd been found. Then I thought she'd been seen but not brought in — which was some relief, at least, to think she was alive. And now I find out it wasn't her at all? No one has seen her this whole time? No one has seen her, in fact, since David put her to bed last night? That was twenty-four hours ago! How is it that we haven't found her yet? How is it possible? It's not right. It's—"

"Elin? What's happening? You've gone completely white."

Even as it was happening, I wanted to reassure her that I was just having a panic attack. Nothing to worry about. But I couldn't speak. I couldn't breathe. I felt, as I always did, that I was having a seizure or heart attack and I was certainly about to die. Then my vision dropped out. The room went black, though my eyes were open. I felt the life had left my body.

"Put your head between your legs, Elin."

But I couldn't move.

"Come here," she said. She grabbed hold of me, forcing my head between my legs, just as your father had done the day I'd come home. I gasped, trying to get air into my lungs. I knew that my heart was beating very fast but I couldn't feel it. My body felt empty and suspended.

"Elin?"

I heard your nain's voice very distantly, like she was in another room. When I came round, she was right beside me, as I knew she had been the whole time. As the feeling returned to my body, I became hot and began to sweat. I could feel my heart again. My sight came back.

"Elin?"

Your nain was clutching my hand, searching my face with her eyes.

"I'm okay," I said breathlessly.

"Good God," she said. "You scared the life out of me."

The phone rang again. I ignored it, trying to concentrate on breathing steadily. Your nain got up to answer it. When she had finished and put down the receiver, I didn't ask who it was. I really didn't care.

"I need to go back out," I said.

But I had lost my conviction, my determination.

"Oh, Elin," she said. "I know you think I'm a terrible nag. But you're making yourself ill. Please will you have some rest? I'm begging you." Tears were running down her cheeks. I wasn't even annoyed with her anymore. In spite of her strange priorities, so out of sync with my own, I felt the sincerity of her despair, as pure as mine.

"Okay," I said.

She made me tea with honey, which I drank, realising I hadn't had anything to eat or drink all day. I had a bath after all. Then I climbed into your bed, clinging to one of your teddies, and cried myself to sleep, overcome with grief and despair and the unendurable pain of feeling, for the first time, that I had lost you.

* * *

You were found by Mr Parry the following morning. He was out at daybreak, the fields faintly lit by a sun yet to show itself over the top of the mountain. His sheepdog was barking urgently, racing towards him then galloping back to the field. Mr Parry put on his boots and looked out to the field where the dog seemed to be taking him. Something was there, splayed in the grass. A dead animal, perhaps. Even with his poor eyesight and the bareness of the light, he knew it wasn't one of his sheep. It was too big to be a hare or a fox. It couldn't be a deer. He wondered if it was a wildcat, down from the mountain, killed or injured by the dog.

He trod through the grass, moving closer. As he approached he saw your dark hair, wild and outspread, and your little face, pale as the light.

* * *

Mr Parry told me all this later, when I went to his house to thank him. At the time I knew nothing. The paramedics weren't aware of the missing five-year-old. When they got to the farm, you were just a little girl, unidentified and unaccounted for. Mr Parry recognised you — he had seen you around — but he didn't know your name and he hadn't heard you were missing. No one called me — and no one called your father — until a nurse at the hospital worked it out. Then I was driving fast through the lanes, overtaking traffic, getting honked at roundabouts, and abandoning my car to run through the corridors to the ward.

You didn't look like you. Your face was swollen. You had grazes on your neck and shoulder, a deep cut on your head and a nasty rash on your arm. You looked like you'd been in a fight with the wild and lost.

"Wasp," said the doctor. As he pointed at your arm, I noticed the pale bump in the middle of the rash. "I'm assuming she's allergic?"

I looked at him. "To wasps?"

He nodded.

"Is she?" I looked at your father, who was standing by the window, his back turned.

"She went into anaphylaxis," said the doctor. "The swelling should start to go down soon with the antihistamine. She was very dehydrated, too, hence the fluids."

I looked down at you, imagining what it had been like, the pain of the sting, your throat closing, not knowing what was happening to you. I had no idea you were allergic to wasps. Neither did your father.

"You're not supposed to give medication without parental consent, are you?" said your father.

He was particularly irritable after a night in the high-dependency unit with Catrin, surrounded by the nurses and doctors who made him feel what he hated most — powerless.

"Her parents weren't here," said the doctor curtly.

Your father looked at him, his eyes menacing. The doctor looked at me. "I'll check in again later," he said, moving towards the door.

* * *

While your father went back to Catrin, I stayed with you, watching you sleep. As well as your injuries, you were exhausted. You had wandered the mountains for almost twenty-four hours. I was heavy with relief and regret, like a bad hangover. It was over but the disturbance lingered, and everything felt wrong. When you woke, the swelling around your eyes prevented you from opening them fully.

"Mummy, I can't see!"

I leaned forward, holding your hand. "You're just a bit swollen," I said. "It'll go down soon."

You frowned. "I got stinged in my arm, not my eyes."

"I know," I said. "But you had a reaction. The doctor says you're allergic to wasps."

You were shocked by this, but rather pleased.

"It was so hurting, my arm. That wasp really stinged me. A dog licked me."

I nodded. "It was the farmer's." I watched you for a minute. "Rhiannon, why did you run away?"

"I didn't."

"Didn't what?"

"I didn't run away."

"What do you mean?"

"I was taking Catrin her inhaler." Accusingly, you added, "You forgot it."

I looked at you. "You were taking it to the hospital?"

You nodded. "And her teddy."

"The hospital is a long way from the house," I said.
You didn't answer.

"You can't just go off on your own like that. Something much worse could have happened."

"Like what?"

"All kinds of things."

You looked at me. "I lost brown bear," you said. Your eyes filled with tears. "The river took my backpack."

"We found it," I said. "And brown bear. The police have him."

You looked at me, smiling. "Is brown bear in jail?"

"They'll give him back. Don't worry. Why didn't you ask a grown-up to take Catrin her inhaler?"

You fiddled with your canula.

"This is hurting me," you said, lifting your hand.

"I know," I said. "But you have to keep it in. Rhiannon?"

You looked at me. "What?"

"A grown-up could have given Catrin her inhaler."

"I make her better," you said.

"Okay," I said. "But sometimes you can't. Sometimes only grown-ups can. And other times, only doctors."

You looked at me evenly. "Daddy said doctors don't know anything."

"He's wrong."

"I want her to be better."

I nodded. "She'll go home today, I think."

"No," you said, angrily. "I want her back to before the accident."

"Oh," I said. I sighed. "I don't think that's going to happen."

"Am I in trouble?"

"No. But we were very worried. And you can't ever do that again, not ever."

"I'm in trouble always," you said.

"What do you mean?"

You didn't answer. Both of us were quiet. This seemed the moment to bring up the other thing I wanted to talk to you about, what I remembered from the accident when I saw the helicopter through the window. It was all related. I could see that now.

"Rhiannon," I said, "when did you start feeling like you're always in trouble?"

"Dunno."

"Is it since Catrin was hurt?"

"It's because I'm a bad kid," you said.

"You're not a bad kid. Not at all. Listen — I need to ask you something. Do you remember when we talked about how I don't remember the accident?"

You nodded slowly.

"I need to know what you remember. It's important."

You looked at me. "Catrin did it," you said.

"Did what?"

"She got out of her cot."

"How do you know?"

"I saw her."

I watched you. "Did you get her out of her cot, Rhiannon?"

"No!" You shook your head. "Not that. She did it."

I knew, now, that it was the only explanation that made sense. Only you, a child, would have let Catrin outside. Why would I have done it when your father had told me not to, and when I knew there was something dangerous out there? Whereas you simply hadn't understood what your father was talking about, at least not the severity of it.

"You won't be in trouble," I said. "I promise."

"She wanted to play with my scooter. Don't be angry with her. She was only a tiny little kid."

"Rhiannon. It's okay if you let her out. No one is going to tell you off."

You looked at me. "Daddy will."

I looked at you, thinking. "I won't tell him," I said.

You recognised immediately the strangeness of this promise, intrigued by the thought of us having a secret.

"Promise?" you said.

"Promise."

202

"If you're lying, I'm going to be so angry," you said.

"I'm not," I said.

You looked at me. "She wasn't asleep when I went in," you said. "She was happy when I went in there. Smiling."

I nodded. "Then what happened?"

"She was standing up and putting out her arms, you know how she does that? She wanted to get out."

"Good. Then what happened?"

You looked at me. "I got a chair."

"And lifted her out?"

You nodded slowly.

"You're very strong," I said. You smiled. "Then what happened? You went outside?"

You nodded.

"Where was I?"

"Sleeping."

"In bed?"

You shook your head. "On the couch."

When you said this, I saw myself as you described, on the couch, my back to the living room. I remembered suddenly and vividly how I had lain down there, taking a break from clearing up after the party. I was utterly and deeply exhausted, that thick and impenetrable tiredness that descends like a heavy blanket. So many times I had fought through it to do the things that needed to be done. But on this occasion, I was helpless, as tired of fighting it as I was of everything else. It didn't help that I had been drinking. Catrin had been asleep. You were playing with your new toys. Your father was getting ready to go to your nain — or had he already gone? I had taken the call from her, gone out to the patio to call him in. He had spoken with her before hurrying around, looking for his phone and keys. I couldn't remember if he was there when I decided to lie down.

I would just rest my eyes for a minute, I had thought.

Then there was screaming. Your screams. That was what woke me. I remembered this now. You were on the patio, banging the glass. This part of the story was harder to grasp, as though the memory was underwater, damp and water-streaked, appearing slowly from the unreachable bottom of my mind. There were others that were opening like quick-blooming flowers, with the colour and clarity of a photograph.

"How did you unlock the back door?" I asked you now.

"It wasn't locked."

"Are you sure?"

You nodded. "I just opened it. That's not lying."

I nodded. "And then you picked up the bucket?"

Your lip trembled. You started to cry. "I thought it was water, Mummy! I didn't know what was inside!"

"Oh, I know," I said. I got out of my chair, put my hands on your face, kissed your head.

"I thought she was dead!"

"Oh, Rhiannon," I said. "I'm so sorry."

"I'm in so big trouble now!"

* * *

Once you and your sister were home from the hospital, there was a fragile calm. Catrin was on antibiotics for a chest infection but seemed to have come through the worst of it at the hospital. Mostly she was back to her carefree self. You were lighter, too, since our conversation. A burden had been lifted, the heavy and solitary guilt of believing you had been responsible for the accident. It was a burden you had carried for almost a year, never mentioning it to anyone. I was making sure to talk to you about it often, reiterating that you weren't to blame — you had never been to blame — and trying to untangle its dark hold on us.

But the calm was fraught, ready to unravel. All of us were suffering. No one had recovered from the upset of the last week. I was disturbed not just by your disappearance and Catrin's illness but by our discussion in the hospital, since when my understanding of the accident was coalescing like never before. I had half a picture — and a hundred questions.

204

The more I thought about everything you had told me, the less sure I was of the things I had assumed to be true. Why, for example, had I never questioned my assumption — everyone's assumption — that I had unlocked the back door and let Catrin outside? This had never made the slightest bit of sense, given I had supposedly been told it was dangerous.

"I don't know," said your father when I confronted him about this. "It just seemed like the only explanation."

"Not according to Rhiannon," I said.

He and I were in the living room. You were in the garden with your sister, playing with the hose. Through the patio doors I could see the two of you running around on the grass. Greta was there, too, sprawled on a deck chair. For once she wasn't holding Deryn, who was asleep in her cot upstairs. I could see Greta was unsettled by her absence, head slightly raised as she listened for her cry, absently watching you spray Catrin with the rushing water. Beti was chasing the hose, barking as Catrin shrieked and trampled the wet grass.

"You're trusting the word of a five-year-old?" your father was saying. "About something that happened nearly a year ago?"

"Her version makes more sense. Anyway, why have you always been so sure that I let her out? You weren't even there."

"I remember locking the door."

"Okay. But why have you never thought Rhiannon might have unlocked it?"

"You just said you think the door was unlocked. Now you're saying you think Rhiannon unlocked it."

"I didn't say that. I'm just asking why did you never consider, for a second, that she might have done? Why have you always been so sure it was me?"

"So you're asking me to explain why I don't think something that happened that you don't think happened either?"

"Yes."

He sighed. "I locked the door and took the key with me. The only other key was yours, which you kept on a keyring in your handbag. It never occurred to me that our five-year-old

205

went into your bag, worked out which was the right key and let herself out the back door. Why would she do that?"

"She wanted to play with her scooter. She had a reason to do it. Unlike me. Why would I wake up the two-year-old I had just put to bed and let her into the garden, knowing there was something dangerous out there? It makes no sense at all."

"You were doing a lot of strange things, Elin. Anyway, this is neither here nor there. Whoever unlocked the door, it was your responsibility to keep the girls in the house. Even if Rhiannon did get Catrin out of the cot and unlock the door, as she claims in her elaborate version, why didn't you stop them?"

I knew the answer to this now — that I was asleep. But there was no reason to volunteer this when your father had proved himself hell-bent on making me responsible. His certainty about this had driven me away from my children. I needed to resist the temptation to admit to anything else he could use against me.

"It's not elaborate," I said. "She was bored. She wanted someone to play with. And she was upset after the party, because of how we'd been behaving."

"How you'd been behaving, you mean."

"All she had to do was bring Catrin downstairs and take her through the back door, especially if it was already unlocked."

"The door wasn't unlocked. I locked it."

"Why are you so sure?"

"Because I remember! I wasn't blacked out on the couch, unlike you."

"But don't you question any of your memories from that day? I mean, with everything that happened — the confusion and trauma of it all — how can you not have any doubt at all?"

I stopped, watching him. Something he said caught in my mind, though I wasn't sure exactly what it was. I turned away from him, trying to focus.

"David?" I said, turning back to him.

"What?"

He appeared not to be listening, looking through a pile of post on the side table. I knew very well that this was a tactic. He hadn't lost interest. He was trying, very deliberately, to make this discussion — to make me — feel insignificant.

"How do you know I was asleep on the couch?" I said.

He sighed. "Elin, I've got a lot of paperwork to do. Do you mind if we put this on hold for now?"

Since you told me your version in the hospital, I was still unsure about whether your father had left before or after I fell asleep. I hadn't thought it was important, except to the extent I wanted to piece it all together clearly. But now, as your father revealed that he had left afterwards, I realised how significant it was.

"David — you have always said that you told me about the acid as you were leaving. We got the phone call from your mother. You locked the back door, taking the key with you. You told me not to let the girls outside under any circumstances. You left through the front door. That's what you told the doctors, the social workers, me."

"Yes. So?"

"So if I was already asleep when you left, how could you have told me about the acid?"

He looked at me, his hand resting on the pile of unopened post. From his expression I knew — and he knew — that he had slipped up. This had all been more deliberate than I had given him credit for. I had been foolish to think otherwise.

"David?" I said.

He sighed, still trying to convey his disinterest. "What does it matter now?"

I stared at him. "What does it matter? This is the reason I left the girls! It's the reason I put them through ten months without me, and missed ten months of their childhood. Because you made me think I had nearly killed one of them. You made me think I couldn't look after them!"

"You couldn't look after them!" he shouted, slapping his hand against the table. "There were accidents happening all the time! You locked our eight-month-old daughter in the car on the hottest day of the year! You took Rhiannon to A & E, bleeding, God knows how many times."

"Twice. I took her bleeding twice."

"You pierced her ears when she was three years old! What kind of mother does that?"

My head swarmed, filling with his poison. But he was twisting everything. He had twisted far more than I realised.

I looked at him. "You never actually told me about the acid, did you? You left the bucket there by mistake. You forgot about it. You left me asleep on the couch. You left Rhiannon unsupervised, the back door unlocked. You left us completely unsafe. After the accident you realised what you'd done. But you couldn't own up to it. You knew I was too traumatised to remember, and would believe anything you said. So you made up a story."

As I talked he was watching me, a stony expression on his face. "Well, it's a good job I did, isn't it?"

"What?"

"I was the only parent the girls had, once you'd gone. Don't you think it was better that social services thought that at least I was capable of looking after them?"

"I only left in the first place because you said it was my fault! I wouldn't have gone if I didn't think that! Even if we could have just shared the responsibility for it, David — I could have coped with that. But you made me think it was all me."

I felt I could kill him. But this was my mistake. I had misunderstood the game we were playing, underestimated the extent to which he and I were working against each other. I should have known he was lying, that he would do anything to make himself the good parent, the capable one, scapegoating me to save himself. He had told this story so convincingly, with all his powers of calm and rationality, I had believed it, never stopping to think how convenient it was for him — and how damaging to me. I had absorbed his version of the accident exactly as he'd presented it: the last crime in

a string of disasters and the final proof of my darkest fear —
that there was something wrong with the way I mothered,
a doubt I had carried since the day you were born, sprung
from the worthlessness living inside me since my own mother's abandonment. As I'd driven away from the hospital that
day, his story was conclusive evidence that I was the mother
I feared, that you were better off without me.

TWENTY-NINE

I left the morning after Catrin's accident, getting a taxi from the hospital back to the house and packing a bag. You were staying with your nain. You weren't allowed to visit Catrin, not yet. Your father was at the hospital. I was still breastfeeding Catrin at the time. She didn't want milk often, weaned except for nursing at bedtime and falling asleep in my arms. Though I liked the ritual she and I shared, I was ashamed. Catrin was two and a half by then. Most people — even many breastfeeding mothers — disapproved of nursing for that long. Even your nain, after all her fuss about the importance of breastfeeding, thought I should have stopped by then, and only a few weeks before I had overheard two mums talking about a friend of theirs. "Once they've got a full set of teeth that should be the end of it," one of them said. "He keeps biting her!"

"Have you seen how he asks, though? He puts his hand up her top and starts grabbing them. She can't say no, I don't think."

Catrin didn't behave that way towards me. But the shame was overwhelming. What those who disapproved didn't say — but I knew they meant — was that it was per- verted somehow, a form of child abuse. And this was what I felt as she fed, a mixture of relief as the milk emptied, pleasure at our closeness, and disgust with a ritual that overstepped hidden boundaries. Looking back, I wish I had known then what I know now: that there was nothing wrong with nursing my two-year-old child, and that how I chose to feed my daughters was no one's concern but mine.

* * *

I drove south-east through the mountains. The weather was wild. The car felt cold. I didn't turn on the heating but kept my coat on. After four hours of driving, I arrived at Jude's, a red-brick semi-detached in a cul-de-sac. It was sunny here. I parked fifty or so yards from the house and watched. Children were in the garden. There was a slide with a long mat at the bottom, spread over the grass, and an older boy was keeping the slide and mat wet with the hose as the younger children climbed the steps then rushed down. There was a double swing — this was new, like the slide — and two kids were sitting on one of them, a little boy straddling an older girl, while the other dangled empty. I never expected Jude to stop fostering, but it seemed incredible to me that these kids were here, after all this time.

A woman walked into the garden. I lowered myself down in the driver's seat, as though she might look behind, into the distance, and spot me. I knew it was her. Even from behind, half a street away, I recognised her masculine height, the bleached-blonde hair cut at her chin and the way she stood purposefully, feet apart, hands on her hips. She was shouting to the children. The girl on the swing climbed down, carrying the little boy into the house. The other kids ran after them. Jude walked over to the tap and turned off the hose. Then she stood for a moment, looking around the empty garden before she walked inside after the children and closed the door. Through the front window I could see her wrapping the children in towels. I watched them for a minute longer. Then I turned the key in the ignition and drove away.

* * *

211

What I remember about all of it — leaving the north, driving to Jude's, checking into a bed and breakfast in the valleys — is that my breasts were slowly filling with milk. It was a sensation I was used to but it meant something different that day. Something awful. When I got to my room it was time for Catrin's bedtime feed. My breasts were full. I ran a deep bath, placed towels soaked in hot water over my breasts and massaged them as your sister's undrunk milk spilled down my belly.

When I was out of the bath, I wrapped a towel around my chest and sat on the bed, which creaked as I lay against the pillow. What I had been trying not to do, this whole time, was not think about what I was doing. But now it came down on me. I had left you.

I needed to go back, I thought. I got off the bed and began gathering my clothes.

Then I remembered your father's words in the hospital. *I told you how dangerous it was to let her outside. You did it anyway. You're not fit to be a mother.*

I sat back down, trying to remember what had happened. I didn't know — I didn't understand — how your sister had got out of the nursery after I had put her to bed, why she had ended up outside when your father had locked the back door and told me not to open it. This was the first time I had wondered — consciously — if I might have been hurting my children on purpose, if I had wanted Catrin to get hurt. When I thought through the past five years — the time I had pushed you off the bed, locked Catrin in the car on the hottest day of the year, pierced your ears against your will, shouted like a crazy person at both of you — I couldn't trust that this wasn't the case.

I lay down again, my mind swirling. I couldn't go back. But as I thought of the night ahead, and the days beyond, a despair came, more violent and frightening than I had ever known. My body turned cold. I ran to the toilet and vomited. Then I went back into the bedroom, got myself dressed and went downstairs.

* * *

The bar was quaint and old-fashioned, a sitting room with grey couches and a mahogany bar. It took me a long time to find anyone to serve me, and when I asked for a glass of white wine the owner seemed annoyed.

"We thought you'd be staying in your room," she said.

As she went to get my wine, I curled up in one of the armchairs. The carpet was grey, like the couch. There were paintings on the walls. Meaningless, pointless paintings. It was all pointless, I thought. The fireplace was deep and black, with gold pokers standing in a wide bucket. The woman came back with the wine, an unpleasant-looking dark yellow liquid filling the glass to the brim. I waited for her to leave before I tasted it. Predictably it was horrible, cheap and unchilled. I drank it anyway. When I met your father I told him I didn't like wine. He insisted I hadn't tried the good kind, and when we went out he ordered cold and crisp glasses of chardonnay. He was right. I did like it. And now I knew how bad this wine really was.

Still I drank until the glass was empty, the sharp edges of my situation beginning to dull. I went to find the woman again, asking her for a second glass.

"We do a half-bottle, if you want," she said.

When I got back to the sitting room, a man was there. He was in another armchair, alone. I wondered if he had been there before and I hadn't noticed. But I felt, if he had, he would have talked to me.

"How's the wine?" he said, as soon as I sat down. He was older than me but not by a lot.

"It's okay," I said.

"Not recommending it?"

An hour later, I was in his room. It seemed the easiest thing. I wasn't attracted to him. I just didn't know what else to do. I couldn't spend the night alone, not this night. But as I removed my clothes and lay down on the bed, waiting for him to climb on top of me, the encounter only increased my sense I had slipped into another world, away from the life I had left behind and the person I had been — or tried to be — as I took care of you. It was then that I realised the extent to which you and Catrin, while causing a certain crisis inside me, had saved me, too. Your predictability and routines, your commitment to the present, your joy and delight in the ordinary — all of it had grounded me even as I was falling apart. Small children didn't think about the past or worry about the future. They were contained in each beating moment of their existence. You had demanded I stay there with you, and it had pulled me back, again and again. What would I do without you?

THIRTY

There was a knock at the door.

I was alone in the house. Your father and Greta had taken you, Catrin and Deryn to the mountain zoo. The night before I had slept badly, shaken by my confrontation with your father about the accident. At first I couldn't sleep at all. When I eventually did, I had a series of upsetting dreams, most of them about you and your sister. Some were about Deryn. All of them featured babies. I was pretty sure one of those babies was supposed to be me. In each dream — or each chapter of the same dream, as they were indistinguishable — the baby was abandoned, left alone on an empty beach or deserted in a pram on the side of the road.

When the morning came, I was disturbed.

You begged me to come to the zoo. I said no, I had things to do at home. As you sulkily put on your coat and shoes, I was overcome with guilt and considered changing my mind. But I knew I needed time to myself. You would have a perfectly nice time without me. My plan was to read a book or watch a film, anything that might calm me down. But I couldn't relax. So I was cleaning.

I had made progress in the kitchen — stacked the dishwasher, swept the floors, filled the mop bucket with hot water

— when the knock came. Beti, who had been observing me from her basket, opening her eyes now and then before nodding back to sleep, let out a loud bark. I sighed, wringing out the mop and resting its handle against the counter. I walked out of the kitchen. Beti trotted after me. It was the middle of the afternoon, the clouds low, wind moving across the mountains.

When I reached the hall, I saw the blurred shape of someone's head through the frosted glass. I opened the door. A woman in a raincoat stood on the doorstep, gold hoops glinting in the recesses of her raised hood. She was very close to the door, as though she had forgotten to take a step back after she rang the bell. Behind her was her car, parked next to mine. I hadn't heard the car on the drive. I was too absorbed in the cleaning, my thoughts.

She reminded me of someone, though it took me a moment to realise who. It was windy outside, the woman's hood protecting her from the gales. The door pushed against me as I held it. In the wide sky behind the woman, the clouds were moving very fast.

When she spoke I realised who it was she looked like. They shared the same timbre of voice, as well as the strong local accent. At first, she spoke Welsh, switching to English when I hesitated.

"Is Greta here?" she said. "I was told she's living here? Do I have the right house?"

"Yes," I said. "I was just thinking how much you look like her."

She nodded indifferently, having undoubtedly heard this a hundred times. "I'm her sister," she said.

"She's out," I said. "I don't know when she'll be back. Do you want to come in?"

I regretted it the second I offered. I didn't want company, particularly from a stranger. And I had no idea when Greta would be back. The woman hesitated, glancing back at her car before stepping inside. She took off her coat. Beneath it she wore a leopard-print jumper and blue jeans. Her ankle boots clipped the tiles as she followed me down the hall to the kitchen.

"I'll try ringing her again," she said.

There was a hesitation in her voice. I wondered about her saying she had been told Greta was living here — if she was her sister, why hadn't she known?

"Would you like tea?" I said.

She paused in the kitchen doorway. "If you don't mind," she said. "I feel bad showing up but I can't get hold of her. I need to speak with her."

I filled the kettle and took two mugs from the cupboard. She stood by the kitchen table, unsure what to do with herself.

"Sit down," I said.

She didn't.

"This is a nice house," she said, looking around. Beti had gone back to her basket but was watching the woman closely.

"It is," I said.

In all the years before I left, I had never said thank you when a visitor commented on the house. I never felt it was mine, even after your father and I were married, even as I was raising our children within these walls. Finally, the woman pulled out a chair and sat down.

"We haven't spoken for months. She hasn't been answering her phone. We used to be on the phone to each other every day. She's upset with me, I think. I don't know."

She looked across the room at me, as though I might have the answer. My main feeling was regret for inviting her in, more with everything she said.

"She hasn't said anything to me."

"She's not the easiest person to get any sense from. I'm Efa, by the way."

"Elin."

"I know. You're the ex. I heard you were living here."

"Temporarily."

"Greta told me about you when she started seeing David. She was worried you'd come back."

217

The kettle boiled. I lifted it from its base and poured steaming water into the mugs, watching the teabags float to the surface. "So you don't live here anymore?"

"I'm in Cardiff now. I thought I'd come back more. It's just finding the time, isn't it?"

I didn't say anything. I thought about how, after I met your father, I lost contact with everyone from my childhood. I didn't return Jude's calls or texts. Eventually she stopped trying. It wasn't intentional. It just happened. I couldn't blame your father for it, either. He had never told me to stop seeing her or anyone else. But there was something about my life with him that they didn't fit into. I wondered if that was why Greta stopped speaking to her sister.

"Do you take milk?" I said.

"Please."

I got the bottle from the fridge and poured a little into each mug. Efa went on.

"It's hard because Mam and me don't speak anymore either."

I looked at her.

"It's a long story," she said. "Mam isn't well."

"Oh. Greta didn't say."

"Greta's got her head in the sand. There's nothing phys-ically wrong with Mam, that's the thing. It's up here." She tapped her head. "Last time I went to see her — this was over a year ago now — she'd asked me to go there, to help her with this issue she was having with her neighbour. Before I had a chance to even look at the paperwork, she was shouting at me, saying I was actually, you know, conspiring with the neighbour. Against her. Totally bonkers. Anyway, I stopped speaking with her after that. I couldn't cope with it. Until today. I needed to know where Greta was."

"I understand."

"It's one thing with Mam but I can't stand it with Greta. We used to be so close. But she hasn't been herself since the miscarriage, you know? That's all I can think. It brought up some issues for her, I think."

"Do you take sugar?"

"One. Please."

I stirred a spoonful into her tea then carried the mugs to the table.

"I didn't know she'd had a miscarriage," I said, putting Efa's mug in front of her. Sitting across from her, I wondered how on earth I would get rid of her.

"You weren't around then, I suppose," she said. "Don't tell her I said anything, please. But, yes, she had a miscarriage when she was twenty weeks pregnant."

"Oh my God," I said. "That must have been awful."

"It was horrendous."

"When was this?" I asked.

"Four months ago," said Efa.

I stared at her. "The miscarriage?"

"Yes. That was when she stopped speaking to me. I think it really messed her up. Maybe she hasn't been able to face me? I don't know. She always relied on me before."

"Are you sure it was four months ago?"

She nodded. "Christmas just gone. She came down to stay with me. She was in a terrible state. The worst I've ever seen her. She hadn't told David yet. She didn't know how to tell him. She thought it was her fault."

My head was spinning. "I don't understand," I said. "What about Deryn?"

Outside the kitchen the wind was gathering, swaying the trees lining the back track. Efa looked at me. "Who's Deryn?"

* * *

The sun was setting behind the mountains, jagged light infusing the sky as the floor of the valley turned black. Wind moved outside the window, making the wide pane of glass tremble. It started to rain. Efa left before you got home. She became upset when I wouldn't tell her any more about Deryn. She hadn't appreciated that. I understood why it upset her, after the relative intimacy of our strange meeting.

But I needed to speak to Greta before I said anything more to anyone. And I had to do it quickly.

I arranged for everyone else to be out. I rang your nain and asked if you and Catrin could stay with her, saying you were desperate to see her, a small and necessary lie. Your father was briefly annoyed that I had arranged this without asking him but he took the opportunity to go to the pub.

Now we were alone in the house — Greta, Deryn and me. I crept over to Deryn, asleep in her basket by the window. I watched her, small and helpless in her layers of blanket. With only the tall lamp in the back corner lighting the room, and darkness falling slowly outside, there was barely enough light to make out her tiny features. People say newborns all look the same, but you can always see a likeness to someone. And it's usually the father. "Nature's way of telling us who Dad is," a midwife told me once. Looking at Deryn in the muted light, I understood now why she didn't look like your father.

In the kitchen I found Greta, standing by the sink with a glass of wine in her hand. She looked dreadful. Her skin was pale and there were dark shadows under her eyes.

"I hardly slept last night," she said.

I looked at her. "The drink won't be helping," I said, harsher than I'd intended.

"It's the only thing that gets me to sleep in the first place! Why do you care, anyway?" She went to the fridge again, topping up her glass before it was even half empty. Her hands were shaking. She took a gulp of wine. Beti trotted over, as though sensing Greta was upset, and gently licked her hand.

"Sorry," she said. "It's not you, it's my sister. She's come up from Cardiff and she keeps ringing me. It's driving me crazy! I don't want to see her."

"I know," I said. "She was here."

She stared at me. "When?"

"This afternoon."

"Why didn't you tell me?"

"I am telling you."

She took another sip of wine. "What did she say?"

I looked at her. "Greta—"

"Listen, whatever she told you, don't believe her. She makes things up. She's always done it, ever since we were kids."

"So you didn't have a miscarriage?"

"A miscarriage?" She looked away, her expression darkening. "No."

"Why would she say you did?"

"Because she's crazy! You don't know her, Elin. I'm telling you. Even Mam doesn't speak to her."

"She said it was the other way round."

"She's a liar. I bet she told you we're such good friends, didn't she? I've never liked her. She just wants to be in my business all the time."

From the living room Deryn began to cry, a high-pitched bleat piercing the air. Greta swore under her breath.

"I'll get her," I said.

"It's fine" said Greta, shoving the wine bottle back in the fridge door.

"Greta," I said. "I'll go."

* * *

Night rolled in, a blanket of black locking in the native stillness of the land. Only the clouded moon and scattered light from the houses and farms broke up the darkness. The rain was coming down thicker, pelting drops on the windows and roof. Wind crashed in the trees. Beti, asleep in her basket, woke occasionally and barked at the storm building outside the house. Deryn was in my arms, hungrily gulping her bottle. When she'd finished, her eyes were wide and alert, staring at the moving shadows in the room as the storm shook the windows.

I held her upright, my palm against the back of her delicate head. The fragility of newborns never ceased to shock me. When Catrin was little, I watched a documentary that explained why human babies were so helpless while every other mammal could walk as soon as it was born. It said that as humans began to walk upright, our pelvises had narrowed and childbirth had to take place earlier than evolution might otherwise have wanted. When I heard this, I felt a little less frightened by Catrin's fragility, how she, like you at that age, was almost unworldly in her dependence.

Greta came into the room, holding the wine bottle in one hand, her glass in the other. She was drunk, walking unsteadily as she approached the couch and stood behind me. She squinted down at Deryn through the shadowy light, taking her in.

"She doesn't even know who I am," she said.

"What do you mean?" I said, though I knew exactly what she meant.

"I could be anyone. She doesn't care if it's me or David or his mam looking after her. Or even you."

"Newborns are like that," I said. "Adaptable. Make the most of it. It won't be long before she won't let you go to the toilet without her."

She smiled happily at that thought and stumbled over to the armchair, sinking down in the cushions as wine sloshed in her glass. With the three of us cocooned in this darkened room, I could almost forget what I needed to say to her, what I had to do. I was sickened by the thought and full of doubt, wondering if I should have talked to someone first, got some advice about how to handle it. But who would want to be dragged into this? And who could I rely on not to call the police before I'd had a chance to talk to Greta? I found myself slipping into denial, too, thinking, *This just can't be true. I've made a mistake.* But however many times I took it all apart, there was no other way to fit the pieces back together.

Abruptly, thunder rumbled outside the window. Electric light flashed in the black sky. Deryn's eyes widened in wonder. Gently I turned her body to face the window.

"About time we had a storm," said Greta. "David will be walking home in this," she added, sounding glad.

"Maybe he'll stay with Ceri," I said.

"I hope so."

For a while the three of us watched the lightning and listened to the thunder, not one after another but rolling layers of light and sound.

"I've been thinking about what your sister said."

Greta tutted. "I told you, Elin. She's nuts."

"But the thing is — it makes sense to me."

"What makes sense?"

"The miscarriage."

"It doesn't make sense because it isn't true. Can we forget it, please?"

I paused. "I never got a chance to tell you this. When I was at the hospital with Catrin, there was a nurse. Anest, her name was."

"Anest Richardson?"

"I don't know her last name."

"It was probably her," she said. "She's a bitch. What about her?"

"She said you didn't have Deryn at the hospital."

Greta was quiet.

I went on. "I remembered you saying you were on the ward the night that baby was taken."

"I was," she said. She tutted again. "Okay. Fine. I had her at home. So what?"

"You had her here?"

"Yeah."

"Why did you say you were at the hospital?"

"I didn't want David to be angry. He never wanted me to have her at home. I didn't want to say I'd done it anyway. You know what he's like."

I thought about this. When I was pregnant with you, I had wanted a home birth. Your father was against it. You'd think he would like the idea, given his distrust of doctors, how he wanted to control things himself for as long as he could. But he had hated the idea of midwives and medical equipment in his home. It was worse for him, somehow, than just going to the hospital. There was no logic, really.

223

The only consistency was that he was right and others were wrong.

"It still doesn't make sense," I said.

"Why?"

"If you had her here, he would've known. Are you saying you cleaned up all the mess, by yourself, before he got back?"

"Yes."

"When you'd just given birth? And you were looking after a new baby?"

"Yes! God, Elin, you're as bad as my sister! This is nothing to do with you."

I paused. My heart was thumping, my hands trembling even as I held Deryn. I had to keep going.

"Your sister said you stopped speaking to her after the miscarriage," I said. "She doesn't understand why. You were close before. It's because she knew about it, right? You didn't want anyone else to find out you'd miscarried. So you cut her out, hoping she would stay away. I'm guessing you've been pretty terrified of her coming back and finding out you have a baby."

"My sister is crazy, Elin. That's why I don't speak to her. That's why I haven't told her about Deryn. I won't have anything to do with her. I don't know why you're listening to her. Why don't you listen to me instead? You don't even know her!"

I turned to face her, placing Deryn against my shoulder.

"You didn't want anyone to find out about the miscarriage because you wanted to keep the pregnancy going. And you didn't want your sister to know about Deryn because she was the one person who would realise she wasn't yours."

Greta shook her head. "David was right," she said. "You are crazy."

"You didn't plan it. I know that, Greta. I understand. You were grieving. You couldn't accept that the baby was gone. You wanted to keep the pregnancy going, just a bit longer. But the longer the lie went on, the harder it was to go back. Right?"

She was quiet, staring through the window.

"So when David left for Prague," I went on, "you pretended to have the baby. You told him you'd had her in hospital. You told your colleagues you'd had her at home. But you didn't have her at either. You didn't have her at all."

Greta got out of her chair. Her glass, which she had forgotten was balancing in her lap, fell to the floor. She looked down at it, letting wine trickle from the glass and form a stain on the carpet. Looking over at me, her eyes were strangely vacant.

"Give her to me," she said.

"Greta," I said.

I stood up, holding Deryn firmly at my shoulder.

"Give her to me now," she said.

"I don't blame you," I said. "I understand."

Through the shadows I saw her eyes fill with tears. "You don't know what you're talking about!" she shouted. "I would never do a thing like that!"

"You have to give her back, Greta," I said. "Can you imagine what her mother is going through? She'll be losing her mind."

It was like talking to a toddler about a toy they had taken, trying to push them in the right direction without further entrenching their position. It had always felt manipulative when I did it with you and your sister. I felt this with Greta, too, that it would be more honest to just call the police, let her face the consequences. How could you reason with madness? But I couldn't do it to her like that. She had been caring for Deryn — or whatever this baby was called — for six weeks. She had convinced herself she was her mother. I had seen how broken Jude was every time a baby in her care was adopted or returned to its birth parents. Besides, Greta was clearly unwell — and I didn't trust the police to treat her as anything other than a criminal.

"I couldn't care less about that woman," said Greta. "She's a drug addict."

This surprised me. It hadn't occurred to me that Greta knew the mother.

"How do you know?"

"Everyone knew! She was tested." She looked towards the window. Rain was hitting the glass hard. "She didn't stop using when she got pregnant. But they were still going to let her take Deryn home!"

"Why?"

"They said the situation didn't warrant immediate removal." She pulled a face. "They were going to send them home under supervision. They were going to let her take her, Elin!"

"Wouldn't she have to do drug tests, if they were under supervision?"

"Oh, who the hell knows what would have happened! They never do their jobs properly. Babies are taken home by the worst parents in the world. Evil people. Look at the news! Kids end up dead because social services want to keep families together. No one cares about anyone, Elin — don't you understand?"

She made a movement towards me, reaching for Deryn. I took a step back. Tears were streaming down her cheeks now.

"I wasn't even going to do it," she said, more quietly now. "When I got to the ward, I was thinking — I can't. I'm just going to tell David the truth now. And then I saw them. Deryn was in the cot, crying. She was only a few hours old and she was crying for someone. And that woman was just sleeping. And I just thought — that baby is better off with me."

"I agree with you," I said. "She is better off with you. I understand how you feel, Greta. I don't know what would have happened to me if I hadn't been taken from my birth parents. I probably would have died."

I found this hard to say. But it seemed important to tell Greta this. She watched me, listening.

"But Greta," I said, "how is this going to go, really? The entire police force is looking for her. Everyone in the country knows about her by now. It can't be long before they work it out. I'm amazed they haven't already."

Even as I said this, I felt unsure. Why hadn't they put it all together by now? At this point, it seemed obvious. But no one else had got there. Not your father, your nain, Greta's mother. None of the midwives at the hospital.

"They don't know what they're doing," she said. "They're not thinking she's here, right under their noses."

"What if someone saw you?" I said.

"No one saw me. They would have said something by now."

"Aren't there cameras at the hospital?"

"Some. I know where they are."

We were quiet. The whole house seemed very still but outside the storm was getting louder.

"How did you hide the miscarriage?" I said. I wanted to know the answer but mostly I felt that, if we talked, it would help keep her calm. She must have been desperate to tell someone. She wasn't the type to bear a secret lightly.

"I wasn't going to hide it," she said, shaking her head. "I started having contractions. I was twenty weeks. I knew something was wrong, obviously. I was at Mam's." She looked away, towards the rain-beaten window, her face full of anguish. "It was the worst thing, Elin. I wanted to die. I didn't know what to do with her. The baby — I just . . ."

I closed my eyes. I didn't want to know what she did with it.

"Greta," I said, "I'm so sorry."

She looked back at me. "I couldn't tell David. I knew he would say we lost the baby because I was drinking. He would have left me."

"Didn't he notice that your bump didn't get any bigger?"

"I didn't let him touch me. I just said I was feeling sick or not in the mood. There are things you can do. But it wasn't how you think — I didn't plan it all out! It was like you said, I was just putting off telling him. I kept wanting to. And it just got harder all the time."

I nodded, looking at her. "If I worked this out, someone else will. Your sister knows something now. I mentioned

Deryn. I didn't tell her who she was, but she must have noticed the baby stuff — and surely your mother will tell her you have a baby!"

"Efa doesn't listen to anything Mam says. She thinks she's lost her mind."

"I think she'll have worked it out already. She might even have gone to the police."

"Well, they're not here, are they?"

I started to panic, realising that if the police did come now, it might look like I had been complicit by not turning Greta in.

Greta was staring at me with a strange expression now, as though noticing me for the first time. "It's too late now, though, isn't it?" she said.

"What do you mean?"

"She's mine now. I've had her since she was a day old. She doesn't even know her real mother. You can't make me tell them, Elin. You know you can't make me, don't you?"

Before I could reply she had moved towards me and taken hold of Deryn. I tried to maintain my grip, but with the suddenness of it, and my fear of hurting Deryn, I let Greta pull her from my arms.

Deryn woke up and began to cry. Greta placed her palm over the back of her head, rested her cheek against Deryn's soft skull. "Shh," she said, rocking her from side to side.

"Greta," I said. "Please don't hurt her."

She stared at me. "I would never hurt her!"

"I'll come with you to the station," I said. "I'll drive you. I'll be there. I'm on your side. I actually am."

"You're insane," she said. "Stay away from us."

She backed away, clutching Deryn to her shoulder, watching me as she moved out of the room. Reaching the door to the hall, she turned and ran. I went after her, watching as she tugged at the lock. As she pulled open the door, wind howled into the house, rain spattering the doormat. She ran onto the drive. She wasn't wearing shoes, only her slippers. She had no coat. Neither did Deryn. She ripped open the back door of her car, her back getting soaked as she leaned in and strapped Deryn into her car seat.

I put on the nearest shoes I could find and went after her, holding up my hand against the downpour. I grabbed hold of the car door, slippery with rain, as Greta tried to close it.

"Leave us alone!" she shouted, pulling my hand away. She turned and shoved me as hard as she could, and I fell back onto the hard stones, watching as she slammed the car door. As I pushed myself up, she climbed into the driver's seat. I scrambled towards Deryn's door, reaching for the handle. It was locked. The engine started. The car lurched back, knocking me onto the ground again. They sped away from me, disappearing down the track.

THIRTY-ONE

"I had that dream again."

"The one where you can't speak? Was it the same as usual?"

"Pretty much. I was with a group of people. I couldn't tell you who any of them were, but in the dream I knew them, if you know what I mean? And it started happening. I opened my mouth but no sound would come out."

"I know I've asked you this before but what do you think this dream is about?"

"I don't know. I've always hated speaking in front of people. Like at school when you had to do a presentation or something. I hated that."

He nodded. But he looked unconvinced. "You say you always feel helpless in the dream."

"Yeah."

"What makes you helpless?"

I frowned, getting the feeling he often gave me, that he was asking me a question with an obvious answer and yet somehow I couldn't answer it.

"Because there's nothing I can do, I suppose. I want to speak but I can't. It's like I'm paralysed or something."

"What about the other people in the dream?"

"What about them?"

"What are they doing?"

"Nothing. They're just there."

He nodded slowly. "The feeling of being paralysed — does that remind you of anything?"

I thought about it. "Not really."

"Which people are unable to move their bodies?"

"Disabled people?"

"Who else?"

I thought about this. Then it came to me. "Babies."

He nodded.

"Babies can speak, though," I said. "Well, they can cry."

"Opening and closing your mouth while the people around you do nothing — when has this happened to you, Elin?"

"Yeah, but—"

"And what about the boy you talked about previously?" he went on, interrupting me. I was surprised by his urgency, and the fact he had cut me off. He had never done that before. "Luke? He was unable to speak except for a high-pitched cry? Why does this stay with you, Elin?"

"But in the dream, I'm not a baby. I just . . . I don't know."

Why was it so important to me that this wasn't what the dream was about? Slowly, my sessions with Ben were teaching me something — when I resisted, we were getting closer to the truth.

Ben sat forward. "Elin, these dreams, these memories — your mind wants you to confront something. That's why you came here."

I closed my eyes, feeling the pressure building in my head, pushing against my skull. The panic came hard and fast. The room went black. Though I was still conscious — I could feel the soft chair beneath me — my vision disappeared.

"Elin," I heard Ben say, his voice floating above me like he was very far away, "I'm here."

* * *

When my sight came back, Ben was gazing at me steadily.

"I couldn't see anything," I said.

"I know. How are you now?"

"I feel sick."

"Would you like some water?"

When I didn't answer — I felt too weak to commit to a response — he got up and walked over to the table where he kept water bottles and boxes of tissue. The bottles were refilled with tap water. You could tell from the softness of the plastic and how easily the lids came loose. When I drank from one, I always wondered who the last person was to use it. I sipped the water slowly. Ben sat down again, folding his hands in his lap.

"Listen," he said, "I don't want to push you."

I was disorientated. Ben was helping me to understand myself in a way no one ever had. I had never had this level — this intensity — of attention from anyone. His commitment and care exceeded any relationship I had experienced. Yet I hardly knew him.

"I know it's important," I said. "It's just . . ." I shook my head.

"I know," he said. He looked at his watch. Matter-of-factly, he said, "That's the end of the session. Next time, I want to give this a try. I'd like you to bring something with you. A comforting object."

I stared at him. "What kind of comforting object?"

He shrugged. "A blanket. An item of clothing. A cuddly toy. Anything you like."

* * *

I wandered the aisles of a discount shop. What I was looking for, I didn't know. There was nothing at home I considered a comforting object. Eventually, I came across some blankets, soft and fleecy. Their labels read: *Super Soft Sherpa Blanket*. I chose a pale-blue one, with white on the reverse, and took it to the till.

When I sat down at the next session, sinking into the armchair, I realised I should have removed the label. Instead, I'd made it obvious to Ben that I'd bought the blanket specifically for this. I hadn't even taken off the price sticker. But I had no choice but to stay as I was, holding the blanket upright on my lap like a bag of flour.

I began talking the second Ben sat down, in the hope this would distract him. "I don't remember anything about that time. Nothing. I don't mind trying. I just don't want you to be disappointed."

I had wanted to say this anyway, but it came out defensively, probably because of the blanket. For a while he didn't speak. "I won't be disappointed," he said. "This isn't about me. And it isn't a test. We're just going to explore and see what we find. There's no pressure. Okay?"

"Okay."

"So why don't you start by telling me what you know."

"What do you mean?"

"Well, I take your point about not remembering. But is there anything you were told about your birth mother, what it was like when you lived with her?"

When he said "birth mother" my mind closed like a blind being drawn. "Nothing at all," I said, though in fact I had had the vision, after I dropped you off for your first day at school, of a woman walking away from me. I had a feeling she was my mother. But I didn't tell Ben about this.

"Remind me how old you were when you were taken into care?" he said.

"Two," I said.

"That's interesting," he said.

"Why?"

"It's the age Catrin was at the time of the accident."

"So?"

"I was just thinking it must have made the threat of Catrin being taken into care much worse for you, given it's what happened to you at that age."

"I don't think I was aware of the parallel. But I don't remember."

"Do you know anything about how it came about?" he said. "That you were taken into care, I mean."

"I know I was abandoned," I said. "They found me in a park."

"That's where you were left?"

"We think they dropped me outside the hospital over the road."

"You wandered across a road?"

I nodded, sucking in a mouthful of air.

"I was lucky. Not to get hit by a car, I mean."

"Do you feel lucky?"

"In a way. Especially because I was fostered by Jude. I think that was lucky."

He watched me. The room was quiet. I tried to keep my gaze on him but I was finding it difficult. There was an intensity that seemed to have come from nowhere, and a scepticism in his eyes that I didn't like.

"What happened to your parents?" he said.

"No one knows."

"How do you feel about them now?"

"I don't think about them."

"What about when you were a child?"

"I don't know. I mean, when the other kids saw their parents, it was always a drama, like with Abi and her mum. So maybe it was better for me, in a way, the way she just cut me off clean."

"She?"

"My mother."

"How do we know it was your mother who left you there, if you don't remember?"

"Yeah, that's a good point. In my head, it was her. Just her."

"That's interesting," he said. "Do you know why that is?"

"I don't know. It seems like the kind of thing a mother would do. Like, if I was in a bad situation, she wanted something better for me and she did something about it instead of just letting me starve."

He looked at me thoughtfully. "Last week, I mentioned how your dream might be related to how you were treated as an infant."

My heart quickened.

"I know you don't like to talk about this."

"I don't even like to think about it," I said.

"Can you try explaining how it makes you feel?"

"I just can't stand thinking about a baby lying there, hungry."

He frowned. "How do you know you were hungry?"

"Jude said I had some medical problems when I first arrived, because of malnourishment. I don't like to think of a baby like that."

"Not 'a baby', Elin," Ben corrected me. "You."

"Okay. Me. But I don't really think of it as me."

"You feel disconnected?"

"I am disconnected. It was years ago. I don't even remember it!"

"Elin," he said, learning forward, "the first three years have a more profound impact than any other time in our lives, whether we remember it or not."

I sighed. "I also don't like to make it seem like I think what happened to me was so terrible. Way worse things happen to kids all the time."

"Worse than being left to starve?"

"I wasn't left to starve. I didn't die, did I?"

"That's true, you didn't die."

"And they didn't assault me, I don't think. I didn't have any injuries. I was just neglected, that's all. Terrible things happen to little kids. Awful things. Sometimes I think I can't live in this world because of the things we do to children."

I began to cry. It was very unsettling. I never cried in front of other people. I had hardly even cried as a child. And in our entire marriage, I had not cried in front of your father.

235

Gently, Ben said, "Elin, all those things, I know they're awful. But do you understand that they feel worse for you because you're one of those children."

"I'm not! I'm not one of those children." I put my fingertips against my temples, trying to ease the pressure in my head.

"Take a deep breath for me," he said.

"That's all you ever tell me to do!" I did what he said anyway. When I opened my eyes, he was still leaning forward, watching me closely. There was no pity in his eyes, nothing to make me feel small or wretched. They were cool and still, like a rock in a storm. Even with the things I was telling him, these ugly stories between us, he didn't look away. Under his calm gaze, a blackness rolled through my mind. When it passed, I noticed that the blanket had fallen flat in my lap and I was clutching the ends in my fists.

THIRTY-TWO

If she was running away from the police, this was a strange way to go about it. She could have turned left at the bottom of the track and it wouldn't have been long before she reached the dual carriageway, a wide and fast road that eventually connected to the motorway and took you across the border. But she had turned right into the mountains. I didn't know what this meant. Either way, she was drunk and driving a six-week-old baby along narrow, often unfenced mountain roads in a storm. Vaguely I could see the tail lights of her car. She was driving far too fast, surging round the bends. The lanes were flooding fast, dips in the road filling to form rivers of rainwater. My wipers moved frantically but made little difference. It was hard to see anything on these lanes at night, even when the weather was calm, with no streetlights and barely any houses.

What I remember most about that night is the fear. It wasn't just the fear of what Greta was planning but driving along those lanes, at that speed, in those conditions. Every bend felt like I would hit an oncoming car or kill someone who happened to be out in the storm. Every second I anticipated something awful, either Greta crashing, or me, or losing sight of her and the baby.

And it only got worse after that, more distressing and disturbing than I could have imagined. I blamed myself for all of it. I had been stupid and naive, thinking I could convince her to hand herself in, and at every point I was aware the decision might be fatal.

Suddenly she turned. I followed her down a dark and sheltered lane, tall trees on either side rising into the black sky, cowering in the wind. The track inclined sharply downward and was barely wide enough for a vehicle. Our cars edged the sides. Greta was forced, as much as me, to slow down. When we reached the bottom, the track opened into a wide space. Greta's car shot ahead but I had to slow down. I had no idea where I was, whether we had emerged onto field or road, whether there were any drops ahead of me. The ground felt rutted and hard. I squinted into the dark and realised we were at the beach, the sea crashing ahead under the rain-washed moonlight. Ahead of me, Greta was bumping across what I now realised was a deserted car park.

When she reached the foot of the dunes, rising beyond the car park, she came to a stop. Her lights turned off. She got out of the car, her figure arching against the rain, and moved round the car to open the rear door and take Deryn from her seat. The state she was in, I wasn't sure if she knew I was there, whether she had noticed my headlights behind her the whole way. I crossed the car park slowly, my tyres bumping on the uneven ground. By the time I parked beside her car, she was mounting the slopes, exposing herself and Deryn to the appalling wind and rain. I turned off the engine. Wind rocked my car. I had to push hard against my door to get out. The second I let go, it slammed itself shut. I felt inside my pocket, checking for my phone, and went after Greta.

* * *

If the wind had been strong in the car park, where the dunes provided some shelter, as I climbed the slopes it became murderous. I could hardly move. I didn't understand how Greta had got over the dunes as quickly as she had, except by sheer strength of will. The storm was at its peak, it seemed to me, unsettling everything in its wake. Rain pelted my head. Wind swelled my clothes and whipped my hair. When I reached the top of the slopes, I was stunned by the sight of the sea.

I knew this beach well. I had brought you and your sister countless times and I had been here a few days earlier, giving my CV to the girl at the ice cream parlour. This was where Tŷ Gwyn overlooked the water and caravans spread for acres behind it, accommodating the visitors who made their holidays here. In the daylight it was glorious, a stretch of sand below a sweep of grey pebbles, mountains in every direction. It was almost always windy and the water was bitterly cold, except in late summer and early autumn. It was late April now, when the sea was colder than December, having been cooled through the winter months. I had never swum here, put off by local stories of drowned tourists who hadn't respected the water. But I had paddled with you and Catrin in the surf.

I had never seen it like this, the beach black with shadows, the ocean rabid and wind-beaten. As the storm unsettled the sea, huge, almost tidal waves were tossed high and broke in every direction. With sheets of rain coming down, and the waves rising and crashing, the whole landscape was awash, sky and sea merged and indistinguishable.

Descending the other side of the dunes, I looked for Greta, scraping hair from my face, searching the wide and wet darkness. It was hard to see anything, let alone a small figure on a vast and stormy beach. I began to feel helpless and stupid.

Finally, I saw her, a tiny moving shape in the distance.

She had crossed the beach and seemed to be climbing over the rocks that formed a promontory out to sea. You and Catrin had paddled there when the tide was out, wading the shallow pools in puddle suits and wellies, trapping shrimp in nets. The seabed, I knew, dropped off at the end.

I ran as fast as I could, the wind beating back against me. I lowered my head, looking up now and then to check I was still going in the right direction. When I reached the promontory, I saw Greta ahead of me, making her way across it as the tide rushed in. Given she was holding Deryn, and using only one hand to climb across each slippery, rain-beaten rock, I felt I must be able to catch up with her. But even with two hands, it wasn't easy. I lost my grip several times, trying not to think about how easily Greta could bash Deryn's fragile head against a boulder.

At my feet the water was shockingly cold, rising higher the deeper I went among the rocks. At least I was wearing shoes. Greta, as far as I knew, was still in her slippers. I was trying not to consider the madness of my situation, focused on getting to them. Later, when I looked back, I would wonder why I didn't call the police at the house, or while I was driving after Greta. Why I didn't give myself the support I needed, rather than trying to do this alone.

Failing to catch up with her quickly enough, I began to panic.

"Greta!" I screamed her name pointlessly. "Stop!"

My voice died in the storm. There was no way she could hear me over the rushing wind, the violent crashing of the sea. Greta was holding Deryn close to her body but I knew she was tiring. She stopped and shifted Deryn to her other arm. The pause allowed me to move a little closer.

"Greta!"

She turned. Her eyes were wild with fear. We were about halfway now. Seeing me behind her, she picked up her pace, becoming more erratic in her movements. Even at that point of high adrenalin, I could feel that I was exhausted. Running over the dunes and across the beach, climbing this long stretch of rocks, and all of it while pushing against the wind — it was a physical ordeal as much as a psychological one. And the stress of it was not only about Greta trying to kill herself and the baby, but being out in these conditions, exposed and alone. I couldn't shake the feeling, the whole time, that I was going to die. That this was the end of my life, in this deathly storm, chasing after a woman I hardly knew and a baby that wasn't hers.

We were deep in the sea now. As it reached my hips, my legs turning numb, I braced myself for the freezing water to encircle my waist. A wave crashed. The water rose. I gasped as it covered my middle, soaking my clothing and shocking my skin. In front of me Greta was up to her waist, too. Her grip on Deryn had slackened and she dangled her loosely over the water's surface. I was not an expert on newborn hypothermia — I had never had to think about what would happen if you exposed a one-month-old to temperatures like this — but I remembered, as a new mother, being told that babies under three months were not supposed to swim in water lower than thirty-two degrees. That was why those little baby pools at the leisure centre were warmer than the main pool. Whereas Deryn was being taken into freezing water that would make a cold-water swimmer breathless. She was already wet. The water had moved and crashed against us many times, barely time to recover from the assault of a wave before another one came. But she hadn't been submerged for any length of time, not yet. I needed to stop that happening.

It is hard to explain what it was like in the water. I was so angry with Greta, furious to be put through this, and that she was putting Deryn through it. I was also very scared. This was when my fear reached its peak and I thought we would all surely die.

At the same time, I felt a huge pity and sadness that Greta was in this state. I wanted to save her and I wanted to kill her.

And I felt I was in a tremendous battle, partly with Greta's stubborn will to kill them both. But also with the storm and the sea. And with myself, strange as it sounds. It seemed like a struggle against everything all at once, and that I would either die or be permanently changed.

I understood with certainty that I would not be able to persuade Greta to give me the baby. For one thing, she was too immersed in her distress. For another, it wasn't practical. She could hardly hear me, even when I was close behind. As we neared the final rocks, only their tips exposed above the rising water, I came within inches of her. Pushing myself forward,

I grabbed her shoulder, moving my other arm around her. Clumsily, I pulled her towards me, my fingers touching her open mouth as she let out an inaudible scream. Shocked, her grip loosened and I felt Deryn slip from her arms. As Deryn's body hit the water, the sea rocked. By some miracle, she was washed against me. I grabbed hold of her tiny body and held her above the water while trying to regain my footing.

It had happened now. She had been soaked in the freezing water. Maybe only for a few seconds. But it was enough to make me feel I urgently needed to get her out of the water. She was sickeningly limp in my arms, her little head flopped against my shoulder. Greta had lost her footing, too, when I pulled her backwards. She was gasping now, flapping her arms to stay afloat. Another wave rose and crashed. Greta vanished. After a few seconds she emerged, spluttering. The water was around her neck. She held on to a rock but another wave came, pulling her under again. She seemed to have lost not only her footing but her ability to keep herself afloat. *She's drowning*, I thought. *She's drowning and there's nothing I can do*. I still had my feet on the ground but the water was rough and rising fast. Trying to keep myself rooted, and Deryn above the water's surface as much as possible, I had no choice but to watch, helpless, as Greta fought back to the surface only to be pulled under again.

With the next wave she was thrown against a rock. I waded towards her, holding Deryn. When I reached her, her head was tilted back. Her body looked limp. Her eyes were closed against the crashing wind and rain. Or perhaps she had been hurt. I couldn't tell.

"Greta!"

Water swirled at my chest. I knew it wasn't long before I would be lifted into the water, along with Deryn.

"Greta!" I shouted again. "Can you hear me?"

She turned her head, almost imperceptibly. She couldn't open her eyes against the rain and crashing seawater but she tried, squinting to look at me.

"Just take her!" she shouted.

"Can you move?" I shouted. "Are you hurt? I need to get Deryn out of this water."

"Just leave me!"

"You're going to drown," I said. "We will all drown."

I didn't say that Deryn might be dead already, though I was terrified that she was. I didn't know if she had hit her head when she was knocked into the water. I didn't know anything. I couldn't see anything. It was chaos. Terrifying chaos. I just needed to get Greta out of the water. But I couldn't support her. She had to do it herself. She had to want to come. I knew that my phone, if it was still in my pocket at all, would not be working. I couldn't contact the police — or anyone — to come and help, not until I got home. Then it would be too late.

"Please just come!" I shouted. "Maybe I can't help you. But if you stay here you will die. You don't deserve to die!"

The water rushed around us. Another wave crashed right over Greta.

"I don't want your help!" she screamed at me. "Leave me alone!"

She was as desperate as I was. Desperate for me to do what she was asking. Desperate for it to be over. This was all she had left, the power to die. I looked at her. It didn't matter what I said. And if Deryn was alive, I had to save her. She had no one else but me.

* * *

As I made my way back across the rocks, the storm seemed to be gathering still, the wind getting harder, the water more violent, as though preparing to take Greta to her death. That was how it felt to me. I was sick with guilt and grief as I climbed back over the long stretch of rocks, my muscles searing with the pain of what I had put them through, what I was continuing to put them through.

Halfway, I stopped. I looked back towards where I had left her. I didn't know if I was looking in the wrong place, or

243

the conditions were blocking my view, or she had been pulled under. I didn't know. But I couldn't see her. I carried on, holding Deryn at my shoulder, patting her back in a feeble attempt to bring up swallowed water. I was forced to stop, more and more, from the exhaustion in my body. As I got to the beach, the tide risen far past the mouth of the rocks, I wanted to cry. I sat down on the slushy sand, breathless. I felt not relief but a deep and terrible despair. I screamed into the wind. Tentatively, I put two fingers against the side of Deryn's neck, her skin raw and water-wrinkled. Her head remained flopped against my shoulder, her eyes tightly closed. But through my numbed fingertips, I registered the faint and rapid pulse of her heart.

Standing up, I vomited, seawater splashing the wet sand. I wanted to lie down and close my eyes, unable to face the walk back over the dunes. I felt inside my water-filled pocket for my phone. It was gone.

"It's okay," I told Deryn. "We'll get you to the hospital. You'll be safe. We'll find your mother."

As I said it, I thought about what Greta had told me about Deryn's mother, how I might now be handing her over to an environment no safer than what she had been put through tonight. I wondered whether she would be taken into care, and what would happen to her after that. I knew how much of it was down to chance. Then I thought about Jude, how lucky I had been to have had a foster home where I was not assaulted or starved or locked away, and yet how I had lived my entire life with the deep pain of my mother's abandonment.

The trek back to the car was even harder than I feared. My legs resisted movement. A few times they gave way, forcing me onto my knees as I climbed the dunes. When I got to the other side, I slid down on my bum. At the bottom I stumbled over the gravel. When I opened the back door of my car, I hesitated. I didn't know if it was safe to put Deryn in a car seat in the state she was in. What if she'd ingested seawater?

I didn't have a choice.

I still had Catrin's seat in the back. I placed Deryn inside it. Her eyes were still closed, her body slack. In the faint light of the back she looked pale. Uncertainly, I removed her sleep-suit, stripping the sopping fabric from her skin. The nappy beneath was swollen with seawater, hanging from her little body. I unfastened it, the lining disintegrating, thick glob-ules from inside lodged in the folds of her skin and spilling all over the seat. In the boot I found an old picnic blanket. It was rough and dusty but it was all I had. My own clothes were as soaked as hers. Hands shaking with cold, I wrapped the blanket around her, threading the straps of the car seat over it, her bald head poking out at the top like a fallen bird.

Through all this, she didn't stir. As I started the car I was reminded, once again, of the doctor's motto on the sanctity of tears. I longed for her to cry. But her body was as slack and still as your sister's on the patio that day, and appalled me just as much.

* * *

It was after eleven when I pulled out of the car park. In the distance I noticed the lights were on at the pub. There was no way they were open in this weather. But if someone was there, I wondered about using the phone, giving Greta a small chance of being rescued by people who might be able to get her out of the water. But I couldn't delay getting help for Deryn. Upsetting as it was, I needed to forget about Greta.

I drove past the pub and back along the road I knew, avoiding the steep lane Greta had brought us down. We were a fifty-minute drive from the hospital, I estimated. With the storm still going, pulling down trees and fences, it would probably take longer. The house was on the way — I would have to pass the bottom of our track to get to the main road. Given the state Deryn was in, I decided to take her home first, warm her up before putting her through the drive. I could call the emergency services from the landline and get some advice. The last thing I wanted, after all this, was for Deryn to die in the back of my car.

That was my decision. But in every situation I found myself in that night, it was impossible to know for sure what was the right thing to do. In one way, I was clear-headed, single-minded in my pursuit of Deryn's welfare, which was by far the greatest thing at stake. At the same time, I felt removed from my reality, so extreme and difficult to process in real time. I felt my mind had, in some significant way, shut down. I knew this disconnection was enabling me to function, preventing me from becoming overwhelmed. But I couldn't be sure it wasn't affecting my judgement, making me hard-headed in some crucial way. In the end I just had to trust myself.

* * *

As I drove up the track to the house, my car shaking in the wind, I saw the warm glow of the living room light and the figure of your father through the glass. He was just standing there, looking out at the bleakness of the storm, no doubt wondering where everyone was.

The sight of him made my heart beat faster.

I parked the car and sat in the driveway, trying to steady my hands. Rain thrashed the car roof. The wind beat the trees. It was too dark to see the ravages, but I knew that in the morning we would find the garden and fields littered with objects carried from afar, trees felled and strewn among the sheep, bins knocked over, children's toys and garden equipment mangled in roadside bushes.

That would be the least of it.

Deryn had remained quiet in the back. I got out, once again, into the lashing wind and rain, struggling against the car door then letting it slam itself closed. I opened the back door and leaned over Deryn, wind howling in behind me. Slowly I unstrapped her, still bundled in the rough blanket. I held her against me, my hand on the back of her head as it flopped forward. When I turned back to the house, your father was gone from the window.

As I moved towards the front door, the light flickered on above it. I rang the doorbell — I didn't bring my key — and waited anxiously for your father. It seemed to take a long time. Everything he did was slow and deliberate, even in moments of crisis, pushing me to deliriums of apprehension at times like this. When he finally unlocked the door, the wind pushed it against him. He stumbled slightly but held on to it. Wind crashed into the house, knocking the post swiftly off the hall table.

I ran past him.

He forced the door shut, clicking the lock then struggling with the iron bolt at the top of the door. He turned to face me, glancing at the back of Deryn's head, the moth-eaten blanket around her. My clothes sagged and seeped water on the tiles. The hall was quiet. Your father smelled of booze. When he opened his mouth, I interrupted.

"I will explain everything," I said. "But I have to get Deryn into dry clothes."

"What the hell is going on? Where's Greta?"

I lied. "She's fine. I'll explain everything. I will. But I need to get Deryn warm and dry. She isn't well. Will you just help me for now? Please, David?"

He nodded, prevented from asserting any kind of authority, or even dishing out a derisive comment, given he had no idea what was going on. This would not last, of course. But for now I seized the chance to do what I needed.

"Can you get her some clothes? And turn the heating up? Which room can we warm up quickest? The bathroom?"

He nodded. I ran upstairs with Deryn and placed her on the changing mat on the bathroom counter. Your father moved around downstairs then made his way up to his bedroom to find clothing. He didn't rush. I unravelled the blanket, pulling it gently from beneath Deryn's naked body. Looking at her in the bright light, her skin was not only water-wrinkled but upsettingly pale, almost grey. Around her

247

lips the skin was a luminous blue. I took her pulse again. Her heart was beating, but slowly now.

Behind me your father moved into the room, getting down on one knee to adjust the knob on the towel rail, then moving over and doing the same with the radiator. I reached towards the rail then changed my mind.

"Are there towels in the airing cupboard?"

Your father stood up. "I'll check."

He moved out of the room. I stared at Deryn as I waited. I would have held her against me but I was so cold, my clothes so wet, it was pointless. I was shivering. Your father came back with a towel. I lifted Deryn gently onto it, wrapping her in its warm layers, and passed her to your father.

"Hold her against you," I said.

He took her from me. "You need to take off those clothes," he said. "You look terrible."

"I know."

"Elin," he said.

"What?"

"Where's Greta?"

"I will explain. I promise. Just—"

I searched my mind for a way to keep his questions at bay. I needed to tell him the truth about Deryn. To do that I needed to keep him calm. There was so much to tell him, so much for him to accept. Suddenly Deryn hiccupped, a small but glorious sound, then vomited water onto your father's shirt. She let out a high-pitched cry.

"Oh, thank God," I said. "Keep holding her, okay? Hold her upright. And pat her back, in case she needs to bring up more seawater."

At the mention of seawater he looked aghast. But he pulled her against him. As he talked quietly to her, the radiator ticked and heat blasted from the rail, slowly turning the small room warm.

"Should we run a bath?" he said.

"I don't think so," I said. "No direct heat."

This was true. But it was also the case that I couldn't bear the thought of putting her back in water. Quickly, I peeled off my wet clothes, took a towel from the rail and fastened it under my arms. I closed the bathroom door behind me, enclosing the heat inside, and looked for the warmest clothes I could find from my suitcase in the nursery. After three weeks home, I still hadn't unpacked. As I removed the towel, putting on dry underwear and thick socks, my body began to shake. None of my clothes were particularly warm. Your father, on the other hand, had all kinds of thermal clothing for when he went shooting in winter. I went into his bedroom and found a fleece in his wardrobe.

In the bathroom, Deryn was crying. Your father glanced at the fleece but said nothing.

"She must be hungry by now," I said. "Let's give her a bottle. Then I'll drive her to the hospital. Better than trying to get an ambulance out in this weather, isn't it?"

Having calmed down a little, my anxiety was rising again as I faced telling your father the truth. But I knew it had to be done before we got to the hospital or called an ambulance. I knew I couldn't deal with paramedics or doctors without telling them who Deryn was. And I couldn't let your father find out at the same time as the authorities. Even after everything, I couldn't do that to him.

"Does she need to go to the hospital?" your father was saying.

"Yes," I said. "She's much better, I know. But she still needs to be seen. She might have water in her lungs."

Downstairs, he prepared a bottle. I sat on the couch with her for the second time that evening. She drank the milk hungrily, still swaddled in the towel. Every few seconds she would pull her head back and cry before chomping down on the teat again with a ravenous shake of her head. Your father sat in the armchair where Greta had been a couple of hours before, watching us.

"Have you spoken to your mum this evening?" I said. "Are the girls okay?"

I felt suddenly worried about the two of you, though you'd likely spent the evening watching television in your nain's living room, warmed by the wood burner and lavished with snacks.

"They're fine," said your father. "Elin?"

I looked at him.

"Where is Greta?"

THIRTY-THREE

My foster sister tried to overdose when she was thirteen. Her name was Abi, the girl who wanted her mother's attention. It wasn't a surprise to anyone when she did it. She had spent the weekend at her mum's and as usual it had ended in a fight. Her mum had said she wished Abi was dead. Maybe Abi was trying to make a point. Or she had genuinely just given up. Either way, it was a Sunday. Pharmacies were closed. She bought two packets of paracetamol from the corner shop, telling the woman who worked there that Jude had sent her. She tried the supermarket but they refused to sell her any. In the end, she had thirty-two tablets that she washed down with a bottle of pink gin Jude had been given as a thank-you present. The gin made Abi violently sick and she threw up most of the tablets. I remember how the vomit — on her bedsheets and pillow, the bathroom floor — was pink and how the tablets had come back up whole, white lumps in chemical-pink vomit. Jude cleaned furiously while Abi was in the hospital. The smell of sick lingered for weeks.

* * *

It wasn't difficult for me to accumulate enough tablets to do it properly. I was an adult. I had a car. Nobody knew me.

But as I drove to the nearest town, I thought about Abi, how she must have felt that day. Defiant, I thought, *I'll show them.* I didn't feel that way.

I left my car near the high street thinking, as I got my ticket, how pointless it was to pay for parking in the circumstances. I did it anyway, sticking the ticket to the windscreen. My head was heavy with last night's drink. There was a stinging in my shoulder where Adam — that was his name — had given me a love bite. I had covered the mark with a shirt.

I left town with carrier bags hiding paracetamol and Southern Comfort. It was an overcast day, a light blanket of clouds shutting out the light. I felt breathless, as though I had walked further than I had. I threw the carrier bags on the passenger seat and drove back to the bed and breakfast. I thought about you, what you were doing, whether Catrin was awake in the hospital, how much pain she was in. My head seemed to close in on itself. *Why not just drive off the side of a cliff?* But I knew I would never be able to do it that way.

As I pulled into the car park, I saw Adam. He had shaved and he wore a blue suit and tie. I expected him to ignore me but when he saw me, he changed direction and walked over.

As I got out of the car, he said, "I've been looking for you."

"Why?"

He glanced at the carrier bags on the passenger seat. You could see that I had been to two different pharmacies, and two shops, but you couldn't see the tablets inside the bags. What you could see, in the off-licence bag, was the label of the liquor bottle. *So he thinks I'm an alcoholic,* I thought. *So what?*

"Last night," he said. "I hope I wasn't—"

"You were fine," I said.

He looked at me for a few seconds, then nodded. "I've got a meeting," he said.

Looking down at his hand I noticed a wedding ring. I was sure he hadn't been wearing it the night before, though I hadn't checked.

"It was nice to meet you," I said.

* * *

Back in my room it was quiet. The bed and breakfast was down in a valley, sheltered by the trees all around. There was no noise outside the window, not even the sound of birds. The cleaners had been already but I hung the *Do Not Disturb* sign on the door anyway. I sat on the bed, looking around the room. Then I emptied out the carrier bags and looked at the boxes. It took some time to remove the strips from the cardboard and push the individual tablets out of their pockets. This didn't happen in films, I thought, when the pills were always in bottles. When I had finished, there was a mound of tablets on the bed. I lay against the pillows, looking down at them, and wondered if my life had always been leading to this.

Slowly, I began to place the tablets in my mouth, a few at a time, then more, washing them down with the Southern Comfort, the only spirit that didn't repulse me when I drank it neat. This had to be easy if it was to have any chance of working. The more I drank, the less I thought about the pills or what was happening in my body. My senses were blunted and although I was afraid, I was removed, feeling that I was already gone, and that the missing part was watching, from afar, the diminishing of what remained.

* * *

The curtains were closed, shutting out the hot light. Little blue elephants were dotted over their cream fabric. Dust rose through the air. A baby lay in a cot, awake but not crying. A girl. The gaps between the bars were wide enough that she could push her hands through, tugging at the bars, pressing her thumb against the painted wood. She was wide-eyed, alert, waiting for something to happen. The ceiling above her was bare and white. A woman came in, walked over to the cot. She reached down with two hands, as though to pick her up. The baby's eyes widened in anticipation. But the woman, hearing something, pulled back and withdrew her hands. She turned her head towards the door, listening. Then she moved out of the room, leaving the baby alone again. Beyond the wall, voices grew louder and the walls began to shake.

* * *

The ground was moving. It was clacking, too. *Clack-clack-clack-clack.* This was dying, I thought. The earth was opening. I was falling into it. I tried to scramble upwards but my body was pulled down.

"Whoa!" someone shouted.

A hand on my shoulder. The ground trembled, shaking as I slipped back down. I opened my eyes to a dizzying light, a stab of pain between my eyes. Sickness rose, a cold shudder travelling through me until it turned to a burning in my throat. There was poison inside me, I thought. The poison erupted in my mouth.

"She's vomiting again."

The ground was moving faster now but the passage was smoother. The shaking had stopped. So had the clacking. This was the afterlife, I thought, this brightness, this pulsing. It was like being born, evicted from the quiet dark into a room screaming with light, your body strangled in the transference. Except this was death, a blinding passage. The poison burned through me again. I closed my eyes, tired of the light.

* * *

When I woke again, the room was still. The sickness was more even, the throbbing in my head dulled. I looked down. There was a needle in the back of my hand, a tube running towards a metal pole, a clear hanging bag. A woman approached, angling a straw towards my lips. She had a soft face and dark hair.

"Have some of this," she said. She threaded the straw through my dry lips. When I sucked, the cold water shocked my throat. I groaned, a surge of nausea.

"Slowly," she said.

"Is there sick on me?" I said. My voice was a whisper. The nurse moved closer, turning her ear towards me. "I can smell it."

She smiled. "There's a bit in your hair," she said. "I'll help you have a bath later."

I felt the need to apologise to her, this poor nurse. I was the last thing she needed.

"How did I get here?" I said.

"No idea," she said. "I only just came on my shift."

I looked at her.

"I don't understand what happened," I said.

"What happened," she said, "is you did something very, very stupid."

* * *

A psychiatrist came. He didn't tell me his name and I couldn't read his badge. He stood as far from me as he could, his back touching the blue curtain encircling us.

"Have you done this before?" he said.

"No."

He watched me. "Why did you take the pills?"

"I wanted to die," I said. I wasn't trying to be difficult. It was the truth.

"Why did you want to die?" he said.

I didn't reply. He wrote something down on his clipboard, his pen scratching the paper unpleasantly.

"How do you feel now?" he said.

"Tired."

* * *

The next day, another psychiatrist came.

"It's the number of tablets that concerns me," he said, pointing scoldingly to the figure on his clipboard. "You're lucky to be alive." Condemnation shaped his voice, just like the man the day before.

"I took more than that," I said.

"That's not what it says here. Anyway, I'm going to give you this." He held out a business card. I took it in my hand. On a green banner were the words *Mental Health Matters* in big text, beneath it a landline number and a local address. "They're expecting to hear from you."

* * *

When I woke again, Adam was there. It was the evening, the sky darkening outside the hospital windows. I didn't know what day it was. For a while I stared at him, trying to remember who he was.

"They brought dinner," he said, nodding at the tray. His face was stricken.

"How did you know I was here?" I said.

"I brought you here."

"What do you mean?"

"I drove you to the hospital."

"Why?"

"Because you'd taken a load of pills."

"How did you know?"

He looked down at his hands. "After I saw you in the car park, I had a bad feeling. I went to my meeting but I didn't feel right, you know? I drove back to the hotel. I knocked on your door a few times. You hadn't locked it so I let myself in. And you were just . . . you were . . ."

I closed my eyes. "You should have left me alone." I felt very angry with him, as though he was to blame for everything.

He didn't answer. I looked over and saw that he was crying.

"You don't need to concern yourself with any of this," I said.

He nodded, wiping tears from his face. Then he stood up and put a card on the table next to me.

"I'm leaving my number here. I'm going home tomorrow."

"To your wife," I said. I didn't know why I said this. I didn't care about his wife. I didn't know him at all and he didn't know me.

He sighed. "Please ring me if you need anything. I'm not saying you need my help. But, please, just . . . Please."

"Before you go," I said, "they're saying I took half the number of pills I did. Do you know why?" For some reason it felt important.

"Yes," he said. "You didn't take all of them. You passed out halfway through. I threw the rest down the toilet."

* * *

When the course of fluids had finished, the doctors wanted to discharge me. I would gladly have stayed there, shut away from the problem of what to do, where to go. It was insulating, like being a child, your life in the hands of the busy adults around you. But I was discharged the next morning. The nurse on shift was the one from the first day. Of all the people who had taken care of me, I liked her best. She had given me a bath, helping me wheel the drip and remove my robe, washing the vomit from my hair. When we got back to my bed, she had said, "Can I get you a cup of tea?" and I had wanted to cry because I couldn't bring myself to ask for anything. I felt too guilty.

She looked tired as she prepared to remove the needle from my hand. When she had taken off the bandage she held my hand in hers, frowning at the bruise that had formed at the needle's entry point. She seemed troubled by it. Finally, she glanced up and said, "Let's get this out of you."

* * *

I collected up my things, putting on clean clothes, throwing away the rancid-smelling ones from when I was brought in. I put my bag on my shoulder and looked around. On the side table were the two cards. I walked over and looked at them, side by side. Adam's was more elegant, the black text italicised on a plain white background. I picked up the other one, with the details of the therapy clinic, and put it in my pocket, leaving Adam's there. Leaving the hospital, I was stunned by a sense of desertion, the same feeling I had always had when you or Catrin were discharged. All this care and expense to be cast back into the world with nothing more than a sheet of paper, the health service vanishing like a forest in a fairy tale.

I sat down on the kerb in the car park, wondering what to do. I had nowhere to go. Even after the course of fluids I felt heavy and sick from the overdose, like there was poison in my blood. I wanted to rest, sleep, hide from the world. But where? The last thing I wanted was to go back to the bed and breakfast, but I needed to collect my car. I went into the hospital reception and called a taxi. Sitting in the back of the cab, I watched unfamiliar streets pass by, strangers getting on with their lives. I hardly knew where I was, which had been exactly what I wanted when I came here. But now I felt frightened and alone. My car was outside the hotel, where I had parked it days before. This struck me as funny, for some reason. Through the window, a woman behind the front desk watched as I climbed into my car. Sitting in the front seat, I reached into my pocket and pulled out the card for the clinic, staring at the number on the front.

THIRTY-FOUR

As I told your father the long story of how I came to understand that Deryn was the stolen baby, starting with Anest Richardson in the hospital and finally getting to the ordeal at the beach, he listened intently, his face sedate and quietly stunned. When I finished, he watched me for a short minute. Then he gave me a disturbed, cynical smirk, and shook his head.

"No," he said.

"What do you mean, 'no'?"

"That's not right."

"It's a lot," I said. "I get that."

"You've got it wrong."

"She admitted to this, David," I said.

He looked at me. "Because you've made her think it's true when it isn't."

I stared at him. I was amazed he could think I had that power. And that Greta would believe such a thing if it wasn't true. Then I remembered how often he had made me believe things about myself that weren't true, and how he had probably done the same with Greta, both of us susceptible to his narrative powers, his self-assured moral authority. Did he think this was what everyone did, all of us casually brainwashing those closest to us? Did he think I would seek to convince Greta of something like this if I wasn't absolutely sure it was true?

"I didn't want to believe it myself at first. But it's the only way to explain everything. I have always felt there was something off about Greta and Deryn."

"Why didn't you say anything, then?"

I hesitated. "I don't know. It wasn't conscious, I suppose. It was more of a feeling. I didn't pay any attention to it. I was busy thinking about the girls. But have you never wondered about the birth? And all the other strange circumstances? Like why did she tell you — and your mother — that she'd had her at the hospital, but tell her colleagues she'd had her at home? Even if she was worried you'd be angry about a homebirth—"

"Stop," he said, holding up his hand. He wrung his fingers in his lap, puffed out his cheeks. He shook his head again. "No," he said. "She wouldn't do this."

"David," I said gently, "it's not her fault. She isn't well."

Deryn had finished her bottle. I removed the towel and laid her on my lap. The pink hue was returning to her skin. Carefully, I dressed her in the clothes your father had chosen — a long-sleeved white vest and a sleepsuit with ducks on the chest. The sleepsuit was new, a tag on the collar that I had to remove. I wondered if it had been bought by Greta, or your nain, or some other family member welcoming the new baby.

"Where is Greta now?" said your father.

"I had to leave her."

"Where?"

"On the rocks. Where I took Deryn from her."

"You left her in the sea? In the middle of a storm?"

"I didn't have a choice. I couldn't get both of them out of the water on my own. It was impossible. I tried to make her come but I had to get Deryn out. She was freezing. It was terrifying, David!"

I started to feel panicked, the way he was looking at me. Maybe he was right. He said nothing. I started to feel awful, again, for abandoning Greta there. I tried to remind myself how certain I had been, at the time, that there was nothing else I could do.

"Please don't turn this around on me," I said to him. "She was trying to kill herself. I did everything I could. I had no one to help me. I saved Deryn's life, David! Don't make me feel bad about it."

"Why didn't you ring someone?"

"I told you — I lost my phone."

"Why didn't you ring someone before that?"

"What do you mean?"

"When she ran off in the first place — why didn't you ring someone then? Why didn't you ring me? I could have gone after her myself. We could have gone together."

I thought about this. "I didn't know what she was doing. She was driving like a maniac. With a baby. There wasn't time to think about anything. I went after her. You're right, I should have rung you. But I was just focused on getting to Deryn."

He closed his eyes, squeezing the bridge of his nose between two fingers. "I need to go and find her."

"It's too late, David," I said. "Either she got out of the water on her own or—"

"Or what?" he said, looking at me. "What, Elin?"

There was a noise outside the window, a flash of head-lights in the dark and the crunching of gravel. The lights went out. A car door opened. I stood up, cradling Deryn, and walked over to the window. Through the rain I could see Greta, rushing towards the house, hunched against the still-thrashing rain.

"David, it's her!" I said.

Your father went into the hall and opened the door. Wind tunnelled through the house. The front door slammed. Greta was sobbing. "I'm so sorry," she was saying. "I'm so sorry, David."

"Shh," he said. "It's all okay now."

I walked to the doorway and watched them in the hall. Greta was soaked, her clothes seeping water on the tiles, as

261

mine had done. She was trembling far more than I had been. Her whole body shook violently. Your father put his arms around her.

"What a state," he said. "What happened here?"

He pushed her back gently and examined a gash on the side of her head. Her hair was matted with blood. He pulled her against him again. "I thought you were dead."

"I should be dead," she said.

"Come on," he said, "let's get you out of those clothes."

They went upstairs, your father leading her by the hand. I went into the hall and listened as they moved around on the landing, going into the bathroom first, then the bedroom, all the while Greta crying and saying how terrible she was, your father shushing her.

I went back in the living room and looked through the window. Deryn was fussing now, becoming restless in my arms. She must have been desperately tired. But she still needed to go to the hospital. And she needed to be handed over to the police — as did Greta. This had been at the front of my mind. But it seemed to be receding. My mind was becoming clouded and uncertain. Your father's reprimands had shaken me, as had his refusal to believe me about Deryn. Doubt seeped in. What if I was wrong? And what was I going to do if your father continued to disbelieve me? What if he managed to convince Greta that she hadn't done this? That Deryn was theirs? What if he persuaded her to go along with his denials?

They came back down, your father still leading Greta by the hand like a toddler. She wore a thick dressing gown, your father's slippers, too big for her, on her feet. The blood had been washed from her hair and face. Her hair had been towel-dried. She looked pale and shaken, but the trembling had stopped. I knew immediately from your father's expression, and the way he was handling Greta, what I was up against.

"Elin," he said, "Greta and I have been talking. We understand how you came to these conclusions. It was a misunderstanding. No harm done, in the end." He moved towards me and took Deryn from my arms. I was so startled, I let him take her. He lifted her gently through the air and gave her to Greta.

My heart began to beat wildly.

"David," I said, looking at him. His face was stone. He wasn't going to listen. I looked at Greta, smiling down at Deryn as she cradled her in her arms. I stepped towards them. Your father stretched his arm out between us, creating a barrier.

I stayed where I was, trying to catch Greta's eye. "Greta?" I said.

She glanced at me for a second then bowed her head again, distracting herself with Deryn.

"You told me this is not your baby," I said. "That you had a miscarriage. Do you remember telling me that?"

"Elin," said your father warningly, "this is not okay. I don't want you confusing her again."

"I'm not confusing her," I said. "I'm getting her to face reality. Greta, do you remember our conversation earlier? How you told me about the night you went into the hospital? You said her mother was asleep and it made you angry?"

"Elin!" Your father moved closer to me. "I'm not going to allow this. If you can't let this go, you'll have to leave."

I looked at him. "Okay."

"Okay what?"

"I'll go."

"Where are you going to go at this time?"

"Maybe your mother's? The girls are there. It might be a good idea to leave you two in peace for tonight."

"It's after midnight. You can't go waking everyone up."

"You just said you wanted me to leave."

He considered me carefully. "What I want is for you to stop this. Why don't you stay, and let's try to forget everything that happened tonight."

"I'd like to leave," I said.

"Why?" he said.

"You don't have to worry. I'm not going to talk to anyone. I just need to think everything through. On my own."

He considered me again. "You need to forget all this stuff, Elin. You made a mistake. You don't need to be ashamed of it. It's been a stressful time. Can we not just move on?"

I looked at Greta, stroking Deryn's cheek with her thumb. I felt suddenly scared.

"You're right," I said. "I jumped to the wrong conclusion. I'm sorry."

"It's okay," said your father. "I understand. It just needs to stop now. We've all been through enough."

"What about the hospital, though?" I said.

Greta looked up, glancing between me and your father.

"She doesn't need to go in anymore," said your father. "She's fine."

"She does seem fine," I said. "I agree. But it would be better if she was checked, don't you think? If she has water in her lungs, she could die in her sleep."

Greta stared at me, her eyes wide and apprehensive. She looked down at Deryn, as though trying to work out if this was the case.

"I don't mind taking her," she said, quiet as a mouse, watching your father fearfully.

"I don't think so," he said. "You know what doctors are like. They'll find some reason to keep her in when she's better off at home. We can keep an eye on her here."

"Okay," I said. "Shall I make some tea? Then we can get some sleep? I'm shattered."

I laughed feebly but felt sick to my stomach. As I moved towards the kitchen, I glanced at the phone on the side table. There was one phone downstairs — that one — and another in your father's bedroom. I went into the kitchen and set about making the tea, lifting the kettle and turning on the tap. My hands were shaking again, not from the cold this time.

In the living room I could hear them talking to Deryn.

"You're okay now, baby girl," Greta was saying. "Mammy would never hurt you."

"You're okay now," said your father. "Everything is fine."

"She's tired," said Greta. "Shall I put her down?" With your father implicitly allowing her delusion to continue, Greta was now behaving as though she needed his permission for everything. "Should I stay with her?" she said. "Do you think that would be best?"

"Yes," he said. "I'll bring your tea. Then I can take over watching her and you can get some sleep."

* * *

It wasn't clear to me whether your father was knowingly denying reality or had convinced himself it wasn't true in the first place, because he couldn't tolerate it. I felt it was the latter, though I also felt, given his intelligence and the evidence I had presented, that he must have, on some repressed level, known the truth. That Deryn was not his child, that she had been abducted, that a crime was taking place. He just couldn't admit to himself, particularly given his pristine moral standards, that he had lived for ten months with a woman who would snatch someone else's child. That a child he believed to be his belonged to strangers. That he would be forced to hand her over to people he'd never met. That she might go into care. And that he had been denied the opportunity to grieve the miscarriage of his actual child, and would have to transfer the love he felt for Deryn to the ghost of an unborn baby, only to have that love thwarted by its absence.

Who could tolerate any of that, let alone all of it at once?

When I had finished making the tea — which I really didn't want — I carried the mugs to the living room. Your father was at the window. The storm still raged beyond the glass. But inside the house it was quiet, the living room silent, Greta creaking the floorboards upstairs as she put Deryn down to sleep.

As I handed your father his tea, he said, "I do understand why you came to those conclusions." He sipped the tea then licked his lips. "I know how it looks. I do. But you have to be careful with Greta." He glanced at me. "She's been through a lot. She doesn't always know what's real. If you tell her something like that — especially if it's something that makes her look bad — she will probably believe it."

"To the point of believing she's kidnapped a baby from a hospital?"

He nodded. "Yes. She gets very confused. But I know her. She wouldn't do that. She might believe it about herself. She might say she had done it. But she wouldn't actually do it. A lot of these things are in her head. Does that make sense?"

"I suppose. But I still don't know how to explain everything else."

"It's just a series of coincidences that seem to add up to a particular explanation. But really those things are unrelated."

"I don't know," I said.

"It's like those conspiracy theorists who take selective pieces of evidence and think it proves a reality they've already decided on. I'm not saying you wanted this to be true — but maybe, in a way, you did? It can't have been easy for you, being here, excluded from this new family I've started."

As he talked my mind ran through it all for the hundredth time: Efa saying Greta had had a miscarriage; the fact Greta had given birth alone then presented a baby on your father's return from a trip that happened to coincide with her going into labour early; the missing baby having been taken the same night she supposedly gave birth; and most importantly, the fact Greta had admitted all of it to me, told me a story about how and why she had done it. How could that not add up to what I thought?

"Why would Greta's sister say she had a miscarriage if she didn't?" I said. "Why would she lie? I don't mean morally, I mean — what's the point? What would she gain?"

"I think Efa has some reality issues, too. Their mam is on medication for psychosis. It's genetic, I guess."

I looked at him, so steadfast in his denial. "But don't you want to be absolutely certain? The police could do a DNA test. There must be some way of confirming — just so you're sure?"

"I am sure."

"So why not check? What is there to lose?"

"I'm not doing that to Greta. Can you imagine how it would go? Suggesting to the police that I even suspect she might have done this? How would that make her look? How would that make me look? And they would take it seriously — with all the irregularities. They would be as suspicious as you. They would treat Greta like a criminal. Maybe take Deryn away, at least temporarily. And what if Greta got confused again? What if she confessed to it — this time to the police?"

"Then a DNA test would prove she was wrong."

"Then they'd have a record of Greta admitting to a serious crime that she hadn't committed. They'd have to involve social services. I've been trying to protect her from all that, with her mother's history and everything she's been through. She doesn't need a social worker hanging around, watching her with Deryn."

I sighed. "Oh, David. I don't know."

I really didn't. I didn't know if he was making sense or talking crazy. I didn't know if he was mad or I was. I felt unsure of everything, awash in the swirling disorientation of his orbit.

* * *

I decided to sleep in your bed. I needed a proper night's sleep; I was utterly exhausted from the ordeal at the beach and everything else. As I climbed under your duvet, the house was silent except for the ticking radiators. Your father was keeping the heating on overnight. I knew he was trying to stay awake in the other room, sitting up in bed to watch over Deryn, just as he had done with Catrin a week before. But he would fall asleep eventually. I closed my eyes, trying to calm the doubt and dread circling my mind. I'm not sure whether I slept. I think I did, briefly. But it was only an hour later that the knocking came, a startling banging that made me sit up in bed. From the kitchen, I heard Beti barking.

I was disorientated at first, sleepy and unsure where the noise was coming from. The doorbell rang. It was after one now. My first thought was that you had run away again, or your sister had been taken to hospital. Your bedroom window overlooked the driveway. I leaned across the windowsill, pressing my face against the glass to try to see who was out there.

On the driveway was a vehicle I didn't recognise, a blue pick-up truck with rain-soaked wood littering the back. The storm still howled, rain coming down on the drive. I got up and went to the bedroom door. Your father was on the landing.

"Stay there," I heard him say.

He was talking to Greta, looking back at her over his shoulder, then moved downstairs in the darkness. The banging continued. So did Beti's urgent barking. I went to the top of the stairs and saw your father at the bottom, standing by the closed front door.

"Open this door!" It was a male voice, rough and local.

Your father looked up the stairway, gazing at me through the shadows. I went down slowly and stood on the bottom step, watching him. I was holding my breath.

"Do you know him?" I said, whispering as though afraid the man outside might hear me. But he wasn't under any illusions that we might not be here. Your father shook his head. The banging continued.

I think I worked out, quite quickly, what was going on. But I didn't say it to your father, who moved past me suddenly, opening the door to the cellar and disappearing down the stone steps. The cellar was barely used. But I knew one thing your father kept down there, and as I waited I heard the sickening and familiar clack of the action. When he came back up, he was holding the shotgun in his fist.

"Why did you load it?" I whispered through the darkness. "There's no need. You only have to scare him."

"Just in case," he said.

He was frightened, I could tell, though he was trying to maintain an appearance of control. Moving close to the frosted glass next to the door, he spoke loudly and clearly.

"You need to get off my property. I've called the police."

The man went quiet, though Beti's barking went on. I went into the living room and looked through the window. On the doorstep was a short, stocky man, hair and clothes soaked by the rain, the sleeves of his shirt pulled to his elbows.

"I'm not scared of you, you bastard!" he shouted. "Open this door before I kick it in!"

He waited a few seconds then moved back from the door, raising a leg and using the force of his body to kick the door as hard as he could. It caused a tremendous bang inside the house. I went into the hall again. The door shuddered as the man kicked it. After several assaults, the wood at the centre of the door began to split.

"You've got the wrong house!" shouted your father. "I don't know who you are!"

The man ignored him. The kicking continued. Finally, the bolt came off its hinges and the door flew open. Wind swept through the house yet again. Your father didn't have time to even raise the shotgun as the man lunged at him belligerently, sending the gun clattering on the tiles. Your father was on the floor, the man straddling his chest. The man pulled back his arm and punched him hard in the face. The shotgun lay beside them. I moved towards it. The man turned.

"Stay where you are!"

When he faced me, I realised who he was. I had seen him on the news, more than once. He turned back to your father, taking him by the scruff of the neck. "Where is she?"

With his head raised, I saw that your father's nose was bleeding. "Who?" he said. "You've made a mistake. I don't know who you are."

"Where's my daughter?"

Your father pulled a face of incomprehension. "Who the hell's your daughter?"

The man let go of him, letting his head hit the hard tiles, and hit him again. Your father cried out in pain, shielding his face. "I told you I don't know what you're talking about!"

The man was quiet for a minute. When he lifted him again, I heard your father's T-shirt tearing. The man moved his face close to your father's and said, "If you lie to me one more time, I'll kill you."

"Jesus — can you listen to me? You're not listening."

He was whimpering now. With the man hell-bent on beating your father, I crept into the living room. Beti was sitting upright in her basket, still barking incessantly, but apparently unwilling to actually confront the intruder. Quietly, I lifted the phone, keeping an eye on the doorway. I could see part of the man's back, and your father's legs splayed on the tiles. The woman at the other end listened carefully as I whispered hurriedly, trying to get across the urgency of the situation without raising my voice. I didn't say anything about Deryn. I just told her there was a man there attacking your father, threatening to kill him, and a loaded shotgun on the floor next to them.

I put down the phone, praying they would come straight away. I moved back into the hall. The man was climbing off your father. He took the shotgun from the floor, gripping the barrel in his fist. He raised it as though he had positioned a shotgun a thousand times, pointing it at your father as a warning, then moved upstairs, making his way through the darkened rooms above. Your father, bloodied and shaken, got to his feet and went to the stairs. I put my hand on his arm. He shook me off, bringing his finger to his lips.

Upstairs, Greta screamed.

"What are you doing! Don't touch her!"

Your father ran upstairs. I went after him. Through the bedroom doorway I could see Greta standing over an empty cot, covering her face with her hands.

"Get back!" I heard the man shout. "Both of you."

The lights were off in the bedroom. But I could see, by the light from the landing behind me and the moonlight slanting through the window, that the man was holding Deryn, his strong arm angled across her back, his hand cupping her head. Deryn mewled and writhed but she wasn't wailing. I didn't think she was frightened. Most likely she was ready to feed, woken in the early hours of the morning.

In his other hand, the man held the shotgun. Even in the shadows I could see how disturbed he was, as likely to break down in tears as he was to shoot anyone. It wasn't clear what he might do, only that he was very upset. He took no pleasure in this. But he was intent, I thought, on righting the wrong inflicted on him and his family. Clearly he hadn't trusted the police to do it for him. I felt he was confused by my presence, too, glancing across the dark room at me now and then, as though questioning my role in all this. It was a fair thing to wonder.

Greta was sobbing, still standing over the empty cot, her hands covering her mouth.

Your father was between me and the man. He had been watching the man intently, and now began inching towards him, holding up his hands. "Listen," he said, "there's been a mistake. A terrible mistake. This isn't your baby."

"I told you to stay back!" the man shouted, lifting the shotgun with alarming clumsiness as he pointed a finger at your father. "There's no mistake. I know everything now."

"What is it you think you know?" said your father.

"I know she did it." He pointed at Greta. "Your own sister turned you in. What does that say about you?"

Your father bowed his head. I couldn't see his expression but he must have been smiling because the man said, "Do you think this is funny?"

"No," said your father, "I don't. I really don't. It's just, it's all so unnecessary. Efa is just stirring. That's what she does. And it's working! You've broken into my house and taken my child from her cot, from her mother's bedside."

It was hard to tell in the darkness, but I thought the man was unsure of himself for a second. But then he said, "No. It's you who's got it wrong. I don't know if you're lying or you're an idiot. But it's her who took my baby from her mother. A midwife! She should be ashamed of herself."

271

Your father shook his head. "I'm very happy to talk this whole thing through. Just give me my daughter and we'll go downstairs and talk, okay? I can explain everything."

"You need to get out of my way," said the man.

The way we were configured — the man having moved with Deryn to the far side of the room, your father and I coming in after him — meant we were blocking his way out. I didn't know what to do. The man had a gun. And he seemed positive — as certain as I had been — that Deryn was his. Perhaps I should have let him leave. But he was also behaving in a troubling and violent way, kicking down the door, beating your father, threatening us with the gun while holding the baby. An unhinged person, for the second time that night, threatening to leave the house and drive off with this poor kid.

What should I do? What would you have done? I needed the police to get here. But there was no sign of them arriving. I also wasn't certain whether it was, as your father kept saying, all a misunderstanding. What if the man was wrong, and I had been wrong, and we let this person leave the house with Deryn? What if Efa had riled this man up but she was wrong or lying about the miscarriage?

But how could she be wrong? And why would she lie?

I still hadn't been given an answer to those questions. It was so difficult to think, so hard to stand up to your father. He had a way of making you question everything, even the things you felt absolutely sure about.

"You need to let me past!" the man shouted. "I don't want to hurt you but I am not leaving without her."

Your father took a step closer. To my horror, the man raised the shotgun. In the moonlight, I watched him position it using his free hand to rest the butt on his thigh, lifting his knee to help steady it. He pointed it straight at your father, his finger on the trigger. Through the semi-darkness I could see that his eyes were wild and his hands were trembling, his grip on the shotgun alarmingly precarious.

"David," said Greta quietly, "let him take her."

Your father turned his head. "What?"

She moaned. "Let him take her! Please."

"Be quiet, Greta!" Your father was trying to keep his cool but I knew he was ready to lose it. A strange man had broken into his house in the middle of the night and was holding his baby hostage. He was not scared now, it seemed. He was just intent on getting her back. This was what frightened me.

He turned back to the man. Gathering himself, he took another step. Now there was only a foot or two between them. Greta, who had been quietly sobbing, was crying loudly now, saying, "David, just stop, please. Please stop." But I didn't move or speak. I just held my breath, watching.

"Just give her back to me," said your father, his arms outstretched to take the baby, "and we'll talk this through."

"I'm not telling you again!"

And he didn't.

THIRTY-FIVE

In my last session with Ben, I thought back to the day, seven months ago, when I had first walked into this light, lemon-smelling room. It had been nine months since I'd sat in my car outside the bed and breakfast, calling the number on the card. When the woman who'd answered the phone had said their first available session was over two months away, I hadn't thought I could hold on. But I'd had no choice. I'd rented a room and waited for my first appointment like my life depended on it. My life had depended on it.

The room remained stark and clinical. White walls, pastel carpets, bland paintings, citronella. It was meant to be like this. A blank slate on which you could create yourself. Between sessions, I thought about Ben often, imagining he was there, talking to me, watching me. Under his imagined gaze I felt like a person, solid and substantial for the first time in my life. Without knowing it I had spent my life slowly choking on the fear that if I asserted any kind of self I might not survive the consequences. But now here I was. I existed. I was learning who I could be, if only I could hold on to this feeling. I didn't want to go back to before.

But what would happen when Ben was no longer in my life? I wanted to ask him about this, but I felt ridiculous saying such things out loud.

As the session started, he got straight to it.

"How do you feel about our sessions coming to an end?"

"Not great," I said.

"What's worrying you?"

I looked at him, feeling I might cry. "I don't want to go back to how I was before."

"How were you before?"

I knew he would do that. "You know what I mean," I said.

"I would like to hear it from you."

I sighed. "I was nothing."

"What do you mean by that?"

I sighed. "I was empty, blank, not really here."

He shook his head. "You weren't nothing, Elin. You were a person. You felt things. You did things."

"But everything just happened to me. I had no control over any of it. I was behind this sheet of glass all the time."

"And now you're not?"

"Sometimes. But not all the time. I'm noticing things I never noticed before."

"Like what?"

"I don't know. I was in my flat the other day and there was this bird on the windowsill. Before I wouldn't have thought anything about it. But I was looking at its wings and feet and stuff and I was just thinking, it's amazing, this busy little bird, right in front of me. That's stupid, I know."

"It's not stupid at all," he said. "It's wonderful."

We watched each other. I didn't avert my eyes, feeling almost comfortable as he took me in. I looked around at the clinical, cocoon-like room. It reminded me of my situation, my life away from you and Catrin. It was clean and quiet and safe, devoid of the difficulty and chaos I had left behind. But it wasn't life.

"I want to go back to my children," I said. "But I'm scared that when I'm with them again, this feeling will vanish. I'll just go back to how I was before. Maybe it's worth it, to be with them again. But it makes me sad."

275

"Why do you think your children will make you go back to how you were before?"

I thought about this. It was another of those questions that should have been easy to answer but somehow I couldn't.

"I suppose just how bad things got when I was with them."

He looked at me. "I wonder if that's because they started you on this path."

"What do you mean?"

"I wonder if this process of — let's say — breaking the glass started when you were with them. Not when you met me."

"I don't understand," I said.

He cleared his throat. "I don't want to impose my opinion here. It's important that you leave here feeling that you control your narrative. Does that make sense?"

"Yes. But I would like you to tell me what you think about this. Especially . . . especially because I'm going back."

He paused, looking at me. He put his hands together like he was about to pray, pressed his lips to his fingertips. "Well, I haven't diagnosed you based on these sessions — I don't particularly find it useful. But if I had to make a diagnosis, I might use the term dissociative disorder."

"Okay," I said.

"Do you know what disassociation means?"

I shook my head.

"It means shutting yourself off from things — the world, your feelings, your body. It's a common response to trauma. You have talked about being behind a sheet of glass, which is a much better description. I think disassociation has been your coping mechanism since you were an infant, when you learned it as a way to tolerate the pain of your parents' neglect."

I flinched a little, pushing out the image that flitted into my mind of that baby — myself, as Ben would remind me — alone in my cot. The despair I had felt then, it was still with me. I understood this now. Perhaps it always would be.

"For a long time," Ben was saying, "it didn't cause any major problems, this disassociated state. In fact, Jude liked having an emotionally shut-down child. You were easier to look after than a child like Abi, who was in touch with her rage. Then you met David, who was drawn to your self-effacement, seeing you primarily as an object."

I shifted in my chair.

"That makes sense," I said. "Though I don't think Jude was exactly happy that I was like that. I think she just didn't notice, you know? It was chaos in that house."

"It's important to you to defend her. I understand that. I'm not judging or blaming her. I'm really not. But from your point of view, Elin, I don't see how you could have interpreted her refusal to adopt you as anything other than that you had no right to personhood, no right to belong."

I sighed. "I don't know," I said. "Maybe. Anyway, what about my children?"

"Your children — they changed everything."

"How?"

"Because they wanted more from you. They wanted the real you. Adults can coexist in emotional disconnection, they do it all the time. But children — babies and young children most of all — cannot tolerate it. You saw this in the Still Face experiment, how babies are hardwired to demand a continuous emotional bond. It is their evolutionary goal. Your children wanted to shatter the glass. And you wanted to bond with them, too. But it required dismantling your entire coping strategy since you were, maybe, six months old. This was very distressing for you. It felt highly unsafe. And who was going to support and reassure you through the transition? Not David, who, on the contrary, dehumanised you endlessly. To make things worse, your daily experience of motherhood was dredging up early trauma."

"Which made me want to disassociate more?"

"Exactly. Your mind was frantically trying to re-establish the dissociative state to protect you from trauma. Meanwhile, your children were demanding the opposite."

"So I had a breakdown?"

"A profound crisis of self. Yes, a breakdown."

I nodded. "It makes sense. But none of it matters."

He looked at me. "Why not?"

"Even if all that is true, no one will forgive me for leaving my children. At the end of the day, I ran away when things were difficult."

"I don't think so."

"Well, you're my therapist. You have to be on my side."

He looked at me. "Do you remember what you said to me about how you were convinced it was your mother who left you outside the hospital? You said that's what a mother would do? Your words."

"Yeah?"

"Why are you so sure it was her? You said yourself, you have no memory of it."

"I don't know. Like I said, I think it's what a mother would do."

"It's what you would do, Elin. It is, in fact, what you did. You came to believe your mental state was causing harm to your children. You did exactly what you claim your own mother did for you. You acted. Not because you didn't want to look after them. Not because you were lazy or blasé. Because you put their safety above your pride, your ego, your claim of ownership."

I thought about this. He had a point, in a way. "No one else sees it like that," I said.

He shrugged. "Maybe not. It's how you see it that matters."

THIRTY-SIX

His name was Tomos Gwyn and he killed your father with a single shot. At his trial, he said he hadn't intended to kill him. He hadn't wanted anything except to rescue his baby, taken from her mother's bedside. He wasn't sure who he was dealing with when he broke into the house. He didn't know what kind of people would do a thing like this. He just knew he had to get her out. For that reason, and not to mention the ordeal he had been through in the weeks preceding the shooting, he was given a lenient sentence. Tomos was, of course, Deryn's biological father. Her real name was Teleri. After Tomos's arrest, Teleri was returned to her maternal grandmother. Teleri's mother, Beca, was being detained on the psychiatric ward at the hospital where she had given birth.

When the police questioned me, I was asked the same questions: did your father know? Had he been involved all along? My answer never changed. I didn't know. And the longer they questioned me, the more I felt that if he was in some way complicit, then so was I. There were many hours between working out what Greta had done and Tomos kicking down the door.

Why hadn't I called the police?

There had been obstacles, it was true. I was under immense stress. I wanted Greta to turn herself in. I was scared. Perhaps I was never, fully, sure of myself. But on those occasions when I had the chance, like after we had all gone to bed and before Tomos came to the house, I did nothing, allowing myself to be taken in by your father's denials.

* * *

What your father did or didn't know became a significant question during Greta's trial, when her barrister presented your father as a controlling and abusive man who had not only influenced Greta through psychological abuse but actively coerced her to take Teleri.

I was called as a witness.

I felt I had little to contribute on the question of his involvement. I told the jury that, on balance, I suspected he hadn't known. It didn't add up, not to me. Why was he in another country when she took the baby, for example? Greta's barrister argued that this had been part of your father's plan, a strategy that protected him from future prosecution, proving him to be the truly manipulative player and Greta his victim.

I didn't believe it.

While Greta had every reason — in her own disturbed and traumatised mind — to steal that baby, your father was not the type. Abusive and controlling, yes. But not this, a crime so erratic and unhinged, with so much risk and so many witnesses. This was Greta's crime, Greta who was, to me, both seriously unwell and basically good. The motive presented by Greta's defence — that your father was himself driven mad by the loss of a late-term pregnancy, and possessed a deep contempt, far deeper than Greta's, for mothers like Beca Gwyn — didn't convince me.

But it convinced the jury.

Greta was sentenced to six months on grounds of diminished responsibility. My testimony about my relationship with your father — his constant belittlements, his judgement and superiority, how he made me believe I had caused the accident — was crucial.

* * *

Greta was incarcerated at a women's prison in the north of England. On her first night there, she was allowed a phone call. She didn't ring her mother or sister. She rang me. When I agreed to go and see her, your nain was appalled.

"I can't believe you're doing this, Elin. She took an innocent child from her mother. She is the reason David is dead. And then she lied about his involvement to get herself out of her own mess. How can you have anything to do with her? She's a monster."

I didn't blame her for feeling this way. She had lost her only child. But I went anyway, leaving you and Catrin with your nain while I drove for an hour and a half along the coastal expressway and over the border. When I hugged Greta in the visiting room, I hadn't seen her for nearly a year, the trial having taken so long to come around; and she and I had not been allowed contact in the meantime.

"There are babies here," she said, sitting down across the table. Her hair was tied back. It was no longer curly, and she wasn't wearing any of her headscarves. "You can hear them crying, especially at night."

"That must be horrible," I said. "Have you talked to anyone?"

"What do you mean?"

"You never got any support with the miscarriage. Not professionally. And then you had Deryn — Teleri — taken. It's a lot."

"Have you heard anything about her?" she said, searching my face.

I shook my head. "Sorry."

The truth was Greta looked remarkably better than she had during those three eventful weeks I lived with her.

She seemed bright and alert, no longer emitting that crazed manic energy that had been masking her fear. The shadows under her eyes were gone. Her skin looked healthier, as did her hair. Perhaps she was getting more sleep in prison than she had been at home with a newborn. But I also knew that giving Deryn up, unburdening herself of that dark secret, had freed her.

"Bet everyone is talking about me?" she said.

"I try not to pay attention."

"Are the girls okay?" I could tell, from the way she asked the question, what she really meant.

"They're fine," I said.

There had been comments at school, particularly at the beginning, when the news about Teleri spread like wild-fire through a community that made a point of knowing everything about everyone. Of course children had said things. You had come home crying, more than once. I comforted you, secretly wanting to march into school and shout at the child in question but knowing it would pass. A year later, it was hardly mentioned. I wasn't worried about you, not the way I worried about Greta, expecting a call from the prison any minute to say she had hurt herself.

"Do you have your own room?" I said.

"Na. I share with this woman. She's okay."

"Have you made any friends?"

"A few. Mainly the girls in the salon. I go there a lot."

"I was wondering what happened to your curls," I said.

"Do you like it?" she said, turning her head.

"You look great," I said.

She did. A lot of pain had left her, I thought. That was the difference.

"Is Beti okay? I miss her."

"We're taking good care of her," I said. "The girls love having her. You know you can ring me whenever, don't you? And I'll keep visiting."

"I know," said Greta. "I get why you're worried. But I'm actually okay. I thought everyone in here would hate me. But

I haven't had any trouble. Most of the girls are nice to me. I stay away from the rest. It sounds weird but I like it in here. It's . . . easier."

I understood what she was saying. It was the same feeling I'd had in the hospital after my overdose, feeling I could stay there for ever if it meant being protected from the pressures of the world and the danger I posed to myself. It was a form of madness, wanting to be institutionalised. Feeling it was worth it to be treated like a child for the sake of making your life easier. But maybe it was what Greta needed for now.

"I have to ask you something," I said.

She looked at me.

"I don't know why it matters," I said. "But I need to know if David was really involved. I've been thinking about it. I don't believe he would do that."

"Not like me, you mean."

I looked at her. "I think the miscarriage made you very unwell. I don't judge you, Greta. I really don't. I left my children and no one will ever understand that, not really. It doesn't matter how much you explain something. People don't understand until they've been through it themselves. Been through the kinds of things we have. I understand you."

"I know you do," she said. "And I know what you mean about David. He's not the type."

"Exactly."

"But doesn't that make you angry?"

"What do you mean?"

"The way he made himself look so perfect to everyone else? And then treated us the way he did when no one was looking? And he always got away with it?"

"Is that why you said he was involved? Revenge?"

She shrugged. "What difference does it make?"

* * *

The following September, Catrin was starting school. As it was a tiny village primary, only thirty children overall,

283

she would be joining your mixed-age infant class. You had turned seven in June, now one of the oldest, and you couldn't wait to show off your little sister to your friends and teachers.

On the first morning, you helped me dress her in a gingham dress you'd never worn yourself and a pair of new white socks and black shoes. When she was ready, I was struck, as I had been on your first day, by how much older she looked in these adult-seeming clothes. I had noticed recently how her scar, though still arresting, had faded a little in recent months. It might just have been the warm weather, browning her skin and obscuring it.

Still, when I tied her hair back, I worried she would feel embarrassed to expose more of it than you could see when her hair was down. But when I turned the brush for her to look in the mirror, she beamed proudly, patting down her shiny clips and swinging her ponytail.

* * *

As we drove along the lanes, Catrin chatted excitedly while you looked quietly out of the window. I couldn't help thinking about when I had taken you for your first day, three years earlier, and what had happened to me in the car afterwards. It seemed a long time ago. I decided to park at the church so we could walk. There were mothers and children, some fathers, too, all heading towards the school. I held Catrin's backpack as she skipped ahead, glancing behind now and then to check I was still there. The trees were green, some of the leaves turning, and when we got to the school the birds were as busy as ever in the bushes along the path to the classroom.

Mrs Williams was standing in the doorway, smiling as we approached. Catrin turned to me, bewildered, wrapping her arms around my legs. As she held on tightly, I sensed her sudden terror.

"I'll be here when you come out," I said. She stepped back, her eyes watering. You moved towards her, holding out your hand.

"Come on," you said, kind but firm.

She put her hand in yours. As you led her into the classroom, she didn't look back.

* * *

Since the previous summer, a counsellor had been coming to our house, talking to you and your sister about the things that had happened. The accident. My leaving and coming back. Baby Teleri, with you for six weeks then taken away. The sudden death of your father.

"There's a lot of loss here," she said.

The summer just gone had been easier than the one before, when your father's passing had been new. Catrin adjusted more quickly, transferring her attachment to me with relative ease. Whereas you found it hard to comprehend the suddenness and finality of his death. You woke up screaming, asking if he was coming back, and I would have to tell you again, no. *I'm sorry, but no.*

Walking back to the car, I took a deep breath, filling my lungs with the cool air. All around me the mountains rose through mist and cloud. More and more in recent months, I had been noticing the life all around me, shrews that scuttled from the hedges then disappeared, the birds calling to each other. Sometimes I felt the trees, rustling in the wind, were talking to me. I noticed the hiddenness that marked the landscape, the insulation from the world beyond and the way in which life was shrouded and still. But how there was exposure, too, in the rough winds, so much of the terrain open and uninhabited. In spite of everything, your innocence tainted by calamity and grief, this was your home. You would grow up here, discover yourselves in this secret, abundant landscape, finding conkers on the ground and woodlice under rain-beaten logs, their bellies golden with eggs.

THE END

ACKNOWLEDGEMENTS

My thanks to everyone at Joffe Books, in particular Steph Carey, who has been brilliant in every respect; also, Suzy Clarke, Matthew Grundy Haigh, Anna Harrisson, Imogen Buchanan and Sam Matthews. The creativity, insight and experience of this dedicated group of people turned my manuscript into a book.

It was my agent, Cara Lee Simpson of Peters, Fraser and Dunlop, who saw the heart of this book from the beginning and directed me to what I was really trying to write about. She has supported my writing through more adversity than either of us banked on. Without Cara I would not be here — it's an understatement to say it means a lot.

Ellie Hawkes, who makes a living reading fiction for a reason, and Alan and Sharon Fraser (who should have their own business doing the same) were generous and shrewd readers of early drafts. This can be a thankless task, but I can at least thank them now.

Thanks to Carys Simon, for kindly sharing expertise in everything obstetrics and maternity, and Imran Howell, for invaluable medical expertise. Angharad Blythe and Manon Wyn Jones — diolch o galon for the translations and answering my random local questions.

Continuing to write through mental health crises, professional failure, early motherhood and a pandemic relied on some perverse determination on my part but also the gentle compassion and infinite wisdom of Sarah Lockley, and before that my previous therapists, Rosa Chillari, Karen Barton and Rachel Akande; and Julia Sweetman and Orla Burchael, whose mindful self-compassion course helped bring me back from a profound crisis to write this book.

Amy — what can I say? Thank you for going back and forth with me on every draft of this story and never making me feel I was getting on your nerves. If I am the mother to this book, you are the devoted live-in auntie. More than that, thank you for being a truly great friend, support and champion since we were eleven.

Speaking of being eleven, I want to thank my Year 7 form tutor and Welsh teacher, then Miss Evans, who introduced me to Toni Morrison, waking me up to not just the all-time master of woman-centred domestic realism but all the black women writers who still inspire me now.

I write in coffee shops and work best (perhaps can only work) with tolerant staff who show compassion to the strange woman sitting at the same table alone for hours. In the case of this book, that was the funny and lovely Carl and Nicole at Costa Coffee, Atherstone, then Anwen Haf at Braf, Dinas Dinlle. Anwen let me in before opening and treated me with nothing but warmth and solidarity.

It's never too late to thank one's parents, in this case especially my mum for generous support with childcare, and both my parents for believing in the legitimacy of a writing life.

My children, Gwilym, Menna and Celyn, kept me grounded and — usually — sane. Their stubborn inability to see me as anything other than their mother takes the edge off this intense, sometimes obsessive vocation.

It's not hyperbole to say I would not be here without Siôn — my love, respect and deep thanks for the honest feedback, intellectual rigour, co-parenting, cups of tea, emotional support — everything.

THE JOFFE BOOKS STORY

We began in 2014 when Jasper agreed to publish his mum's much-rejected romance novel and it became a bestseller.

Since then we've grown into the largest independent publisher in the UK. We're extremely proud to publish some of the very best writers in the world, including Joy Ellis, Faith Martin, Caro Ramsay, Helen Forrester, Simon Brett and Robert Goddard. Everyone at Joffe Books loves reading and we never forget that it all begins with the magic of an author telling a story.

We are proud to publish talented first-time authors, as well as established writers whose books we love introducing to a new generation of readers.

We won Trade Publisher of the Year at the Independent Publishing Awards in 2023. We have been shortlisted for Independent Publisher of the Year at the British Book Awards for the last four years, and were shortlisted for the Diversity and Inclusivity Award at the 2022 Independent Publishing Awards. In 2023 we were shortlisted for Publisher of the Year at the RNA Industry Awards.

We built this company with your help, and we love to hear from you, so please email us about absolutely anything bookish at feedback@joffebooks.com

If you want to receive free books every Friday and hear about all our new releases, join our mailing list: www.joffebooks.com/contact

And when you tell your friends about us, just remember: it's pronounced Joffe as in coffee or toffee!

Made in the USA
Columbia, SC
13 August 2024

40398784R00176